The
Watchmaker
of
Dachau

BOOKS BY CARLY SCHABOWSKI

The Ringmaster's Daughter

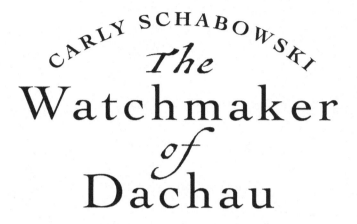

CARLY SCHABOWSKI

The
Watchmaker
of
Dachau

Bookouture

Published by Bookouture in 2021

An imprint of Storyfire Ltd.
Carmelite House
50 Victoria Embankment
London EC4Y 0DZ

www.bookouture.com

ISBN: 978-1-83888-641-7
eBook ISBN: 978-1-83888-640-0

For my father, who loved the first book and I hope loves this one too!

PROLOGUE

Cornwall, England

1980

The window was open, letting the cold winter air seep into the bedroom, chilling her as she lay asleep.

She woke, her nose cold, and pulled the covers over her head. She could, she knew, climb out of bed and simply close the window, yet she had never closed it, not even when it rained, or when it snowed and ice appeared in spider-web patterns on the glass. It was the freedom she loved – to make her own choice of whether to have the window open or closed. It was silly, but it had become such a habit – almost a compulsion – and she could not let it go.

Eventually, she turned in her bed to face the window, allowing the covers to slip away from her face. The room was a muggy grey that came with an early winter morning, when the light was late to find the earth, and purple and grey snow clouds muffled any sun that could find its way through.

It was time.

She shivered, not from the cold but from the realisation that it was actually going to happen, and she would have to face it, face them all and let them see who she once was.

Bracing herself, she swung her legs out of bed, as elegant as a dancer, and flexed her toes to get the blood moving. Bit by bit, she dressed herself in a slim cornflower-blue dress which nipped in at the waist, and gathered her hair into a loose chignon. She stood, staring at herself in the full-length mirror. She squinted at her reflection, seeing herself as a young woman again. Then she stopped and opened her eyes fully, to see herself as she was – the fine lines on her face and the wisps of grey in her hair showing the time that had passed, the minutes, seconds even, each part of her had been marked by time.

She slicked on some light pink lipstick and rouged her pale cheeks, concluding that she was done. As she was about to leave the bedroom, her right hand suddenly gripped her left wrist, feeling the soft skin under her fingertips. *How could I forget?*

She opened her jewellery box and took out a gold watch, the gemstones in the strap winking dully in the light.

Fastening it, she looked outside.

It had started to snow.

CHAPTER ONE

Isaac

January 1945

The sky looked as though needles had been sent through velvet, causing pinpricks of light to glitter from above. Isaac watched the stars, waiting to see if one would shift its anchor and speed across the thick void, leaving a trail of light and a year's worth of wishes.

His breath hung above him, curling upwards like dragon's breath, and he soon had to admit defeat and lower his gaze to concentrate on his deep steps through the crunch of the iced snow.

All around him was silence, and that did not unnerve Isaac – it soothed him. In silence there was no menace, no death. Only in silence did he know he and others were safe.

He reached the corner of the street he had known all his life, now blanketed with snow, causing it to look like another world; a cleaner, perhaps brighter one. As a young boy he had played on these streets with his friends whilst his father had worked in the shop, fixing clocks, locks, and anything that anyone else could not. He had taken pride in his ability to figure out the complex workings of a carriage clock, or perhaps a locked puzzle jewellery box. His face was always aglow in the evening, as he related how he had finally managed to compete his latest quest – a watch sent from England by a man who had been recommended his excellent services, or a carriage clock, with its tiny roundabout of little gold mice underneath, from a lady in Munich. Isaac had sat many a night, listening to his father's tales of the mechanics of time, of locked treasure chests, making him feel as though he were on an adventure, not merely repairing the broken items of those around him.

He shook the memory from his mind as he crossed the street towards the shop that was now his. He looked left and right and stood for a moment, checking that the silence was still his friend. He brushed the snow from the keyhole, and as he did, his arm caught a veil of the icy powder on the door, uncovering the corner of the star, one he now wore too.

The click of the latch seemed too loud in the street, and Isaac hushed it as if it would obey, like a baby soothed by hearing its father's voice.

Upon opening the door, a thud of snow fell from the low-hanging roof and Isaac felt his heart beat faster. He closed the door behind him slowly, carefully, seeing his tracks in the white being covered already.

He dared not switch on the light – a bare bulb that hung in the middle of the room – and instead lit a candle, its milky wax melted and bent to one side.

The shop had been closed now for almost a year; the dust long settled into thick grey grime that covered the glass display cases, obscuring the gold, bronze and silver watches and clocks that lived inside. A grandfather clock that stood in the corner dully ticked the seconds away, echoing in the stillness.

Isaac walked to his chair behind the counter, the floorboards creaking underneath his feet, and sat down, placing the candle on the worktop. He rubbed at his leg; the cold had made the stiffness from his childhood injury worse, and the muscles and tendons tensed beneath his skin with the same knot of fear Isaac felt in his heart.

He bent down and slowly got on all fours. With bent arthritic fingers he prised away a small floorboard, revealing the prize within – his grandfather's pocket watch. He sat back on the chair and pressed the tiny clasp. With a quick snap, the plain gold cover opened and the watch face could be seen, the hand frozen in time at 3:20. Isaac tapped the glass, as he had done as a child, as if this tiny tap would make the hands start moving once more.

'Silly,' he said into the quiet. 'Silly old man.'

He wanted to put the watch into his pocket and take it home, but he knew he could not. This was just a visit to an old friend, to a memory, to one part of his family that was still close by. Hannah, his wife, had died ten years before; before the world had gone mad, and before the rest of her family in Berlin had been rounded up and disappeared into the night.

Isaac knew now where they had gone, but then it was as though they'd simply disappeared. He was glad now that Hannah had died when she did.

He closed the watch and ran his hand over the smooth metal circle. He had wanted to engrave it one day, but he had never known what to draw or write on it. Now he laid it on the countertop, and found his tiny needles that pounded up and down to engrave. Slowly, methodically, he began to write his name – *Isaac Schüller* – and then, *remember me, January 1945.*

Once he had finished, he blew on the gold plating, the dust clearing to reveal his handiwork. He wiped it and then wrapped it in a cloth and placed it back into its hiding place, securing the wood with a gold-tipped nail.

He did not linger once his task was complete; he did not look at the treasures he was leaving behind, nor even glance at the photograph of Hannah that sat next to his ledgers bound in blue leather.

Isaac blew out the candle with one breath and opened the door slowly, checking the street for anything, anyone, before leaving.

He did not lock the door as he normally would have – what was the point? Instead, he placed his hands in his coat pockets and, bowing his head to the icy wind, he walked towards home, his left leg leaving a slightly larger print in the snow as it painfully tried to keep up with his right.

Isaac's house was a small affair, nestled in the valley between rolling hills that sprouted springy green grass in the spring and summer, where bright red poppies, blue wheels of fluffy cornflower petals and tall daisies would bob and weave in the breeze. He stood and looked at those hills, his house a dark silhouette below, and hoped he would see another spring. Perhaps he would, he thought. This village was small, only a few hundred souls spaced between farmlands, and other than the local police insisting upon the Star of David stitched onto their clothing, and that any Jew give his business to the Reich, no one had come to take them away yet. Even his shop had been left untouched – the Reich clearly uninterested in the small treasures it held.

As he began to walk again, he felt a tickle on the back of his neck, just like when Hannah would quickly kiss him there when he was bent over a dim light, fixing and tinkering with the pieces of a watch.

He turned, almost expecting – stupidly – to see her there, her head wrapped in her cream woollen scarf, her lips bright red with cold. But he was alone.

'Silly old man,' he said aloud, then laughed. The cold and tiredness was tricking him, he decided. He was about to turn away when two yellow headlights appeared, and came barrelling over the potholes towards him.

Isaac dreamt he was a child again. Summer had woken the valley into a thick carpet of wildflowers and trees of all shades of green against the clear blue sky. He was lying on his back, feeling the tickle of blades of grass underneath him. Hannah was by his side and he reached out his hand to take hers. He could feel the warmth of her skin, smell the sweetness of her, but he daren't look at her in case she went away.

He could hear the caw of crows and magpies in the trees as they screeched a warning to protect their young, whilst the chirp and chirrup of sparrows and blue tits interrupted them, allowing a mellower song to ring out.

'You have to get up now,' Hannah told him.

'I don't want to,' he said.

'Don't be like that, Isaac. You can and you must.'

'But where will you go?' Isaac finally turned to look at her, and instead of seeing her face – her beloved face that was round like a child's, with plump cheeks and a tiny snubbed nose, her almond-shaped eyes wide like a cat's and sparkling with green and amber – the face he saw was that of a man, with a thick moustache and slanted grey eyes.

'Wake up!' the man shouted.

Suddenly, Isaac opened his eyes fully.

'Where am I?' he mumbled.

'You've been leaning on me for hours. My arm has fallen asleep. I'd let you sleep longer, really I would, but I couldn't move,' the man said.

Isaac's legs were asleep, his knees tucked under his chin, and trying to move them sent pins and needles shooting under the skin.

'Stand for a minute, but not long as you'll lose your spot,' the grey-eyed man said.

Isaac stood unsteadily, leaning against the cattle cart's wooden slats, and shook each foot. As he did, he looked around. The meek daylight that seeped through the slats illuminated little, but he could just make out people lying on the carriage floor, covered in coats and blankets, bags underneath their heads as pillows. They were packed tightly, like litters of kittens nestling into their mother to find warmth.

Isaac blew into his cupped hands. The air that filled the cart was freezing, and though it blew through the slats, it didn't take away the musty smell of dried human sweat and dirt.

'You got on late.' The grey-eyed man stood up beside Isaac. 'I'm Elijah. I'd shake your hand, but it doesn't seem right.'

'Isaac.' He blew into his cupped hands once more.

'Lucky, that's what you are,' Elijah said.

'Lucky?'

'Like I said, you've only been on here, what, a few hours? Me, it's been days I think, but I was lucky too – some of these have been on here a week.'

Isaac looked around him. He caught the eye of a woman, her face gaunt and pale, her arms wrapped around two smaller sleeping figures, their eyelids fluttering in dreams. Isaac hoped they would stay asleep; he could not bear to see their eyes.

'Although,' Elijah continued, 'they're lucky too. Other carts, I saw people standing, no room to sit. Imagine, standing for a week?'

'Where are we going?' Isaac whispered, the warmth of his breath causing a puff of white smoke to hang in front of him.

'Who knows? I started out near Cologne, but this lot, from what I can gather, are from Czechoslovakia, a few French too. Your head is bleeding, did you know?'

Isaac felt the back of his skull where a lump had grown, and a small cut had left dried blood down his neck. He drew his hand away and saw a smear of crimson.

'It was bad when you got on – they threw you on and we all thought you were dead. Me, I was jealous of you. I thought to myself, I'd like to be like that now – you know, dead.'

Isaac's hand shook a little and he flexed his fingers to alleviate the stiffness in his joints. 'I can't really remember what happened. There were headlights – I remember that. I was near home and then – nothing.'

'Better that way,' Elijah said, his body pressing into Isaac's as the train rounded a bend, the click-clack of the wheels speeding up once more as it hit a straight. 'I was awake the whole time. Marched to a school and told to bring a bag of belongings. They told us we were going to be repatriated somewhere else.'

'We're not…' Isaac said.

'No. We're not. They think we are stupid, you know? They think we don't know about the camps. I know where I'm going. Like I said before, I would rather have died than go through this.'

The train suddenly began to slow, the brakes lurching the cattle carts as steam billowed from underneath the chassis. Isaac held on to Elijah's coat, and he did the same as around him the bundles of people began to sit up straighter, rubbing at tired, scared eyes.

Once the train had shuddered to a stop, people began to stand, clutching on to children, on to bags and empty hands that needed some comfort.

'We've stopped,' Isaac said stupidly.

A child pushed forward and pressed his face against the slatted door, trying to see through the thin gaps.

'You see anything?' a voice called from the back.

'Think it's a platform. I don't know. There's feet. I can see feet!' the boy shouted back excitedly.

'Bare feet?' another child asked.

'No. In black boots. They're walking, I think.'

'Come. Come, sit back down!' the child's mother admonished.

'You have no belongings,' Elijah said, looking at Isaac's empty trembling hands.

Isaac looked at the others who clutched their small carpet bags and leather suitcases, then placed his hands in his coat pockets, finding them bare save for the cold iron key that opened his front door at home.

'Don't worry,' Elijah said. 'What does one bring on a trip like this, anyway? Books? Clothes? Food? I was given such a small amount of time to pack, I placed the most random things in my bag – a magazine, of all things, a magazine about woodwork! I doubt I've ever read it in my life, yet that's what I grabbed – can you imagine that?'

Isaac felt comforted by the stream of chatter that came from Elijah. He could imagine nothing was really happening as long as Elijah continued to talk.

'I thought of taking my sheet music, but then I thought to myself, I doubt I'll get another piano where I'm going, so I left it. But now I'm thinking maybe I should have brought it – it was my mother's, so maybe it would have been nice to have it now.'

Isaac thought of his own belongings; his green dressing gown that hung off the back of the rocking chair in his bedroom, the silver brush and comb set that had belonged to his wife, which still sat on the dresser along with small perfume bottles he would sometimes smell, just to get a scent of her once more.

He wondered who would take care of his home now – would someone live in it, side by side with his clothes and books?

Suddenly the carriage door began to slide open, and Isaac craned his neck to see what was outside.

One by one they were ushered out onto a stone and dirt track that sprouted weeds and grass in between cracks, as if life were still trying to show its face. Grey slush that had frozen overnight lay in mounds and the sky overhead matched it in colour, thick and heavy with the promise of new snow.

Within seconds the tracks were full of scores of people, with guards standing in front of them, pushing and shoving them into smaller groups, then dividing them by male and female.

'Put your belongings over here!' A man stood in front of Isaac, wearing a brown woollen coat, the Star of David stitched onto his breast and an armband on his left sleeve, his cheeks rosy from the cold. 'You deaf? I said, put your belongings over here! Now! On the cart!'

Elijah stepped forward and placed his small tan suitcase onto the cart that was quickly becoming a heap of luggage.

'Don't worry, don't worry,' the man repeated. 'You'll get it back. You – I asked you to place your belongings on the cart.' He turned once more to Isaac.

'I have nothing,' he simply said.

'Nothing? A Jew with nothing?' The man stared at the yellow star on Isaac's coat.

Isaac held his hands open.

The man smirked at Isaac as if he had been waiting for someone just like him. He walked three or four steps towards a tall SS guard who stood aside, smoking a cigarette, his thick black coat wrapped around him, the lapels pulled up to keep his neck warm. He reminded Isaac of a crow.

The black crow listened as the man spoke to him, his moustache twitching, perhaps in a smile. He flicked his cigarette with expert fingers so that it flew into a pile of slushed snow. Isaac imagined that it extinguished with a hiss, like the candles he used at home.

The pair walked towards Isaac and he looked to Elijah, who was mumbling to another man about his magazine and whether he was indeed right to have brought it rather than the sheet music.

'Name?' The moustached man stood in front of Isaac, easily a head taller or more.

'Isaac. Isaac Schüller.'

'My Kapo here says you have no belongings?'

'No.'

'Not one thing?'

Isaac could feel sweat colleting under his armpits, even though his breath hung in the frigid air.

'No. Not one thing.'

The moustache twitched again, then he turned to his Kapo and whispered in his ear, making him smile.

Suddenly, the butt of the Kapo's baton was pounded into Isaac's stomach. He hit the ground and curled himself up into a ball as the man struck him on the back, the kidneys.

'Straighten out!' the Kapo commanded. 'Move your legs!'

Despite the pain, Isaac unfurled himself and lay flat on the ground, his breath quick and ragged.

The Kapo kneeled over him, his hands rummaging in the inside pockets of Isaac's coat, his face set and disappointed at the lack of jewellery, watches or wallet. Then, he smiled. Slowly he drew out a leather pouch, just larger than an envelope. He held it up to the moustached man like a prized trophy.

'Ah now, nothing you said,' the moustached man said. 'Stand up.'

Isaac placed the palm of his hand on the stony ground and heaved himself up, standing slightly doubled, wrapping his arms around his stomach where the brunt of the blow had hit him.

He looked left to see if Elijah was there, a face, someone who could help him, but he was lined up with thirty or so other men, their eyes facing towards a line of barracks and barbed wire that lay ahead.

Isaac looked back to the moustached man who was now unwrapping the leather pouch, revealing the tiny gold and silver instruments that lay within. He pulled out a miniature screwdriver, and held it close to look at the tiny engraving of Isaac's name.

'What are these?' he asked.

'They were my father's,' Isaac managed to gasp the words, his lungs feeling bruised. 'They are mine now.'

'Yours? And what do you do with them?'

'I fix watches, clocks. Sometimes music boxes and jewellery puzzle boxes. Sometimes toys.'

'Toys?'

'Yes, children's toys.'

'Steam engines?'

Isaac nodded.

'And clocks, you say? What about grandfather clocks – can you make them work if they are quiet?'

'They take time, they are tricky, but yes, I can.'

The moustached man seemed interested and placed the tiny screwdriver back in its pouch. 'What else?'

Isaac tried to think about all the things he had mended through the years. 'Locks, sometimes, but not always… radios, but mostly watches and clocks.'

The moustached man lost interest and pocketed Isaac's pouch of tools. 'Get in line,' he said, and nodded towards the shorter line of men that Elijah stood in, away from the others who were now marching towards the black gates and watchtowers of guards and guns.

'Wait in that line until someone tells you to move.' The Kapo pushed Isaac towards the men who stood shivering with cold, their hands in their pockets, their eyes focused on the camp ahead where smoke billowed out in thick blasts from the buildings within.

CHAPTER TWO

Friedrich

By the time the car crunched over the gravelled driveway, the snow had turned to grey sleet that sludged down the car windows. Friedrich wiped his palm across the condensation that covered the inside of the glass and peered through at the distorted image of a three-storey red-brick house, its bay windows overlooking the driveway. He looked to a window to see if anyone had noticed his arrival, but all he could see was the dim orange glow of lamplight from inside.

'We're here.' The driver turned to Friedrich. 'Wait here and I'll get the umbrella.'

Friedrich ignored the driver and immediately opened the door, the iced rain dripping into his collar and tracking its way down his spine, making him shiver. He ran to the black lacquered front door and heaved the brass knocker up and down.

'Friedrich!' His mother smiled at him as she opened the door.

Friedrich went to embrace his mother, but instead she simply placed her hand on his head as if in benediction. 'You're wet,' she said, and wiped her hand on her cream skirt.

'Where's Father?' he asked.

'You brought all your things?' She looked over his head as the driver brought in three brown leather suitcases. 'Your books? You'll need them.'

'I did. Where's Father?'

'At work.' She directed the driver to the second floor: 'Second room on the left.' Then, she turned her attention to him. 'What are you doing?'

Friedrich wasn't sure. He stood dripping on the lacquered wooden floor next to a silent grandfather clock. He held on to the hem of his school blazer, and looked around him as if the answer could be found in the hallway.

'You're making the floor wet.' She looked at his feet. 'Go and get changed. Dinner is at seven, you'll hear the dinner bell.' She moved towards a door that led to the room with the large bay windows, stopping at the threshold and looking back at him. 'It's so good to see you, Friedrich. I am glad you are home.'

When she had closed the door behind her, Friedrich let out a long sigh as if he had been holding his breath for the entire time. She hadn't smiled when she had said she was glad he was home. She wasn't glad, he knew. He had hoped that maybe, just once, she had wanted him with her.

He climbed the staircase to the second floor and found his room – a single bed facing a narrow window that looked out onto the gravelled driveway, a thick green rug on the floor with matching green curtains, and a small framed photograph of his parents on his desk. He had had more at school – pictures on his walls, books, toys. He looked at the cases on the floor. He had brought as much as he could pack in the time he had been given, but it had been so rushed that he had left most of his things behind. His dressing gown, he knew, was still hanging on the back of his door in his dormitory, next to Otto's, who had been called home too.

'What do you think is happening?' Otto had asked him as they packed quickly, their faces flushed with effort.

'Nothing. Maybe because we missed the Christmas holidays with them, now we will go home and there will be a tree and presents?' Friedrich had said hopefully, though he didn't really believe it.

'Doubt it. Half the school are going, you know. I think it was those bombs last week – scared our parents silly.'

'Not mine.' Friedrich had sat back and drawn his legs to his chest, his arms wrapped around them. 'They don't care. I bet they'd be happy if a bomb landed right on the school.'

'Don't be like that.' Otto's pudgy hand play-punched him on the arm. 'They're busy. I mean, your father is like the Führer's right hand! He has to travel and do all those jobs. And your mother, well, she has to go with him, right? She has to set up a nice home for him wherever they go. My mother says that's the most important thing for a wife to do, to look after her husband. I want one like that someday.'

'What about her son?'

'Come on, Fried. It's really not that bad. You'll go see them, and then we'll be back here in no time.'

'And if we're not?'

Otto shrugged. 'Then we'll write to each other and see each other in the summer. Let me know what your new house is like, and maybe I can come and stay for the summer with you?'

'It's hardly new. They've been there nearly two years and I've never seen it.'

'Well, it's new to you! Think of the adventures you can have. Gosh, I hope they've got you a garden. We can build a treehouse!'

Friedrich now stood at the slice of a window in his new house in the countryside outside Munich, looking at the grey gravelled drive, the grey stone walls that surrounded it, and the black gates that kept them firmly inside. Was everything grey here? Where was the garden?

He left his room and tried the doorknobs across the hall from him – surely, they would have a view of the garden – but all of them were locked. He tried each of the three doors – once, twice – and even pushed his scrawny eleven-year-old body against the heavy oak as if it would yield to him.

Exasperated, he returned to his room, lay on his single bed, and fell into a fitful sleep, tears silently working their way down his cold cheeks.

The dinner bell woke Friedrich with three gongs that seemed to echo off the empty walls of his room and down the corridor with its locked doors. He sat on the edge of his bed and rubbed the sleep from his eyes, then opened his valise and took from it a clean light blue shirt and navy trousers.

Once dressed, he descended the staircase, noticing the pictures hanging on the wall – a watercolour of the seaside that his mother said she had painted as a child; a mottled brown photograph of his grandfather and his father as a child, their coal-black eyes seemingly dead and yet staring at him as he passed by.

'Hurry up!' his mother's voice rang out to him, and he took the rest of the stairs with quick steps until he reached the foyer, looking around him to see where the dining room lay.

'In here. I can see you dawdling, you know.'

Friedrich looked left and there, through the half-open door, he could see the white linen tablecloth, the silverware, and his father.

He went in and took the place that had been set for him near the window, his father at the head of the table, his mother opposite, dressed in a plum taffeta gown that clashed with her white-blonde hair.

'Sir,' Friedrich said to his father, as he draped a napkin over his lap.

His father looked up from the stack of papers he was reading. 'You made it back then.'

'I did.'

'No reading at the table, Peter.' His mother's voice was high and light. She giggled when his father patted her hand.

'You are quite right, my dear. Quite. A new dress?'

She smoothed the creases on her lap. 'It is modelled after a picture of Eva's dress when she was at the theatre with the Führer. I think it is almost the same!'

'You look perfect, my dear. Absolutely perfect.' He patted her hand again.

Friedrich shifted in his seat.

A maid entered the room, dressed in a striped dress of blue and white, her head covered in a piece of cornflower-blue cloth. She did not look at Friedrich as she moved around the table, ladling the soup into their bowls.

When she reached Friedrich, he could smell her – she smelled of the dirt he had played in as a child, of sweat and a stale smell, like the dampness in the cellar, as if she had been hidden away amongst the dusty bottles of wine and boxes of old clothes. Her hand shook a little as she spooned in his soup, and a splash left the bowl and splattered on the tablecloth.

'Really! Anna!' his mother exclaimed.

Anna did not look up, did not speak. Her hand shook more, and Friedrich could see the spidery blue veins through the tight white skin of her wrist.

'Anna, go! Get Greta. Don't come back in here tonight, I cannot bear you today.'

Friedrich looked to his father, who seemed not to notice the servant woman and was heartily spooning soup into his mouth. Now and again it got caught on his moustache, and he stuck out his tongue like a snake to quickly lick the drops away.

'You really can't think this is a good idea, Peter?' his mother asked when Anna had left. 'Why can't we get a local girl like the last time? This is not going to work, it really isn't.'

His father ignored her and turned his gaze to Friedrich, his eyes so hooded by bushy eyebrows that Friedrich was never sure what exact colour they were.

'You brought all your books back with you?' he asked Friedrich.

'I did, Father.'

'Good. You'll have a few weeks before the tutor comes, so I expect you to teach yourself for a while.'

'A tutor? Will I not be going back to school?' Friedrich stirred his soup with his spoon and thought of Otto.

'No.'

'Why not?'

As soon as he had asked the question, Friedrich wished he could take it back. His mother sucked in her breath and his father placed his spoon by his bowl. 'I said no. That is enough for you.'

'I'm sorry,' Friedrich said, feeling as if he were small again and asking questions – *why is the sky blue, why can't I have cake?* Questions were not permitted – not then and not now.

'You'll keep to your room, read, learn. Keep out of your mother's way too – she has things to do.'

The dining room door edged open and a short man entered, his stomach drooping over his black belt, his thick thighs straining against his grey trousers. Friedrich watched him walk towards his father, not asking permission to be in the room, his tiny wisp of a moustache, so much like the Führer's, twitching on his lip as he finally found the words to speak.

'I have them here,' he managed to say to Friedrich's father, white globs of spittle immediately forming in the corner of his mouth, making Friedrich wipe his own with his napkin.

'Schmidt, good work.' His father took the papers that this Schmidt handed him.

'He's here,' Schmidt observed, nodding in Friedrich's direction but speaking now to his mother.

'Arrived today,' she answered, her voice edged with tiredness.

Schmidt made a noise that reminded Friedrich of his mathematics teacher when one of the students got an answer wrong.

His father looked up. 'Friedrich, this is my assistant, Herr Schmidt. He will sometimes be in the house when I am not home and will work in my study. You will not get in his way, you understand?'

Friedrich nodded.

'When I am not here, and when your mother is busy, he is in charge and whatever you do, he will tell me about it.'

Friedrich looked to the fat Schmidt who was now smiling with thin lips, the spittle still edging the corners of his mouth.

'Yes, sir,' Friedrich answered.

'Good. Very good. He'll be here tomorrow?' his father asked.

'I'll collect him myself,' Schmidt answered, then turned from the family, walking quickly towards the door, his heavy footfall echoing on the wooden floor as he strode purposefully away.

Friedrich shuddered at the thought of being in the house alone with Schmidt. The way his dark piggy eyes had looked at him with no emotion, and the way that man spoke to his parents, gave Friedrich the feeling of having a teacher about the house who was not afraid to use the cane.

Friedrich ate his soup slowly, trying not to think of the spittle that had decorated Schmidt's lips, the silence in the room only interrupted by his mother beginning to chatter about Eva Braun, the fashion, her hair.

'Is there a garden?' Friedrich asked, when there was a pause.

'There is,' his father said. 'At the rear. It stretches out towards a small stream and a few trees. You can play up to the trees but not beyond. Is that understood?'

'Yes, sir.'

'Good.'

'Can I build a treehouse? That way, maybe if Otto can visit…' He trailed off, seeing the look on his father's face.

'Otto won't be visiting,' his mother said. 'No treehouses.'

Friedrich wanted to ask why not, but knew better. Instead he asked, 'Did you bring my train set with you?'

'Oh, Friedrich!' His mother played with the pearls at her neck. 'You've been here less than a day, and the number of questions coming out of your mouth is exhausting!'

'Now, now, Liesl.' His father stood and kissed the top of her head. 'You know your mother gets tired, Friedrich. You must let her be.'

'I tried to look for it, but the other rooms were locked,' Friedrich said.

'I have already found it for you. It is in the spare room and I will bring it to you tomorrow.'

'If you give me the key, I can get it?' Friedrich ventured, wanting to see the view from the house, the garden and the stream, imagining what it would be like to one day build a treehouse and sit high in the branches, almost touching the sky. 'That way I won't upset you or Mother.'

His father sat back in his seat. 'I said I will bring it to you. I don't know why you want to play with it anyway – the engine is broken, and besides, you are too old for that now, almost a man!' His father forced out a bark of a laugh, and slapped his hand on the table as if he had made a wonderful joke. His mother laughed heartily along with her husband and Friedrich excused himself, walking away from his parents, who seemed to relax as soon as he left the table and fell into a conversation which he could not hear as he left the room.

He unpacked his cases, stacking the books on an empty shelf, and tacked a photograph on his wall of himself and Otto, dressed in their white shorts, t-shirts and black plimsoles in front of the running track. They were both smiling at the camera, their arms slung around each other's shoulders, a slight mark visible on each of their hands where the night before they had pledged to be blood brothers, and used a letter opener to slice away the soft skin of their palms – only a centimetre – before they shook hands.

Would he see Otto again? Surely in a day or so he could broach the subject once more and invite Otto to come for spring. They could perhaps make a secret treehouse that his parents would never find.

He heard soft steps outside his door, and a light knock, and climbed off his bed hoping to see his father with his train set, or maybe his mother, to say goodnight.

Yet on the other side of the door there was no one, save for a small plate of meat, bread and cheese on a silver tray with a glass of milk. As he looked down the hallway, he saw the cornflower blue of Anna's cap disappear down the stairs, towards his parents and the empty echoing foyer of the house he did not know.

CHAPTER THREE

Anna

Anna walked with her hands stuck under her armpits to fend off the biting air that nibbled at her fingertips, turning them first white and then blue. She followed Schmidt who walked in front, wrapped in a thick coat, his hands encased in leather gloves. He smoked a thin cigar as he walked, humming a tune that Anna did not know and did not care for.

Her feet burned as they crunched through the frozen snow, the holes in the bottom of her thin soles leaking iced water into her already damp socks. The small track was hemmed in by thick pines and for a moment, underneath the light of the full moon and the prick of stars, she imagined that she was simply walking in the woods, her hand safely encased in Piotr's as he told her which type of owl had just screeched through the air, what it ate, where it slept. If he were here now, he would know how to run and hide in the trees, dig a hole underground to shelter in, and forage for food.

Schmidt suddenly stopped in front of her and raised a hand to halt her. His head jerked from side to side, as if he were trying to hear something in the still air.

'What is it?' she whispered.

'Shhh!'

As they stood, Anna's legs trembled with cold, fatigue and hunger, her teeth knocking against each other – her whole body seemed to be alive and working independently of her.

'I said to be quiet!' Schmidt hissed at her.

She tried to still the chatter of her teeth and held her breath, waiting.

Then, as if all was as he had expected it to be, Schmidt continued to walk, puffing at his cigar once more.

Although the camp was only a mile from the house, Schmidt seemed to take pleasure in making Anna hurry to work, so that she arrived breathless, her face covered in sweat, and when it came time to take her back so she could eat and sleep, his pace became leisurely.

She tried to slow her steps to match his, her face now downturned, looking at her sodden brown shoes – shoes that did not really belong to her. She wondered who had worn them before her – were they young, old? Then she remembered the bodies being carried, dragged and piled upon carts, to be buried in a large pit not far from her bunkhouse, and she felt sick at the thought of whose shoes they had been.

Piotr's face came to her; his dark green eyes that showed his smile, his happiness when he was with her. She thought of his shoes: the clunky boots he wore, a lace missing, when they walked together in the countryside; the shiny brogues he wore when he took her to dinner or dancing.

She imagined his feet by the side of hers now, matching her stride like a mirror image, as if they were walking down the aisle, their families smiling at them.

'*Guten abend.*' Schmidt's voice broke into her thoughts and she looked up, the wrought-iron gates in front of her, the gatehouse and guards with guns slung on their shoulders.

Schmidt spoke to the guards, who ignored Anna until finally Schmidt nodded in her direction. She took the ten or so steps forward that brought her through the gate, towards the shadows of the camp.

*

No one was sleeping when she arrived in her bunkhouse; all were undressing for bed, their thin arms and legs on display as their skin goose-pimpled with the cold. Anna made her way to her bunk, her friend Nina already in her bed above, the blanket pulled up to her chin and eyes closed.

'You're back!' Nina's voice was as excited as if she hadn't seen Anna in weeks, when it had simply been a day.

'I thought you'd be asleep.' Anna sat on the edge of her bed, removing her shoes then her wet socks.

'I was waiting for you. How did it go? Was it better today?'

Anna remembered the soup, spilling it, and Liesl's scolding. 'Not good.'

'Do you think you will get to go back there again? It must be better than the laundry, surely?'

Anna lay in her bunk and pulled the thin blanket over her freezing body.

'Your socks are wet.' Nina had climbed down and hung the threadbare socks on the edge of her bunk, the drip-drip of water splattering the wooden floor. 'Was it really that bad?'

'I'm just too nervous around them, it's like I can't control my hands.' Anna held out her hands to Nina, to show how they still tremored – whether from the cold or the evening, she was not sure.

Nina took Anna's hands in hers, warming them. Anna smiled gratefully at her friend, whose face, although much younger than hers, bore the scars from almost a year in Auschwitz before being transferred to this camp, her cheekbones jutting from the thin stretch of skin as she smiled to comfort her.

'You know the others are jealous.' Nina sat on the edge of Anna's bed now, still holding her hands, teasing some warmth into them.

'They have no reason to be,' Anna replied.

'I think it was because you missed roll call tonight, so they were grumbling afterwards. We had to stand in the snow for three hours. They counted us once after two hours, but then found a way to see their counting was wrong, and made us stand and wait for another.'

'And yet here you are trying to warm me,' Anna said.

'Well, the way I see it is that you helped me when I arrived. You gave me your own food and helped me to survive, so maybe it's my turn to help you a little, if I can.'

A shout from the doorway alerted the women that it was time for sleep, and within seconds the bunkhouse was plummeted into darkness.

Anna felt Nina move away from her, the creak of the wood as she climbed above her into her own bunk, and then a whisper of 'goodnight' as the room fell quiet with the deep breathing of sleep.

Anna woke with her head facing the wall. She opened her eyes and looked at the slatted boards of the bunk that had engravings etched into the wood. She ran her fingers over a few, feeling the names and dates under her fingers, not daring to say them aloud.

She closed her eyes once more and wished for sleep, yet all she could see in the dark of her eyelids was the young boy from the night before, Sturmbannführer Becher's son, Friedrich. He was a slight boy, wiry, yet she could tell from the way he moved, the way he sat, that he would grow tall and strong. His blue eyes were as bright as the cap that she had worn, and she had almost wanted to laugh and tell him that they were matching – like twins. Spilling the soup had angered Liesl Becher, and Anna had spent the rest of the evening in the larder, sorting and stocking, until Greta had given her some bread and cooked potatoes to eat before Schmidt came to take her back to the camp.

She had heard the boy talking carefully to his parents, and imagined that he looked like a small fawn with two tigers ready to pounce – carefully measuring his movements, his sounds, as if at any moment they would leap at him. When he had left the table after only eating a small amount of his soup, Anna made up a plate for him, even though Greta had warned her not to – his mother would see to it if she wanted to feed her son – yet Anna knew Liesl would not bother now her husband was home. Instead, she would talk to her husband even though he did not hear her, then they would sit in the salon and drink wine or whiskey, whilst listening to the music that came out of the polished brass horn of the gramophone.

Friedrich remined her of Elias, her younger brother, shy and yet brave – a look in his eyes as if at any moment he would surprise everyone with a joke, a song or a dance. She shook the image of Elias away, wishing now she had not thought of him at all.

'Are you awake?' A whisper from the bunk above – Nina.

'I am,' Anna whispered back.

Nina climbed down into her bed and lay behind her, her body warmth a welcome addition as they squeezed into the bunk together.

'I was thinking about Kuba,' Nina said, her breath tickling Anna's ear as she spoke.

'I know. I was thinking of Elias.'

'But you know what happened to Elias. At least you have that.'

Anna felt like scolding her for her thoughtless remark, but her friend was only nineteen, and Anna knew she sorely missed the older brother from whom she had been parted when she had been first sent to Auschwitz and he somewhere else.

'Do you think he is here? I keep asking but no one has heard his name before.' Nina's voice was small, like a little girl.

'It means that you can keep hoping.'

'You think he could still be alive?' Nina's voice pleaded for it to be true.

'I know he is,' Anna said. She turned to face Nina, their noses almost touching, Nina's chocolate-brown eyes wide like a rabbit's.

'I miss you in the laundry,' Nina said.

'I miss you too.'

'But then, when I am there, washing clothes, my hands raw, I think of you in that house and I wish they had picked me. I think I would be a good maid.'

'You're good at everything.' Anna smiled at Nina and touched the tip of her nose with her own. 'You work hard and that's what you must do. Then one day, you can do whatever you want to do.'

'Like be a dancer.' Nina closed her eyes for a moment, and Anna imagined that she was picturing herself twirling in front of an audience applauding her.

'What do you want to be, Anna?' Nina opened her eyes.

'I'm too old for that now.'

'You're only twenty-nine, you can still decide.'

'I feel older than that.'

'Me too. I feel old. My bones and my legs – everything hurts.'

Anna flexed her toes in response and felt the pain as she did. It was as if all her muscles and tendons had tightened since she had arrived, like her bones had been broken and put back together again, the skin shrinking over her as the fat that had filled her breasts, her thighs and her stomach had seemingly melted away, leaving little else than a structure to hold her head and make her work.

'I don't know. For now, a maid is what I am, and then maybe one day things will be different.'

'They will be, isn't that what you always say? Don't you think they will be different?'

'Maybe for you, dear Nina.'

'Why not for you?' Nina's face in the darkness looked pained, as though she was going to cry.

'Maybe for me too,' Anna said, taking her arm from under the thin blanket and stroking Nina's hair, which was beginning to grow back after being shorn at Auschwitz, reminding Anna of downy baby hair. 'Maybe for me too.'

Anna's hand soothed Nina to sleep and back to a dream, where, she hoped, Kuba was waiting, telling his sister that all was well, and that they would be together again.

The second time Anna woke that morning was to the sound of Aufseherin Margarete Lange's voice booming around the bunkhouse, alerting them that it was the beginning of their day.

Nina was no longer in Anna's bunk but making her own bed, pulling the blanket over her pillow, taking as much care as if she were at home.

Anna swung her legs out of her bunk and placed her feet on the wooden floor, feeling the freezing cold seep through her soles. She dressed quickly in her work dress, tying the blue scrap of cloth over her greasy brown hair, made her bed and then quickly got in line for breakfast.

In front of her was Joanna, a woman she had met at the camp, but had since found out was from the village next to her.

'It's not even light,' Joanna said, as the other women woke and dressed. 'You'd think they wouldn't want to get up before dawn just to wake us up.'

'Lange seems to enjoy it,' Anna said, as the Aufseherin wandered the bunks, pushing women aside, swatting them with the back of her hand now and then if she thought they were moving too slowly.

Anna watched as Lange made her way to the back of the bunkhouse and shouted at the lump that was Marguerite, still huddled in bed.

'Up! Up, you lazy pig!' Lange shouted.

When there was no movement, Lange hit the lump with her baton, waiting for some reaction, but there was none.

'You – you there.' Lange pointed her baton at Anna. 'Come here.'

Anna walked over, knowing what she would see when she was made to remove the blanket from Marguerite.

'Pull the blanket back,' she ordered.

Anna did not want to. She imagined what was underneath and could not bear to see any more death. It was daily – either in this bunkhouse or others – as each stream of new prisoners arrived from other camps, their bodies already frail, sick and failing. They were dying before Anna's very eyes.

'Pull it back, I said!' Lange swatted at Anna's arm, causing her skin to sting with pain.

Anna slowly peeled the blanket back, and there beneath it was the pale, skeletal body of Marguerite, her eyes closed, her lashes so black against her porcelain skin. Anna gently touched her neck to find a pulse, even though she knew there wouldn't be one.

'Dead?' Lange asked, raising an eyebrow.

Anna nodded, her stomach turning at the sight of Marguerite, her mouth slightly open as if she'd died in the middle of taking a deep breath.

'Bring her to roll call after you've eaten.'

Anna looked at Lange's face – her eyes sunken in her fleshy face, her bulbous lips always moist and too red, as if she had just eaten – for some sort of emotion, but all she could see was disgust.

'Did you hear me?' Lange asked, pushing Anna hard in the shoulder.

'Yes, Aufseherin.' Anna looked at her feet.

'Useless. All of you are useless!' Lange's voice bellowed and bounced off the bare walls.

Anna shuffled back in line as each woman stepped forward to wash quickly in cold water at the one washstand, then take their tin cup to one of the camp kitchen workers to ladle in weak coffee.

Anna took her small piece of almost stale bread out of her work dress pocket and sat on her bunk, accompanied by Nina, whose own hands were empty, save for the coffee.

'Where's your bread?' Anna asked.

'I ate it last night,' Nina said, and sipped at the coffee.

'You know you need to keep half now – that's what they said – it's supper and breakfast.'

'I couldn't help it,' Nina said.

Anna looked at her own piece of bread. Saliva had already gathered in her mouth in anticipation, and her stomach churned and bubbled with hunger.

'Here.' Anna passed the bread to Nina.

'No! I can't. It's yours.'

'I had some potatoes last night and some bread – I'm fine.'

'They give you food?' Nina was already reaching out for the bread.

'The cook, Greta, did last night – maybe she will again.' Anna pressed her shoulder against Nina's.

Nina nodded as she ate, devouring the black bread and washing it down with coffee.

As soon as Anna had gulped down the last of her breakfast, she saw that Lange was motioning for her to bring Marguerite to the roll-call square, where each of them would be counted and checked.

'I'll help you,' Nina offered.

'You save your strength, I'll ask Joanna.'

Joanna was less enthusiastic as she helped Anna manoeuvre Marguerite's body out of the barracks towards the square; Anna carrying her legs and Joanna her arms, her limbs already becoming stiff.

'What's the point of counting her?' Joanna huffed. 'She's dead. We can just say Marguerite is dead, and be done with it.'

'At least she went in her sleep,' Anna said, looking over her shoulder to see where she was going as she shuffled backwards.

'Typhus is next. Hit the gypsy barracks two days ago with that last lot that came in. They're in quarantine now. I bet Marguerite got it too.'

'She wasn't sick.'

'Apart from coughing and sputtering all the time, no, she wasn't sick,' Joanna said wryly.

They stood in rows – Marguerite's dead body on the floor beside them – and waited for the numbers that had been sewn into their uniforms to be called. The roster was taken; a few more had joined Marguerite in the night.

Lange walked amongst them as their numbers were called, checking each one of their uniforms for a mark, a rip, anything that would give her an excuse to use her truncheon.

Anna stood straight, her eyes ahead, focusing on the backs of women's heads that were illuminated by the spotlights that came from watchtowers. The warmth of their breaths hung in the still air, their bodies twitching and shaking with the cold.

Suddenly, the roll call stopped.

'Over already?' Joanna whispered to Anna.

Before Anna could respond, a cry rang out and all the women turned to the right, to see who Lange had found as her victim.

It was a young woman, perhaps Nina's age or younger. Lange was screaming at her for fainting. Anna saw Lange bent over the woman, her arm rising to get traction with the truncheon that she hammered into the woman's body, making it jump like a fish out of water.

With each blow, Anna flinched – *One, two, three, four.* It couldn't go on much longer. *Five, six.* Anna bit down hard on her lip, tasting the metallic blood in her mouth. *Seven, eight.*

The woman's body had stopped moving. She was as still as Marguerite.

Nine. Ten. Then, Lange stopped. She stood and straightened out her jacket, then wiped sweat from her brow.

'Let that be a lesson to you all,' she said, then nodded. 'Let's start from the beginning, shall we?' she said with a smile, as the women froze to the spot and the counting began once more.

'Two hours today,' Joanna said as the women began to disperse, making their way to their work detail. 'I counted. Each second, I counted. Two hours. In the other camp it was longer – sometimes five. You're lucky, you know, to have come here and only here. I was in two other camps before this one.'

Lucky, Anna thought. She was lucky to have only been here five months. She was lucky not to be as thin and fragile as the others. She picked up Marguerite's legs once more as Joanna heaved her up by the arms.

She looked at Marguerite's face as they walked towards a cart already laden with the dead from the morning. She had always imagined that when people died, they looked at peace – at least, that was what her mother had told her when her father had died; he was at rest. Marguerite did not look at rest. Her skin wasn't skin anymore, it was like tightened leather that had been left to bleach in the sun; her top front three teeth were gone, leaving gummy, gappy holes; her lips were dry and cracked and brown. She was not at rest.

They hauled her body onto the cart where it rested on top of two other women, their ages indistinguishable, their eyes still open, glassed over and dry.

'If I go next, make sure you are the one to carry me to roll call – will you do that, Anna?' Joanna asked, as she wiped her hands on the skirt of her dress.

Anna nodded. Joanna walked away, leaving her with Lange to be taken to the gates, where Schmidt would be waiting to rush her to the Bechers' home.

*

When Schmidt left her at the kitchen door of the house, Anna could hear the call of the young boy Friedrich as he shouted for his mother.

Anna entered into the kitchen, where Greta, a local woman from the village, sat on a small wooden stool peeling potatoes, letting the washed skins fall into a bucket at her feet. Anna had the sudden urge to take a handful of the peelings and gorge on them until her stomach would silence itself.

'She's at it again,' Greta said by way of greeting, her grey wiry hair caught back in a bun that seemed too tight on her scalp, so that her eyebrows were always pulled up in surprise. 'Shouting this and that as soon as she woke. The young boy can't even find her – he's been at it too – asking for toys, food. It's not even breakfast and I'm worn out by both of them. Here, make the coffee, will you?'

Anna moved to the polished silver coffee pot engraved with the Becher family crest – an eagle perched atop a cliff. Anna doubted it was really their crest; it was more likely that Liesl Becher wanted to show off to her friends when they visited.

'You eaten?' Greta stood by Anna's side, and silently placed a lump of bread from the counter into Anna's pocket. 'You finish the coffee and I'll take them breakfast. You pop into the garden and fetch some carrots, eh? Help me make the lunch.'

Anna smiled at Greta. She wished she could hug her for the kindness she had shown her since she had been given this work detail, just a few days before.

'Of course,' Anna said, her hand already in her pocket, feeling the warm bread under her fingertips.

CHAPTER FOUR

Isaac

The line of men moved slowly towards the high fences of the camp, which were topped with barbed wire and soldiers with guns who leaned over lookout towers, watching as the silent trudge of the new prisoners came closer.

Isaac's hands shook as he walked and his teeth chattered, knocking against each other, making his head hurt. He could not see the others from the train as they walked under the black iron gates that welcomed them with the words *Arbeit Macht Frei*.

The sky seemed to hang lower inside the camp, so that Isaac wasn't sure where the ground ended and the clouds began. It reminded him of strange, frantic dreams he had had as a child, where he would be walking through smoke, seeing shadows, yet he could never find a way through to clear air, to being able to see properly again.

He followed the man who wore a star like his own, the man who had been called the Kapo, who pushed and shoved at the new arrivals as they walked, seemingly delighting in their fear.

The men were marched into a room towards a desk where three soldiers sat, ledgers in front of them, demanding to see their identity cards, then telling them to go through to the room next door.

One by one, the line of men in front of him disappeared until it was only Isaac left, standing in front of the panel. The Kapo approached the soldiers, mumbling something in their ears.

'*Kennkarte*?' one of the soldiers asked.

Isaac handed over the curling yellow card that stated his name, his date of birth.

The man scribbled the details into the ledger. Then, Isaac saw, he added an exclamation point next to his name in the margin.

He wanted to ask what it meant, what all of it meant, but no one looked at him, only ushered him onwards.

There was a queue to go into the next room and, as each man waited, his head was shaved, the locks of hair falling to the floor in swift heaps.

Isaac removed his cap and held it between his fingers as the clippers moved over his scalp, taking away the pebble-grey hair that he had always allowed to grow long, letting the natural curls take over; mostly to delight Hannah, who had loved to twirl her finger in them in the evenings as he read a book.

'In you go,' the barber said, his own head bald, his clothes a striped uniform.

The room next door was tiled in grimy white, showerheads fixed to the wall. All of the men now stood in the centre of the room, unsure of what to do. As soon as Isaac entered, followed by four SS guards, the door crashed shut. He made his way to Elijah who was running his hand over his newly stubbled head, as if he were trying to figure out what had just happened.

'Undress!' a guard said. He had a large scar above his eyebrow and was tapping his black rubber baton impatiently against his leg.

At first, none of the men moved to do as they were asked. Instead, they looked at one another, like baby birds – no feathers and big eyes – waiting to see if they should really do as they had been told.

'Undress!' the lieutenant shouted again, and to make himself clear, he thwacked the baton against a young man's leg, making him fall to the floor and cry out in pain.

The men quickly undressed, their jackets, trousers, shoes all heaped at their feet. Some men covered their private parts with their hands, as Isaac did, but some stood ramrod straight, their hands at their side, a look of defiance in their eyes.

'Shower! Now!'

They stood under the showerheads, each one waiting for the rain of water to come.

At first nothing happened.

Isaac looked at the guards who were kicking at the bundles of clothes, waiting to see if anything of value came from them. One bent down and picked up a watch, turned it over in his hands, then placed it in his pocket.

Suddenly, the water came – an iced stream. All of the men immediately jumped out of the way. The guards shouted, and pushed them back under the water, so that soon all of them were goose-pimpled and white with cold.

Isaac made the motions as if to wash himself; then, as suddenly as the water started, it stopped. No one was handed a towel or their clothes; instead they were marched out of the shower room into another, where each of them was handed a blue and white striped uniform with a number stitched onto the lapel and a pair of worn shoes.

They dressed quickly. The rough cotton clung to Isaac's damp cold skin and offered little warmth. He noticed a stain on the trousers and a hole in the elbow of the sleeve – someone else's clothes.

'I'm glad I didn't bring the sheet music now.' Elijah was at Isaac's side, watching as Isaac's hands shook when he tried to fasten the buttons of his shirt. 'Bet you're glad you didn't bring anything. Nothing to miss, nothing to wish for back.'

'I want to go home,' Isaac said quietly, suddenly feeling like a small child again, wishing for his father and mother, wishing that they would come and tell him it was going to be OK.

'I know, I know.' Elijah patted him on the shoulder. 'Me too.'

'This way!' The lieutenant was back, flitting between the men like a ghost – one minute gone, the next he was back – his baton twitching and his thin smile offering no comfort.

The men were ushered into a line again, and like ants they followed one another, no one daring to look anywhere but straight ahead.

Down the corridor they walked, their shoes squeaking on the tiled floor. Then they were stopped, and one by one they were photographed: from the front, side, back.

Isaac had only had his photograph taken once, on his wedding day. Now, when he stood in front of the box camera, he stupidly wanted to smile. And then he looked at the guards, at the line of men, and his silly idea flew away. He set his eyes forward, his mouth in a line.

The bunkhouse was a short walk from where the men had been registered, stripped of their belongings, their hair and their names, across a large concrete square, past another brick building, then another, to a long shed, again encased with more barbed wire, more watchtowers, more men with guns.

Each was given a thin blanket and pillow and assigned an empty bunk, told to make it, and then they were shut in for the night.

'No food, no water?' Elijah was in the top-tier bunk one over from Isaac, a younger man called Jan below him, who had been in the camp for some time.

'You'll get something tomorrow,' Jan said from the bottom bunk. 'Not much, mind you – but something.'

'So what do we do now?'

'I'd sleep if I were you,' Jan said.

Isaac lay back on his straw mattress, feeling the pricks of the stalks in his back. His leg ached and he rubbed at it, staring at the ceiling, trying to calm himself by imagining Hannah's face.

'You awake?' Elijah asked.

'I am.' Isaac turned on his side to look at Elijah, who was doing the same. All around them were the whispers of the men as they asked questions, forged friendships, and tried to make sense of the reality they now found themselves in.

'Are you married?'

'I am – I was… My wife died ten years ago,' Isaac replied.

'I was never married. Not once. I thought perhaps I had some more time, but I'm not sure I do now.'

'How old are you, Elijah?'

'Forty-five, you?'

'Almost sixty.'

'I know what will happen to us here, I know. They'll not let us out. I doubt I'll get married.'

'Things can change. I never thought Hannah would die, I never thought this would ever happen. But it has. So, things can change again, you know? The British and Americans will find us,' Isaac said hopefully.

'Quiet down!' Jan's voice came from below. 'Keep thinking like that if you want, but I'll tell you now, in a day or so, you'll be so tired, so hungry that those thoughts will disappear.'

'There's no harm—'

'Shh, quiet now,' Jan interrupted Isaac. 'Get your sleep, you'll need it.'

The morning had not yet broken when Isaac was woken by the Kapo from the train tracks. His name was Adam, Jan had told him, a Jew, a prisoner just like them who slept in other barracks and was given better food, better clothes, as long as he helped keep them all in line.

'How can he do that?' Isaac asked Jan as they left the bunkhouse. 'How can he turn on his own people?'

'You say that, and I agree with you, but Adam was in three camps before this one. He is just trying to survive.'

'So, you think it is right?'

'I think it is wrong. I think he will have to live with this for the rest of his life if he does survive. We hate him, of course we do, but there is a fine line between the hate that we feel and our jealousy at the privileges he has. You'll see. Give it time – you'll see how this place can change a man.'

Jan fell silent as they marched outside into the sleet that now fell from the dense clouds. Each man was counted, then counted again. Now and again, for no reason, one or two men were singled out and walked away by a guard.

After more than an hour, Isaac could barely feel his toes or fingers, and the pain in his leg throbbed from standing for so long. He couldn't understand why they had to count again and again. Then, he realised. As the time passed the men became weaker, colder, more tired, and this was when some would find their legs crumbling beneath them, and this was when the guards and Kapos found delight in meting out punishment.

With each beating of each man, the roll call began again.

Those who were new to the camp were made to stand longer whilst the others were sent to their work – none of them had eaten. Isaac stood with Elijah and a few others from the train.

'Your work details.' A guard stepped in front of them, a boy it seemed, perhaps no more than eighteen, whose blond hair and blue eyes were the epitome of the Reich. He called out each number, and the men had to look at their shirts to check if it was theirs that was called. Each one was assigned their place of work – labour, factory, morgue.

Isaac checked his own number multiple times, but his was never called. Soon he was the only one left standing as each of the others were marched to work.

'Schüller.' The blond guard stood in front of him. 'We've a special job for you.'

Isaac wasn't sure whether to ask what it was or to say thank you; instead he nodded.

He shuffled after the blond guard who led him towards a watchtower and gates, where a short, fat man waited on the other side, puffing at a thin cigar.

Isaac stood in front of him.

'So, you're him, are you?' the fat man said, eyeing him up and down.

Isaac looked over his shoulder at the blond guard who was now walking away.

'You want to go back inside?' the fat man asked through a thick plume of smoke. 'I doubt it. Follow me.'

The fat man turned from him and walked quickly away, so Isaac had to half run to keep up with him, his leg painful and slowing him down.

The trees along the track bowed under the weight of the snow, the only sound Isaac's fatigued footsteps as he tried to keep up with the fat man, who would turn around every few seconds to bark at him to hurry up.

Isaac stopped to catch his breath and rubbed at his thigh, the muscles feeling torn underneath. He looked about him and imagined himself running into the safety of the trees.

'Don't even think about it.' He was by his side, and Isaac felt the cold metal of a pistol on his temple. Isaac slowly straightened and he lowered the gun. 'I'd almost dare you to try and run. It would be like hunting a wounded rabbit. Not much sport, I grant you, but I do love the thrill of a hunt – don't you?' He grinned at Isaac.

A whump of snow hit the ground from a low-hanging branch, causing a bird to flap its wings in fright.

'Get moving.'

Isaac began to walk once more, his leg dragging a little behind him. He licked at his cracked lips and quickly stooped down to grab a handful of snow, shoving it into his mouth, the icy freshness a quick comfort.

They rounded a bend and in the distance Isaac could see the chimney pots of a house, the smoke billowing from them as those inside warmed themselves against the morning's chill. A memory suddenly assaulted him – a morning like this one, where the clouds, grey and purple, were laden with snow, when he sat by a fireplace warming his hands as Hannah sat across from him, a bundle in her arms to which she softly sang.

He shook his head to make the memory go away, but it sat, stubborn, willing him to remember the warmth of the fire as the wood hissed and crackled with heat, the caramelised, nutty scent of fresh coffee that he had just brewed, the sound of Hannah's voice as she sang a lullaby.

'Are you deaf?' The fat man's voice broke into his reverie. 'I said go in.'

Isaac realised that they had reached the house, and the gates in front of him were opened by two armed guards who eyed him as he walked past.

Isaac followed him down a gravelled driveway that led to the house, where large bay windows still had curtains shut against the early morning. They turned away from the black lacquered front door towards the side of the house, round a pathway that led to the rear. Here, the man stopped and opened a door, the blue paint peeling from the woodwork.

'Another one, Herr Schmidt?' An old woman with grey hair appeared as if she had been waiting for them.

'He was asked for by Sturmbannführer Becher,' he replied.

The old woman shook her head. 'She'll not be happy, you know. She wasn't happy about the girl and she won't be about this.'

'Put him in the shed, that's what I was told.' He nodded towards the half fallen-down garden shed nestled between a row of fir trees.

'Out there? He'll freeze, it's too cold.'

'Not your problem.'

Isaac felt as though he was not really there. Neither looked at him, yet they talked of him as if he were a stray dog. He wanted to say something, wanted to do something so they would look at him.

'Well, all I'm saying, Herr Schmidt, is she won't be happy...' the old woman said.

'Sturmbannführer Becher has asked to see him. I must get back. You know how it is – there is always someone who is not doing as they should. It's my job to make sure they learn.' He smiled then turned, humming a tune as he walked away.

The old woman stood in the doorway, watching Schmidt as he left footprints in the slush smattering the ground.

'Come in, come in.' She ushered Isaac into the kitchen and closed the door. 'Sit, sit.' She pointed at a chair next to the stove. 'Warm yourself for a minute, you look like death.'

Isaac sat next to the stove, feeling the heat seep through his damp clothes, and finally reaching the skin. He blew into his hands and flexed his fingers, teasing the blood to flow.

'Take this.' The woman gave him a tin cup of coffee and some warm bread. 'Eat quickly now, and don't tell a soul, eh?' She tapped the side of her nose conspiratorially. 'What's your name?' she asked, one hand on her hip, the other placed on the kitchen table as if she were propping herself up.

'Isaac, Isaac Schüller,' he replied between hungry mouthfuls.

'I'm Greta. I was brought in from the town to cook and manage this house. I see what's going on, I see it.' She looked out of the window as if the camp was right there in the back garden. 'Now I'll mind you. But you can't say anything about the food or that

I let you in for the warm, or I'll find myself where you are. Do you understand?'

Isaac nodded then drank back the coffee.

'Here, take some more.' She refilled the cup. 'They're still in bed, see, so it's all right. But you never know, so be quick.'

Isaac drank once more and she handed him another piece of bread, then a bell tinkled in the kitchen.

'He's up!' She took the cup from Isaac and beckoned him to follow her out of the kitchen, down a passageway that led to double oak doors, ornately carved, with brass handles. Isaac wanted to reach out and trace the pattern that a carpenter had made in the wood, imagining the feel of the flowers and curled leaves under his fingertips.

Greta knocked, then waited.

'Enter!' a voice boomed from within.

Greta nodded at Isaac then opened the door and let herself in. 'The man you asked for from the camp is here,' she said.

'Good, let him in.'

Greta opened the door wider and again nodded at Isaac for him to enter. As he did, her eyes went to the soft cap on his head and Isaac reached up, took it off and held it in his hands.

She closed the door behind him, and Isaac saw that sitting behind a mahogany desk was the moustached man from the train tracks, Isaac's leather pouch of tools in front of him.

'Ah, the watchmaker!' The moustached man beckoned for Isaac to come closer, but not to sit.

'I think you are wondering why you are here, are you not?'

Isaac nodded.

'Do you know who I am? No, I don't suppose you do,' the man answered his own question, then smoothed at the hairs under his nose, tracing them to where they ended, just as they reached the corner where his top and bottom lip met.

'I am Sturmbannführer Becher,' he said. 'I have the pleasure of running the camp you now find yourself in. Is it to your liking?'

'Yes, sir,' Isaac answered, unsure what game was being played.

'Good answer – the only one I would want to hear. Well, watchmaker, I have asked for you personally. I very rarely ask for anyone from the camp, but you, when I saw you, when I saw this,' he held up the leather pouch, 'I knew you were a man of talent and that I should utilise your talent whilst you stay here. Does that sound agreeable to you?'

'I – yes, yes, sir,' Isaac stuttered.

'You see, I have a grandfather clock, gifted to me by the Führer himself. One of the many treasures that now belong to the Reich. Sadly, it does not chime. Many have tried to fix it, and all have failed. But you, you, good sir, I think may be the man for this very job. Do you think you can fix it?'

'I can certainly try.'

'Try? No, no.' Becher stood. 'Trying is not doing. You will fix it. Say it.'

'I will fix it,' Isaac parroted.

'And if you do, then perhaps I can find other things for you to fix too. Perhaps it will be a nice job for you to have.'

'It will.'

'Good. Very good. Now, I will take you to look at the clock, but you cannot fix it in here. Take a look, let Greta know of any parts you may need, and she will show you to a suitable place in which to work on them. My wife, you see, would not like you to be around the house, so you must find a way to fix it without actually touching it often – is that clear?'

Isaac tried to understand what was being asked of him. He had never before tried to fix anything without it sitting in front of him, so he could look at it, imagine how the parts moved, see where the problem might lie. Yet he simply replied, 'Yes, sir. It is clear.'

Becher walked out of the study and had Isaac follow. He led him to the hallway where the grandfather clock sat, regal and yet silent.

'It is rather beautiful,' Isaac said.

'Take a look, get closer,' Becher said. 'See there in the clock face, tiny gemstones in Roman numerals, and then, see the ornate carvings – a cherub, a vine with grapes. It is a work of art, is it not?'

Isaac nodded, then crouched down to look at the chime that hung still within its glass house, all the cogs and mechanisms on display, a joy to watch if they were all working together, pushing and pulling against each other to make the time pass.

'May I?' Isaac asked.

Becher nodded and Isaac opened the glass door, inspecting the sleeping cogs inside.

'It is magnificent,' Isaac said as he looked, forgetting where he was for a moment. 'It is meant to chime the hour, and when it does, a smaller chime should ring out afterwards, sort of like in a music box – a tune that marks midnight and midday. I have heard of such clocks but never seen one before.'

'What is your suggestion of what ails it?'

'It could be that the two are not synchronised. The time is ticking, yet the mechanisms stay still. I will have to draw it to take the drawing away with me and inspect it – would that be possible?'

'Quite!' Becher smiled and seemed excited at the prospect of getting the Führer's gift working once more. He bounded into his study and returned with a pencil and paper in one hand, and Isaac's leather pouch with his tools in the other. 'You'll be needing these.' He handed them to Isaac.

Isaac sketched quickly, trying to be as precise as he could. He could see a worn cog, a spoke missing, which could be the problem, yet there was something else that wasn't quite right...

'I think someone has tried to mend it before. They have placed the wrong screws in the cogs – they are too large – and that is perhaps what is hindering it.'

'Get a list to Greta by the end of the day as to what you may need, and I will see to it that they are brought to you by tomorrow.'

Isaac stood, the sketch, his tools and his cap in his hands. 'Yes, Herr Becher.'

'If you go to Greta, she will show you where to work.' Becher smiled at him once more then returned to his study.

Isaac followed the passageway back to the kitchen, unsure of what had just happened. Becher had been nice to him – or if not nice, cordial – as if Isaac were in his shop once more, and Becher were but a customer.

'I see you made an impression,' Greta said to him as he reached the kitchen. 'Come with me, I'll show you where to work.'

Greta took him down the wet grass to the dilapidated shed at the edge of the garden.

'I'm afraid it's got the gardener's things in here still, so you'll have to make a space for yourself.'

Isaac looked about him. The shed was filled with odds and ends – pieces of furniture, planks of wood, gardening tools and above, old spider webs that stirred as the air blew through them. In a corner he spied an old chair with three legs and a wooden box – a makeshift workspace perhaps.

'It'll get cold in here,' Greta said, then leaned forward and whispered in his ear, 'there are some blankets at the back, in the corner. Don't let anyone see you using them. There's also a small gas lamp – it will give you some warmth and light.'

With that, Isaac entered, and Greta closed the wooden door behind him with a creak, leaving him in semi-darkness and with only silence for company.

CHAPTER FIVE

Anna

In the side garden, Anna tried to forage for carrots in the frozen soil whilst she ate the bread Greta had given her. She was cold, yet glad she did not have to be in the house – Liesl had made the distaste she felt for her clear the previous evening and Anna was only too glad to stay out of her way for the time being.

As she made her way towards the kitchen door, she noticed footprints in the icy mulch leading to the shed at the rear of the garden. She stood and looked, and there in the small window a warm yellow light lit up a figure inside.

The figure turned at the same moment and, through the misted glass, looked at Anna. She turned and hurriedly made her way back to the kitchen, where Greta was filling trays ready to take into the dining room.

'There's someone out there,' Anna told her. 'In the shed. I saw a light and a figure.'

'Shhh.' Greta turned to her. 'That's Isaac. New – here to fix that blasted grandfather clock they're always moaning doesn't work. Get the butter, will you?'

Anna did as she was told, and helped slice the butter into pats and place them onto a china dish, the toast chestnut-brown and hot.

'I'll take this through – can't have you going in there again just yet.' Greta lifted the tray, but her hands shook with the weight, the plates rattling. Anna made to help her. 'Leave it, I can do it. Let's not start her off in a bad mood. You do the lunch, and for goodness' sake when you are cleaning today, make sure you make yourself invisible!'

Anna let Greta deliver the breakfast and turned to look out of the window, the glow of the light from the shed beckoning her towards it.

'Isaac...' she muttered to herself. Then she wiped the condensation away from the window, looking for a moment at her handprint on the pane.

Anna spent most of the morning doing as Greta had advised, trying to make herself as invisible as possible. Every time she heard the click-clack of Liesl's heels on the wooden floors, she dipped into another room, polished dust from surfaces and laid fires.

'Why are you so scared of her?' Anna whispered to herself. 'If you weren't here, you wouldn't be scared of her, you know, you would—'

'Who are you talking to?'

Anna turned in shock to see the small boy from dinner standing at the door, a train engine in his hands.

'I'm sorry,' she said.

'Why are you sorry?' he asked, and took a step inside the parlour.

'I don't know. Perhaps because I shouldn't be talking to myself.'

'I talk to myself,' the boy offered. 'Not at school, but here I do.'

Anna knew she shouldn't speak to him, knew she should leave the room, yet it was the first time anyone had looked at her – not her uniform, not her religion, just her – and seemed interested to hear what she had to say. 'I used to when I was young, like you. I used to talk to my imaginary friend.'

The boy sat in a chair and leaned forward. 'What was his name?'

'He was called Bobo.' She smiled. 'I would tell him about my day and about the girls at school who teased me.'

The boy laughed. 'Bobo! That's a silly name. But I like it. I don't have an imaginary friend – I just talk to myself, sort of the same way I speak to my friend Otto. He lives far away, and we can't see each other at the moment,' he babbled.

'Friedrich!' Liesl was at the door.

Anna saw the fear in Friedrich's eyes upon hearing his mother call his name, and she knew her face must look just the same.

'What on earth are you doing in here? Why are you talking to *her*?' Liesl's nose crinkled as if she had smelled something rotten.

'I was just looking for Father. My train…' he said limply, and held up the engine to show her.

'I'll take you to him. Come with me.' She held her arm out for Friedrich to take. 'And you,' Liesl looked at Anna, 'do not talk to my son.'

Anna nodded and as soon as Liesl left, she exhaled. She tried to polish the side tables but her hand shook. Would she be punished? If so, she did not dare think what the punishment might be.

She looked out of the window at the gravelled driveway, the slurry mix of melted snow and dirt edging it, and in contrast, the patches of clean, pure snow that covered the lawn. Although the camp was a mere mile away, she felt as though she could be anywhere, perhaps at home, simply looking out of the window, waiting for Piotr to come to take her for dinner, a walk, perhaps even to a dance.

Piotr – he was there, back in her mind once more. She remembered the day he left, a bag slung over his shoulder, with a promise that he would survive, that this was the right choice – he had to do what he could to stop what was happening, he had to resist.

She had wanted to go. Embarrassment surged through her as she recalled the scene when she had begged him on her hands and knees to please take her with him – she could help, she could.

But he had kissed her and told her to stay safe, and left her on the floor, tears streaming down her face. It was Elias, her brother, who had picked her up from the floor, Elias who had promised to keep her safe. And now she was alone.

A click-clack of heels on the floor alerted her to Liesl's presence once more. She turned away from the window and gathered the feather duster, the cloths and the wood polish, and scurried away to seek refuge in the kitchen with Greta.

'I knew having that boy here was going to cause trouble, I could sense it. Just say – politely to him, mind – that you cannot talk to him and leave the room next time it happens, and mark my words, it will. He barely gets any attention, let alone affection from them, so he'll seek it out. I've seen it before,' Greta told her.

Anna nodded. 'Should I take their lunch through?'

Greta shook her head, 'I'll manage today, we'll try again with you tomorrow. For now, go out to see that Isaac fellow. Herr Becher wants some sort of list from him – tools and whatnot; he's waiting for it. I thought Isaac would bring it to me, but I suppose he realises he shouldn't really leave the shed. Go and see him, but don't be too long. And here,' Greta passed Anna some hot soup in a tin mug, 'take him this, it will warm him a little.'

Anna made her way towards the shed, feeling the warmth in her hands that the soup offered. She had to chastise herself for wanting to drink it, and hoped that Greta would have saved something for her too.

She knocked gently on the wooden door, then, feeling silly, opened it.

The shed was no longer cluttered. The gardening tools and junk were lined up, as if waiting to be used. The man, Isaac, was wrapped in blankets and old pieces of cloth, and sitting on a chair over a makeshift desk of a few boxes and crates, the lamp settled in the corner.

He did not look up at first from the piece of paper that lay on the desk, his head bent. He was muttering words and making small movements with his hands as if he were fixing something.

'I've brought you soup,' Anna said.

Isaac looked up, his green eyes bright, white stubble across his chin and above his lip. He did not smile.

'Thank you,' he said.

'Greta said you had a list for her?' She placed the cup on the desk and he immediately picked it up and held it in his hands, his face above the rising steam, closing his eyes as if savouring the warmth it provided.

'Is this it?' Anna picked up the piece of paper in front of him.

'No!' he shouted and grabbed the paper back from her, then placed it back on the desk and smoothed the crease out with one hand whilst still holding the cup with the other. 'I don't need anything.'

'But Greta said...' She trailed off.

'Everything I need is already here. I have decided how to fix it, and there's nothing I need.'

'What should Greta say to Herr Becher?'

'She should say that Isaac will fix the clock and that he does not need anything.'

She waited a second, then two, then three. He bent his head to study the paper once more, then picked up a pencil and began to write notes against it.

'I'm sorry,' he mumbled as he wrote. 'When I am working, I get stuck inside my head a little. It makes me grumpy – at least that's what my wife used to say.'

'I get stuck inside my head too. But not because of work,' she said.

He looked up at her now, as if she had just walked in. He studied her face, almost as if he were trying to place where he had seen her before.

'I think of silly things,' she said, the silence and his stare unnerving her. 'I think of walking in the woods or of reading a book in an armchair next to the fire.'

'Memories,' he said. 'We are all full of them.'

He was still staring at her, so she looked away from him, towards the neatly lined-up tools. 'You've been busy,' she said.

Finally, his eyes left her face. 'I can't work with clutter. I never could. I like things organised.' Then, he drank back the soup and held the mug out towards her. 'You're waiting for this?'

She nodded and took it from him, his fingers brushing against hers, soft and feathery.

'I'll leave you to your work.' She opened the door.

'Come back again,' he said softly – so softly that when Anna turned to look at him and his head was bent over his piece of paper once more, she wondered if she had imagined it.

In the kitchen Greta was sitting next to the oven, staring at her hands.

'Are you all right?' Anna asked.

Greta looked up. 'Fine. My hands are failing me. They saw... they know that I'm not what I used to be.'

'I'll serve dinner.'

'No. That Liesl will start again.'

'Just let me try. I'll be quiet.' Anna crouched down and took Greta's hands in hers. She could not lose her; she could not risk someone else overseeing her.

'Just make sure you don't talk to them, don't look at them. Perhaps...' Greta's eyes lit up.

'Perhaps what?'

'What if I ask Herr Becher if you can wear an old maid's uniform instead of that? That way perhaps Liesl won't notice you as much?'

Anna looked down at her dirtied smock dress, the blue stripes dull against the grubby white. 'We can try.'

'Did you get the list?' Greta asked.

'He says he doesn't need anything, that he can do it without.'

Greta stood, ladled soup into a bowl and handed it to Anna. 'Go outside and eat quickly – see if you can find carrots again. I'll speak to Herr Becher.'

Anna gladly took the hot soup to the garden and burned her throat as she drank it down, barely chewing the soggy vegetables, until she felt the warmth reach her belly.

When she finished, she looked once more to the shed, the light still burning brightly, the figure of Isaac hunched over his piece of paper, a flutter in her stomach as she thought of his fingers touching hers and the way he studied her face like Piotr had once done – searing it into his memory, he had told her.

She licked the bowl, taking every last smear of soup, and turned away from the shed, from Isaac, from a memory of Piotr that did not belong here.

CHAPTER SIX

Isaac

Isaac could not concentrate after Anna left him. He thought of her watery brown eyes staring dolefully at him, reminding him of the way Hannah would sometimes look at him. Her lip was cracked, revealing a small smear of bright crimson, begging her to lick it or for someone to wipe it away.

'Silly old man,' he chastised himself. And yet, he could not settle completely into his task, his ear keen for the sound of her at the shed door once more.

He took his pouch of tools and opened it, laying them in front of him as if he were about to fix a watch. He picked up a tiny screwdriver and held it up to the light, seeing the tiny engravings of his initials on the stem, and then two more letters, H. S. He placed it back down and closed his eyes, letting his forefinger run over the tiny letters, first his and then the others.

It had been a summer day when he had engraved the second set of letters, a day in July when the heat had swamped the village, causing everyone to fling open windows and wedge doors ajar to let any wisp of a breeze cool the inside. He knew he had to be quick that day – Hannah had told him not to be late, not today of all days, yet he had wanted to do this first so he could show her at dinner.

He had hurried home after closing the shop, ignoring the cries from his friends who sat outside the tavern with half-filled tumblers of beer, the pouch of tools in one hand and a small box in the other – a pocket watch his father had given him, and now it was time to give it to someone else.

Before he reached the crossroads, ready to turn left towards his home, he saw a figure running towards him, stirring up the summer dust with their heels, their hands in the air, waving. He stopped, waiting for them to reach him – he knew he had to wait. As they came closer, the pouch of tools and the gift fell from his hands, ready to take them in an embrace.

'You look deep in thought.' A voice woke him from his reverie.

He looked up to see Herr Becher, wrapped in a thick black woollen coat, wearing black leather gloves and a hat with the insignia of the Reich – an eagle – glowing in plated gold from the centre.

'I'm sorry,' Isaac said at once, standing quickly, assuming that he had done something wrong already.

'Whatever for? I got your message – you need nothing to fix the clock? I must say, I am impressed so far – I will be more so when you have completed the task.'

Isaac nodded, his eyes darting to the pile of blankets on the floor, hoping that Becher had not seen them and confiscate them.

'I have another task for you to do today. A small task, but one which will help my wife immeasurably. My son Friedrich has a train set, and the engine is not working. I have tried myself to fix it with him this morning, but it will not run. I have to leave this afternoon and my wife has many things to do, thus the boy needs some entertainment to keep him occupied. I had a thought that you may be able to help?'

'Of course, Herr Becher.' Isaac held out his hands, expecting Becher to give him the toy engine.

'No, no, it is up in the boy's room. There are bits of the track that need fixing too and I haven't the time to bring it all to you. I have forewarned my wife that you shall be in the house, and my assistant, Herr Schmidt, will oversee you. Once you are finished, you will leave and come back to the shed immediately – is that understood?'

'Yes, yes, of course.'

'Wonderful. Wait here, Herr Schmidt will collect you shortly. I wanted to ask you myself, as it is a personal request, very personal indeed, and I would be disappointed if it were not completed to my son's satisfaction.' Becher smiled, and Isaac caught a brief glimpse of his teeth, the incisors long and sharp, the rest of the teeth neatly worn straight so that they looked as though they were not entirely real.

Becher left Isaac for a moment, and Isaac felt fearful suddenly. The smile, the request, there was something about it – a threat perhaps – almost as if Becher were toying with him as a cat plays with a mouse, just before he is to snap its neck.

Schmidt came soon afterwards to collect Isaac, and as he followed Becher's assistant towards the house, he could hear the swish-swish of Schmidt's plump thighs chafing as he walked.

'Up there,' Schmidt said. 'I will be in the study and will come to collect you in one hour.'

Isaac climbed the stairs slowly, not daring to use the polished mahogany stair railing to aid him. As he climbed, he noticed family photographs and paintings of distant relatives adorned the wall, as if with each step he were to be reminded whose home this was. He could feel Schmidt's eyes on his back, and he lowered his gaze to his feet, ignoring the pictures, ignoring the pain as he walked.

A long landing greeted him at the top of the stairs. A rug of scarlet with gold flowers ran the length of it, as closed doors left and right hid the family's rooms.

'Second one on the left,' Schmidt's voice shouted from below. 'Don't touch anything. Be quick. When you're finished, I'll get the maid to clean the room again.'

Isaac nodded and grasped the weighty brass knob, feeling the cool metal under his hand click as he pushed it open then closed it gently behind him.

Isaac looked about the room. On the floor was the train set, completed as he was told it would be, the neat rows of red and green trains lined up at the station where tiny figures waited for their journey. Fake trees were dotted about the landscape, then another station, this one with small cars waiting for the new arrivals outside. The picture in front of him made him smile – as if he were here to play and not to work.

'Shhh,' a voice said.

Isaac, to his surprise, saw a boy, perhaps ten or eleven years old, sitting cross-legged on his single bed, a book by his side, his golden hair shiny and forming a curtain of a fringe over his bright blue eyes.

'I'm here to fix the train,' Isaac said.

'Mother told me to go and play outside,' the boy whispered. 'But I don't like the outside in the cold, so I hid under my bed when she checked.'

'I should come back later…' Isaac walked backwards, his hand feeling for the doorknob.

'No! Don't!' The boy jumped off the bed. 'Please. Mother says you can fix it. Even Papa said you are going to fix the grandfather clock – he says you can fix anything. Please. It's just the engine, the red one, it won't go, and they'll make me study or practise my music if I've nothing else to do. Please?'

Isaac took his hat a few inches off his shaved head and ran his hand over the stubble. 'Let me see,' he said.

He bent down and picked up the engine. Underneath the chassis he unscrewed the plate that held the engine's insides in place, then sat on the floor as he tinkered with the parts.

'Do you live in the shed?' the boy asked him.

'No.'

'Where do you live then?'

'With the others,' he said.

'Which others?'

Isaac sighed – did the boy really not know? 'How old are you?' he asked.

'Eleven. Just.'

'I'll fix the train and then you can play.' Perhaps he was too young to realise what was happening around him.

'I came from school yesterday. They closed it and I had to come here. It's boring here, there's no one to play with.'

'Quite,' Isaac muttered, as he concentrated on the tiny mechanisms.

'You have the same clothes as the maid,' the boy said.

'I do.'

'Her name is Anna, and your name is Isaac – I heard Mother and Father talking. They always think that I cannot hear them – but I think it is because they don't see me – they forget that I am there.'

Isaac smiled to himself; he knew what that felt like too.

'Are you a Jew?'

Isaac nodded.

'I thought so. You're supposed to have long noses though, and sometimes just one eye, and long teeth and long scratchy nails and—'

'Enough!' Isaac slammed the engine down hard on the floor. The boy was startled. 'Do I look like that to you? Look at me,' Isaac demanded.

'No,' the boy said in a quiet voice. 'No, you don't look like the pictures on the posters.'

Isaac picked up the locomotive engine once more, his hands shaking again – not with the pain of arthritis, but with anger.

'I'm Friedrich,' the boy started again. 'I think you should know my name, because I know yours and that's polite, isn't it, to introduce yourself when you meet someone new?'

'It is polite, yes. It is good to meet you, Friedrich.'

'And you, Isaac.'

'Here, I think it is done.' Isaac placed the engine on the line, then moved the broken slats away and re-joined the tracks together. 'It will be a little shorter for your train to run, but it will work.'

Friedrich jumped off his bed where he had been sitting and watched as the engine started to crawl slowly forward, then, picking up speed, it chugged along. Friedrich clapped his hands together in joy and Isaac found himself laughing along with him.

'It works! It really works! You are a magician! Father couldn't fix it and I couldn't fix it, and then you come and it's all fine!'

Isaac stood and watched Friedrich play for a moment, connecting the carriages to the engines, placing the small figurines of passengers at the station to await their train and their onward journey. He wished he could stay and watch the boy forever, the simple joy of playing with a train and naming the stations, the people, and the conversations they would have as they travelled to a foreign land.

'You're welcome, Friedrich,' Isaac said. The boy looked at him and smiled.

Isaac left the bedroom and walked slowly down the stairs, trying to stretch the minutes before he was once more sent to the cold shed, or even worse, back to the camp.

The day disappeared quickly beneath the winter sky, plummeting Isaac into a cold darkness in the shed, with only the thin light of the lamp to aid him. He scribbled more notes on the paper, ready to fix the clock when beckoned, but no one came for him.

He was not used to having no work. He sat and stared at the shed walls, the thin gaps in between each slat that let the icy air creep in so that his warm breath was forever hanging in front of him.

Work would help – it would keep his mind off the hunger that chimed in his belly each minute, causing a rush of saliva to culminate in his mouth, expecting a meal that would not come. Work would also keep his mind away from the camp, from the life he now found himself in. He chuckled to himself in the quiet – he had been so lucky so far – so very lucky. Years of hiding away in his village, in his work, and no one had come for him, and, just as news reached them about the Americans and the British who were drawing closer each day, he was taken.

He chewed at a piece of skin next to his thumb as the door was flung open and Schmidt entered.

'Time to go,' he said, already turning away. Isaac made to stand, his legs feeling wobbly underneath him.

He turned off the lamp and hobbled after Schmidt, the hunger replaced with nausea as he remembered the high fences, the soldiers with guns, and the cold stares of the guards.

But then, it all disappeared – Anna exited the house through the kitchen door, smiling weakly at Isaac as she noticed him.

As Schmidt walked Isaac and Anna back to the camp, Isaac looked behind him at the house, the lamps glaring from the windows, as if the house had sucked in all the light, leaving Isaac in the inky stillness of the night. The sleet from the morning had turned into thick flakes that settled quickly, layering one on top of the other, weighing down branches that creaked and shifted with the load.

Schmidt walked behind them, humming a tune and smoking his cigar, now and again asking them to stop – Isaac was sure for no other reason than to slow them down and keep them in the cold for as long as possible.

Isaac's arm bumped into Anna's and she flinched.

'I'm sorry,' he whispered to her.

'No. I'm sorry. It's not you. It's this place – every time I hear something, or someone touches me, my body just can't help itself.'

'You have been here long?'

Anna shook her head. 'Since September last year. You know, they only opened the women's block last year – I was one of the first. I often wonder, why me, why now?'

Isaac chuckled. 'I have just been wondering the same thing myself. Almost five years of freedom and now here I am.'

'Piotr would have called it fate,' she said. 'Kismet. Like we have no choice.'

'Piotr?' Isaac asked.

'My fiancé. He believed in destiny and even that dreams could tell you things.'

'And you don't?'

Anna shrugged, her shoulder now brushing his comfortably, adding a smidgen of warmth to his body. 'I don't know what to believe anymore.'

'Hush!' Schmidt commanded from the rear. 'You think I can't hear you two whispering? Do you think I am stupid?'

'No, Herr Schmidt,' they answered, almost in unison.

'Stop walking. Stand here for a moment, seeing as you are so keen to be in each other's company.'

Isaac stopped and Anna moved closer to him, her body trembling with the cold. He wished he could put his arm around her to warm her, but instead he did only what he could and leaned back into her, so that they looked as though they were conjoined twins, both of them feeding heat off each other, both of them calming their fears.

CHAPTER SEVEN

Friedrich

'Eat your food, Friedrich, stop playing with it,' his mother admonished, as they sat around the shining dinner table for their supper.

The silverware had been cleaned that day, Friedrich could tell; there was still a lingering scent of polish in the air.

'He fixed it then?' his mother asked his father.

'He did,' his father responded, through a mouthful of potato.

'I don't like him being in the house. What if he hurts us?'

'He won't, my dear, why would he? Besides, I will have Schmidt watch him tomorrow when he works on the clock. He says that he has figured out the problem and will need only a few hours.'

'A few hours!' his mother cried, and Fredrich looked at her, expecting her to have had one of her fainting spells.

'Now, now, Liesl.' His father stood and poured her a measure of dark liquid into a heavy crystal glass. 'Drink this and calm your nerves.'

'I can watch him?' Friedrich offered. 'I can. I can stand next to him.'

'You'll go nowhere near that Jew!' his mother shouted at him. 'Who knows what diseases he has, or what he likes to do to young boys.'

'He's not like that—' Friedrich began.

'And how would you know what he is like?' his mother asked, narrowing her eyes at him.

Friedrich stopped himself from saying more, from telling them that he had spoken to Isaac about being a Jew and that perhaps they had got it all wrong. Instead, he cut into his meat and ate.

'You need to understand, Friedrich,' his father began, 'that people like that man, and the woman who sometimes serves us, are not like us. They are here to do as we ask them, and it makes them happy – they want to make us happy. So, you don't talk to them, you just tell them what to do, and if they will not, you tell me or your mother.'

Friedrich nodded and swallowed the meat.

'Father, can I ask a question?' he ventured.

'You can. I will decide if I answer.'

'Where does the man live? Does he live in the shed?'

His mother and father looked at one another, and Friedrich saw his mother shake her head ever so slightly.

'They live in a town,' his father said. 'Not far from here. They live all together in a place that keeps them away from us and keeps us all safe.'

'Can I go there?' Friedrich asked, forgetting to ask if he could, in fact, ask another question.

A wail escaped his mother and she went limp for a moment in her seat. His father rushed to her side and helped prop her up, her eyes already open and alert once more. He pressed the glass of brown liquid to her lips, which seemed to revive her quickly.

'Friedrich, you may not go anywhere but this house, is that understood? I will not say it again to you. You may go in the garden, but only use the side gardens, not the rear now that the watchmaker is using the shed. And as you've upset your mother, you may go to your room.'

Friedrich stood, his legs shaking a little. He could see the anger in his father's eyes, hear the words that had come out of his mouth, so clipped and threatening that he knew to disobey would mean a severe punishment.

'I'm sorry, Mother,' he said at the dining room door.

She looked at him briefly and gave a weak smile, then waved him away, the rest of his dinner growing cold on the table.

As he left, he saw Schmidt sitting in the living room, a foot propped up on a footstool, a glass of amber whiskey in his hand. Friedrich watched him for a moment as he drank, as if he were the man of the house.

'What are you looking at?' Schmidt barked, as his red face turned to look at him. He stood, placed the glass on the polished table, and walked towards Friedrich.

'What's the matter?' His father appeared behind him.

'Nothing,' Friedrich answered, his head turning from his father to Schmidt.

'He was staring at me, almost as if he wanted something. Tell me, Friedrich, what do you want?' Schmidt bent down, his face close to Friedrich's so he could smell the liquor, the stale cigarette smoke and Schmidt's sweat.

'He's been difficult since he got home,' his father said, and pushed Friedrich towards the staircase. 'Go to bed!'

As Friedrich took each step, he could hear his father asking Schmidt to come and have some dinner, his mother's voice singing out that she, too, wanted Schmidt for company.

Why did they make me come here? he wondered as he opened his bedroom door. *What was the point?*

He sat on the edge of his bed, imagining Schmidt eating the rest of his dinner, his stupid fat face shovelling the food in like a pig that scoffs at the trough.

Friedrich looked about him – at the train set, at the few books on the shelves – and wondered what he could do. His room was beginning to tire him already. The train set had provided some relief that afternoon from the boredom he felt, but he could not fathom spending all his time in this room, or in a side garden, and since he was told not to go to the rear garden, where the shed was, it was all he could think about.

He left his room and tiptoed across the hallway, tried the doors opposite once more. The windows here would provide a view of the shed, and at least he could watch Isaac, and perhaps see the town in which they lived – maybe even see some children playing. But the doors were still steadfastly locked and there was no way that he would be able to pick a lock.

'Otto could do it,' he mumbled to himself, as he sat on the edge of the bed. 'I should have asked Isaac – he could have done it, and he would have had to do as I told him, just like Father said.'

Then he realised he was talking to himself like Anna, and he giggled.

He picked up a book from his dresser and lay down to read about the ancient Egyptians, and how they made their mummies and pyramids. He was halfway through the first page when there was an almighty crash downstairs.

He went over to the door and opened it a crack. He could hear his mother's voice, loud, sobbing, screaming at his father. 'How can you ask me to bear living here, day after day? No one wants to visit me here – my friends will not come! And who can blame them! With that place just a mile or so from us, with them infecting our very house!'

Then Schmidt's voice, soothing, trying to calm his mother when it was usually his father who would do this.

Friedrich could not hear what his father said in response, only the rumble of his voice as he spoke. He didn't dare leave the bedroom, didn't dare peek at the scene unfolding below.

Within moments, there was quiet, and then the sound of a door closing. He heard his father's footsteps and then his voice, more clearly now. 'She's broken the damn phone,' he said.

Friedrich lay back on his bed. 'Father is talking to himself now too. Perhaps we are all going mad.'

CHAPTER EIGHT

Isaac

The morning broke as it had done the day before. Adam the Kapo screamed a wake-up call at them as they lay half asleep in their bunks, huddled into balls to try and find warmth.

As Isaac dressed and washed his face in the scummy water that others had already used, and took his piece of bread and weak black coffee, he noticed Jan looking at him and then whispering to another man whose large round eyes were bloodshot, his cheeks hollowed.

Isaac sat on the edge of his bunk and ate slowly, trying to pretend he was simply at home, having breakfast before going to work.

'You got yourself a nice job then?' The man with the hollowed cheeks stood in front of him, leaning his arm on his bunk.

Isaac looked at Jan, who sat on a lower bunk across from him, an unlit cigarette between his fingers.

'I hear our Kapo singled you out – you know him, do you?' the hollow-cheeked man asked.

Isaac shook his head. 'I don't know anyone.'

'You see that cigarette Jan has? You know, there are better ways to get things you want, or things you need, in ways that don't make you a traitor.'

'I'm not getting anything,' Isaac said. 'Nothing.'

'Apart from a nice little job with our Commandant? Maybe an extra meal or two? And what do you do for that exchange, eh? Tell him about some of us – what we do? You know, last night, two of our friends were beaten to death, right out there at roll call – which you missed. Don't you think that's a nice coincidence?' The man came closer to Isaac, then took the last of his bread from his hand and ate it.

'That's enough.' Jan stood now. 'All my friend is saying, Isaac, is that if you are perhaps helping them for your own good, then it's not too late. You don't have to be like Adam, you understand?'

Isaac saw Adam, the Kapo, shoving an elderly man, whose arms were over his head in expectation of a beating, from the bunkhouse.

'Do you understand, Isaac?' Jan repeated.

Isaac nodded. 'I'm not helping them. It's just a job. It's not my fault.'

Jan patted Isaac's hands. 'I believe you.'

'I don't,' the hollow-cheeked man said. 'I'll be watching you, Isaac.'

The pair walked away from him and Isaac looked at his hands, which were now shaking from fear as well as the cold.

That afternoon, Isaac found that he wasn't alone in the shed. After he had fixed the grandfather clock, Schmidt took him back to the garden and handed him a small bag containing wristwatches and pocket watches of all sizes and shapes, all of which were silent.

'I'll let Herr Becher know that you were successful,' Schmidt said, as he left Isaac outside the shed. 'He requested that once you completed your task, you fix what is in that bag.'

'To whom do they belong?' Isaac asked, opening the bag to peek inside.

'None of your business. Fix them.' Schmidt walked away, leaving Isaac feeling somewhat lost. He had hoped for something more when the grandfather clock had begun to chime once again, ticking away, the cogs and wheels moving perfectly together, the chime for midnight and midday ready for the hands to strike the hour.

If he had been at home, he would have taken a drop of whiskey to celebrate, and if it had been when Hannah was alive, he would have told her all about it, feeling as proud as if he had cracked a safe that held the King of England's crown.

He opened the shed door and was startled to see a hunched figure wearing the same uniform as himself, sitting on his chair, his head bowed as he napped.

Isaac coughed, once, twice, then a third time, louder.

A man, perhaps the same age as Isaac, with heavy eyebrows that almost obscured his eyes, and lips white with cold, raised his head.

'You're new,' the man said to Isaac.

'I was going to say the same thing to you,' he replied.

'I'm not new. Rather, they had little work for me lately, but now I hear they can't bear all the dead leaves and would like them to be removed. They like to remove things.' The man stood and smiled at Isaac, which unnerved him as the smile reached the man's eyes – no one he had known in this place so far could claim such genuine happiness.

'What have they got you doing, then?' the man asked.

Isaac lifted the bag. 'Fixing these.'

The man did not wait for Isaac to show him; instead, he grabbed the bag from Isaac's hands and began to take out each watch.

'You know where these are from, don't you?' the man said.

Isaac shook his head.

'From the camp. From our belongings. They'll sell them, or gift them to the guards, you'll see.'

Isaac took the bag roughly from him and began to place the watches back inside.

'I'm Levi, by the way.' The man did not seem upset at Isaac's briskness. 'And you are?'

'Isaac. Are you going to be in here much longer? I've work to do.'

Levi suddenly laughed. 'My, my, you sound as though this is your shed, your workshop. Good for you, Isaac, good for you.'

Levi picked up a rake and, whistling a tune, made his way out of the shed, leaving Isaac with the bag of inmates' belongings.

Isaac had been working less than an hour when Herr Schmidt came to the shed and handed him a telephone, the base broken and the wires escaping like octopus tentacles. 'Fix this,' he said, and placed it on the homemade table. 'They'll need it today, so be quick.'

Schmidt left as quickly as he'd entered, and Isaac heard him shout something at Levi, who did not reply.

The phone was dented in the base, a crack along the stem. He had never fixed a phone before – had never owned one either.

He stood and opened the shed door, calling out to Levi, who ambled over, the smile on his face once more.

'What can I do for you?' Levi asked, leaning on the rake.

'Have you seen a telephone before?' Isaac showed him the mess that he had in his hands.

'I actually had one myself. Two, if you count the one in my office. I'm not so sure I know how they work, mind you.' Levi looked closer at the wires, the base. 'Seems to me those wires there need to be connected to the base – see where they have come away. Then, I suppose, check the earpiece and the speaker, make sure they are all connected too – I can't see how else you could do it.'

'They need it by today,' Isaac said worriedly, looking at the foreign object.

'You'll do it, I can tell,' Levi said.

'And how can you tell?'

'You just look like you can.'

Isaac did not look at him, his gaze on the telephone, imagining using it, calling someone for help – but who?

'You need to smile more, you know,' Levi suddenly said.

'What are you talking about?' Isaac raised his head.

Levi was staring at him as if he could read Isaac's thoughts and see his memories, his brows knitted together as he spoke. 'I mean it, you need to smile more. Start smiling and soon you'll feel happier. It works.' Levi bent down to pick at some weeds.

'There is nothing to smile about.'

Levi stopped pulling at the weeds and propped himself on the wooden rake once more. 'You have known me what, an hour or so at best, but have you seen me without a smile?'

'You look as though you are simply having a rest from tending your own garden; leaning on your rake as though you have all the time in the world.'

'And I do. Have all the time in the world. You didn't answer my question. Have you ever seen me without a smile?'

'No,' Isaac answered. 'It makes you look simple. As if you don't see what is going on around you.' He lowered his gaze and began to look at the mess of wires once more, Levi's questioning unnerving him – reminding him a little of Hannah, who always told Isaac to stop being so serious, to try and look at the world through kinder, happier eyes. 'You can't find happiness here,' Isaac said simply.

'You know, Isaac, my home was taken from me. My business. My wife and children sent to a different camp, where I expect they are dead or dying.'

'And yet you smile.'

'Yet I do. Can't you see, Isaac? They have taken everything from me – everything. But this – my humour, who I am – they cannot. I was happy before in my life. Always joking, playing, smiling. I decided that no matter how I feel, no matter what they try and take away from me, I will keep this humour, I will keep who I am. Who were you before you came here?'

Isaac stopped and looked up once more. 'Does it matter?'

'Of course it matters. Come on, who were you before?'

'I was Isaac, with a dead wife. I was alone with my workshop and my watches. I had friends who I ate and drank with. I had God. But now, I have nothing.'

'You still have God,' Levi said, opening his arms towards the sky as if God Himself were visible above him.

Isaac looked at the grey mulch of clouds overhead and tried to see through them – above them – towards the heavens. 'I do. But I am not sure he can hear me anymore. Not from here.'

'He can hear you anywhere, my friend.'

'You should work. If they see you not working, what do you think they are going to do? Share a joke with you?'

Levi suddenly laughed. 'See, I knew you were funny! Share a joke with me, I like it. Do you think they would like my joke about Hitler – here.' Levi leaned towards Isaac and said quietly, 'Hitler and Göring are standing on top of the Berlin radio tower. Hitler says he wants to do something to put a smile on the Berliners' faces. Göring says, "Why don't you jump?"'

Despite himself, Isaac felt himself smile.

'You'll laugh one day – one day, I promise you, you will laugh again. And in the meantime, I will keep you company and try my best to make you see some humour here.'

'You need to keep that joke quiet,' Isaac said. 'If anyone hears you…'

'Then what? They'll kill me?'

Isaac watched Levi as he resumed raking the dead leaves off the grass, his eyes bright, his movements swift like a dancer. Just a man tending his garden, who looked as though he had all the time in the world.

He returned to the shed and set about trying to understand the mechanics of the phone, yet Levi's grin, his voice, seemed embedded in his mind. He replayed the joke Levi had told and allowed himself to laugh. He remembered, then, a time when Hannah had told him he would smile again and laugh again, when the engravings that he had made on his tools would not haunt him so much. Had she been right? Had he smiled since then?

He thought of the grandfather clock he had fixed in the Bechers' home, that now neatly chimed and called the minutes and hours. All the time that had gone before, all that had happened to him, each minute ticking quietly by, and he had not laughed in years, not felt a ball of joy grow in his stomach as he went about his day, his life. He had surrounded himself with the ticking of time, yet had paid no attention to it as it had propelled him forward.

But Levi – Levi who had had just as much despair in his life, still swore to cherish the time, to smile and to find some measure of joy.

He thought of Hannah once more. She had been right – he would smile and laugh again one day, but he never thought it would be here.

He shook his thoughts away and began his new task to fix the telephone. After some time, he felt he had a grasp on what each wire might do, and where it should be connected. Oddly, he felt content. It was a new, strange task, but he was engrossed in fixing something he had never seen before.

It was not long until he was interrupted again. He didn't look up when Levi entered but continued concentrating on his task.

'What are you doing?'

Isaac looked up, surprised to see the boy there, his hands in his pockets, a miniature image of his father.

At first he smiled, happy to see him, and then his smile disappeared. 'You're not to be in here. Go back to your train set,' he told the boy.

Friedrich ignored him and his eyes moved about the shed, as if he were looking for treasure.

'It's cold in here,' he said.

'It is. That's why you should go back to the house and keep warm.'

'What are you doing?' Friedrich asked again.

'Fixing this.' Isaac sighed and showed him the telephone.

'Mother threw it last night,' Friedrich said.

'She did?'

'Yup. She threw it at Father. They think I don't know but I heard them.'

'How's the train?' Isaac asked.

'It works. But Father says I can't play with it too much. He says that I am almost a man and can't play with toys much anymore, so Schmidt told me to find something else to do. He sent me to the side gardens, but there's not much there – nothing to play with. He said I have to keep out of his way because he has important work to do for Father, but I saw him sitting in the living room with Mother and they were laughing at something, so I don't know if that's what he meant, or…' Friedrich raised his arms as if in question.

'So you came here – nothing to play with here either.'

Friedrich sat on the floor of the shed in front of Isaac and crossed his legs. He picked up a small golden screw. 'What's this?'

'A screw.'

'What's it for?'

'To hold the base of the telephone together.' Isaac felt something – a memory trying to resurface, but he pushed it down; the boy's questions reminded him of someone else.

'I always want to use the telephone, but I don't. I don't have anyone to call. Father says it's for business.'

Isaac nodded and gently tried to coax a wire out of the speaker, to connect it to another thread of wire. His hands shook. 'You should go and play. If your mother finds you here, you will get in trouble.'

'She's busy with Schmidt.'

'Your father then.'

'He left this morning for Munich.'

Isaac sighed and lifted his gaze to the boy, who now had his chin balanced in cupped hands. 'You'll be bored here.'

'Teach me to fix something,' Friedrich said.

'I can't.'

'You can and you have to. I know who you are, and you have to do as I say.' Friedrich stood now, his hands on his hips. 'You have to. You are the Jew who can fix things, but Father says that does not mean you are not an animal like the rest.'

Isaac placed the tools on the small table next to him. He looked Friedrich in the eye. 'I am no animal.' His voice was firm, cold. 'You need to leave now.'

The boy's bravado left him as soon as it had arrived, and he dropped his hands from his waist to hang limply by his side.

'Go. Now.' Isaac pointed to the door.

Friedrich began to walk away, then suddenly he turned and kicked at the phone base that Isaac had placed to one side on the floor. He sent it across the dusty boards where it cracked against a metal jerry can.

'Fix it,' Friedrich said angrily, then left.

Isaac waited a few minutes after the boy had left, until he stood to fetch the base of the telephone from where he had kicked it.

The boy hadn't meant what he said, he knew. He could tell when parents had put words into children's mouths, and he could hear the boy's father speaking through him as he told him what to do.

His bad leg almost gave way underneath him as he tried to kneel to pick up the phone base. He rubbed at it and wished he could sit in a warm bath, letting the water lap over the muscles and tendons, releasing them and allowing him some relief.

As he picked up the base, he knocked over the jerry can. Isaac crawled towards it to set it right again and saw that it had fallen into a small hole in the ground, where a floorboard had come away. He picked up the can and then he placed his hand in the hole, out of curiosity, almost as if he expected to find his grandfather's pocket watch inside, as if he were back in his shop once more.

Instead, his fingers found a cloth bundle. He pulled it out. The red cloth was cut from a piece of one of the old blankets he had been using in the shed, and it was bound and tied with a shoelace. Isaac looked behind him at the door, then back at the cloth bundle. Slowly, he untied the shoestring and uncovered a sheaf of papers, each one covered with diary entries, journaling, letters and drawings, the initials J. A. L. written in each corner.

'Isaac!' Levi's voice was coming from outside. 'Can I come in? I know you are busy, and I'm scared to interrupt you!' His voice was almost jovial.

Isaac quickly wrapped the pages back inside their makeshift cover and placed them inside the hole, moving the plank of wood on top.

He stood and opened the door to Levi.

'May I?' Levi grinned at him and doffed his cap, as if he were wearing a bowler and the two of them were going to sit in an office and have a cordial business meeting.

Isaac smiled. 'Come in.'

CHAPTER NINE

Anna

'You need to stop staring,' Greta warned.

Anna turned from washing the pots in the sink, realising that once again her eyes had strayed to the kitchen window, watching the lamplight in the shed.

She had not seen Isaac that morning when Schmidt had walked her to the house – her workday beginning an hour or so before his, it seemed. She had wanted to speak to him again, just like they had when they had walked back to the camp; she wanted to hear his soft voice and precise words, as if she measured them out before saying them, each one important. Just like Piotr.

'He fixed the clock this morning. Madam has just been taken out by that Schmidt in the car – I heard him telling her that it would cheer her up after having Isaac in the house all morning.'

Anna turned to look at Greta who was kneading a ball of dough, her hands floured white, a smear of it on her cheek where she had brushed strands of escaping hair from her face.

'Where did she go?' Anna leaned towards her and wiped away the dusting of flour from her cheek.

'Shopping, I imagine. Doubt we'll see her until tomorrow. Herr Becher is in Munich for two days too.'

'Did Friedrich go with her?'

'Ha! No.'

'So she'll have to come home today, to take care of him.' Anna opened a tin that held the last of the cake, and readied it on a blue china plate to give to the boy when she found him in the house.

'She's forgotten she's got a son. She won't be home today – you mark my words; she'll stay at one of her friends' so she can moan about her difficult life.'

Anna turned to finish the washing up, cleaning the last plate, and then began to dry them, feeling suddenly weary, as if her legs were going to give way from underneath, leaving her in a heap on the floor.

'Once you're finished in here, get the bedrooms and bathrooms cleaned whilst she's out. We'll tell her I did their bedroom, all right?'

Anna did not answer; it took all her energy to keep drying the plates and pots.

'Did you eat that bread I gave you yesterday?' Greta eyed her as her old hands stopped kneading the dough, wiping them now on her apron.

Anna nodded. She had meant to, but once back in the camp, the large lump of bread in her pocket began to feel like a selfish treat. The other women were completing harder tasks than her, kept out in the cold, whilst she was in the warmth of a house. Despite her own hunger, she'd given the bread away.

'Here, sit for a minute.' Greta pulled out a chair for her, poured her some coffee and went to the larder. She came back and placed in front of Anna a lump of cheese, a slice of cold chicken and some more bread.

'Eat it. I want to see that you eat it.' Greta sat on the chair opposite and watched Anna take each bite.

'I can't feed you all. God knows I wish I could.' Greta wrung her hands as she spoke. 'What with Levi and that Isaac and you, it's hard to get you much without it being noticed. I've been making more bread, but Frau Becher has noticed how much flour I am asking for, so I had to lie and say I spilled a bag. You can't keep giving it away, Anna – you have to eat too.'

'I felt guilty,' she said as she swallowed a mouthful then drank back some coffee, her head feeling less woozy, her eyes becoming alert once more.

'I'll make a soup.' Greta suddenly stood. 'I can do that. There's leftover vegetables and some meat. It'll be watery, mind you, but I can do it, and that will keep you three in some food for a few days.'

With that, Greta began to gather the carrots, onions and potatoes, and set them down to chop. Anna stood and placed her hand on Greta's shoulder. 'Thank you,' she said, leaving Greta to cry over the onions that stung her eyes.

Anna started in the Bechers' bedroom – a room she had never been in before. The bed dominated the room; a four-poster with drapes tied back with tasselled, woven purple ropes.

The bed was unmade, covers half on the floor, even a pillow, as if Frau Becher had fought with herself in her sleep. Anna opened the curtains, letting the weak light filter in, then opened the window a crack so the fresh air could take away the cloying scent of rich perfume that Frau Becher must have sprayed on herself before she left the house.

Her dressing table was full of small glass jars, some holding cream, others perfume, each topped with a silver monogrammed lid. Anna smiled, thinking of her own set, which her mother had put away for the day she got married. She traced the curlicued L and B on a powder lid, then took her hand away quickly, as if Frau Becher would know what she was doing.

She began by making the bed, enjoying the sensation of the soft cotton sheets in her hand, wishing she could lie back and feel the feather-stuffed pillows under her head. She picked up Liesl's silk dressing gown and nightgown, both pink, with a matching pattern of tiny birds and flowers. She placed the nightgown on the end of the bed and the dressing gown in the wardrobe. As she straightened the silk robe on its hanger, Anna could not tear her eyes away from the other clothes in the wardrobe. She took her index finger and touched the edge of each dress, shirt and skirt, feeling the soft textures. Her finger stopped when she reached a cornflower-blue dress with small yellow flowers. It was like her mother's – almost identical, right down to the darker blue belt that slipped around the waist. The wind was knocked out of her as a memory took hold. She was young, maybe four or five, and she was sitting with her mother, brother and father on a picnic rug. Her mother wanted to dance, and Anna took her hands and the two of them twirled around and around, singing a song her mother had learned from the radio.

Even in the bedroom she could smell the flowers, the clean water from the stream that rippled nearby. She could feel the wind in her hair as she twirled, and her mother's soft yet firm hands in hers, never letting her fall.

A loud shot peppered the air outside, bringing her back to the room. She looked out of the window. She knew where the gunshots came from, and her heart beat faster as they continued to ring out. Then, silence.

As if someone else had taken over her body, she reached out and took the dress from its hanger, quickly undressing herself and stepping into the flowery gown.

She did not button it; she did not tie the belt. She simply stood, the dress large over her thin frame, and ran her hands over her hips, her breasts, as if seeing them for the first time. They had changed, she had changed.

She turned and looked at herself in the full-length mirror, the cap still on her head. She removed the cap, held it limply in her hand and stared at her reflection. Her head seemed too large for her body now, her hair dull, lank, and stretched over her scalp into a tight bun. Her eyes were larger too, flecks of green in the brown, deep black rings underneath them, and her lips were chapped and raw. Anna spoke to the reflection: 'Who are you?' The girl in the mirror matched her movements. 'Are you really me?' she asked.

Suddenly a ball of anger rolled in her belly, and her hands lashed out and knocked all of the bottles of cosmetics from the dressing table, sending them rolling onto the floor. One smashed, and as soon as it did, emptying its liquid contents on the wooden floor, Anna came to her senses.

She wiped away the tears that had wetted her face, and the mucus from underneath her nose. She had broken something. She kneeled down and picked up the shattered bottle, not knowing what to do with it.

Then she quickly found her own clothes and began to undress. It was then that she saw a pair of eyes in the mirror that were not her own. A reflection of the boy – of Friedrich – standing in the doorway. She turned quickly, but he was gone.

'I broke this.' Anna's hand shook as she showed Greta the perfume bottle.

Greta looked at Anna's face intently. 'I'll tell her I did it.'

'But you'll get in trouble,' Anna said, knowing that Liesl took every chance to complain about Greta's age, how the plates rattled, how slowly she moved.

'And what will they do to me? Send me back to my home, that is all. You would face much worse. It's all right.' Greta patted Anna's hand and took the bottle away. 'It'll be all right.'

That evening, Anna was back in the camp early as there was no one to serve at the house.

She sat with Nina and Joanna, who looked ready to fall asleep in their bowls of soup, which was clear and held a piece of carrot.

Anna had eaten Greta's soup earlier, and allowed Nina and Joanna to share her meal.

'You're not hungry?' Joanna asked.

'I'm all right.'

'You look really pale,' Nina said, her eyes wide with worry.

'I was busy all day, that's all. I just need to sleep,' Anna looked down at her hands, not daring to raise them to her nose to check if she still smelled of Liesl Becher's scent. She picked at a ragged nail and tore it off so it bled, the pain a welcome distraction.

'You're bleeding!' Nina reached over to take Anna's hand in hers, but Anna drew it away and placed it on her lap, allowing the blood to drip onto the rough cotton.

Merely a minute later, the women were ordered out of the mess hall, all of them walking slowly as if their legs had been filled with lead.

Anna was glad to get to her bunk for the first time since she had returned to the camp. She wanted the solitude, the quiet.

She lay down and pulled her blanket over her, turning to face the wall, thinking of the boy's reflection in the mirror, his expressionless face. She felt sick. She knew he would tell his mother, and she in turn would tell her husband, and then – she couldn't bear to think.

Nina's body was next to Anna's, curling around her as soon as the other women had silenced themselves into sleep.

'What's wrong?' Nina asked.

Anna did not turn to look at her friend. 'Nothing.'

'Tell me, Anna, I know something is wrong. Please.'

'I did something stupid.'

'What? What did you do?'

Anna shifted so she was now face to face with Nina. 'I made a mistake. I don't know what happened – one minute I was fine, and then the next it was as though there was someone else in my body, making it move and do things, and I couldn't stop it.'

Anna told Nina of wearing Liesl Becher's dress, of the perfume bottle and of the boy who had seen her in his mother's bedroom, dressed in her clothes.

'Maybe it wasn't someone else who made you do those things. Maybe it was you.'

'I don't know what you mean,' Anna replied, sniffing as silent tears ran over her face once more.

'I mean that maybe you, the person that's deep inside, which we have to keep hidden from everyone, maybe she came out, and for a minute you were yourself.'

'I was angry. I was so angry, Nina, and I don't know, I felt a kind of disgust when I saw myself, but it was more than that – I just can't find the words to explain it.'

'That's *you*, the deep-inside you.'

'No. I was never like that – never – I was always happy, and I never had feelings like that before.'

'But the secret you, she's changed. After this you won't be like before, you will be different.'

'My darling Nina.' Anna wanted to laugh. 'You do surprise me sometimes. Perhaps you should study philosophy when you are free.'

'And not dance? I hardly think so!'

'You could be a dancing philosopher!'

The two women giggled, and someone hushed them. They lay in silence for a little while.

'I keep thinking of my brother Kuba.' Nina's whisper was barely audible. 'I can't help thinking that maybe he is dead.'

'Hush. No, he is not. You know he was working just months ago, and was safe.'

'The pyres were burning again. I have nightmares that he was in them.'

'Things have changed, Nina. The guards seem on edge, the work is harder and the hours longer. How could he possibly get word to you at the moment? It would be impossible. Trust me. He is fine, Nina. He must be.'

Anna allowed Nina to turn away from her so she could place her arm around her waist, the two of them fitting together like two pieces of the same puzzle.

There was silence, then Nina whispered, 'Tell me about Elias.'

'You know about him.'

'I know. But if you tell me maybe it will help, maybe you will feel close to him again and that will help you through to the end?'

'There is nothing to say, Nina.'

'You never talk about how it happened. It's as if he just disappeared.'

'He did.'

'But how?'

'Why do you want to know, Nina? Why?' Anna's voice was harsh now.

'I just – I miss Kuba. I don't know. I want to know so if he is dead, if he isn't coming back to me, then I'll know I can cope, because you did.'

Anna's mind had been trying to avoid her brother for months, yet it was as if he were always just on the periphery, waiting for her, begging her to think of him. She scrunched her eyes closed. 'I can't, Nina, I can't say it out loud.'

Nina did not answer, and Anna waited until she could hear Nina's breathing settle; only then did she allow herself to remember her brother.

Elias had been funny. He always joked – trying to find the humour in things. Even when they came for them in the middle of the night, and they had to pack just one bag each, he still tried to make Mother smile and make Anna laugh.

'It's like an adventure,' he had said, as they walked towards the train station amongst a throng of others that shuffled along the pavement like ants, simply following the leader. 'Just think, we can tell this story when we are old and grey, Anna. You will tell my grandchildren how I did a funny walk to try and make Mother smile, and I will tell your grandchildren how you were so brave.'

Seeing that her mother's eyes were downcast, as if she could not bear to look ahead of her to see where her journey would take her, Anna had held her mother's hand.

'Remember that day when we were flying kites on that hill?' Elias asked, trying to get her to think of something else.

She did remember.

'It was that red kite we had drawn a face on, and the wind took it so I ran down the hill as fast as I could, trying to catch it, and I fell. Do you remember that, Anna – how I fell and tumbled and you came running after me, and when you reached me I was in a heap, laughing and laughing, and you laughed too… remember that, Anna?'

She looked at her brother then and realised how scared he really was, how the memories he was trying to locate were not really for her or Mother, but for him.

'I remember,' she told him, and forced a smile. 'And remember that time you ripped your trousers on a tree branch, and we had to walk through town to get home and everyone was staring at you? Yet instead of being embarrassed, you told anyone who would listen it was old man Müller who had gone rabid and tried to bite you, ripping your trousers in the process?'

Elias grinned. 'He never forgave me for that.'

'I think he would now,' she told him.

They soon reached the train station, but were not allowed on the platform. Instead, they were herded into a pen of sorts, with a high fence topped with barbed wire. Once they were inside, the gate was locked, and the guards lit cigarettes and talked as if they were not even there.

Anna, Elias and their mother sat on the dusty floor until the sun rose, and were still there when the sun began to set again. They shared what food they had with the others, and water that someone had thought to bring, but soon it was gone, and they still sat in the pen, still not understanding what was happening.

Her mother was ill – her heart, which had plagued her with palpitations for years, was succumbing to the stress, her face pale, and she clutched at her chest, her lips turning a strange blue.

Anna screamed, her own heart racing, her eyes already glazed with tears as she watched her mother struggle for breath. She looked for Elias who was on his feet, running towards the gate, shouting at the guards for help, but they turned to him, then laughed and turned away.

He ran back to Anna, looked at his mother and ran back to the gate once more, this time frantically pulling on it, yelling.

'We need help!' he screamed at them. 'She's dying!'

Someone in the crowd was a doctor and had come to their aid, trying to breathe life into her, but Anna could see it was too late; her eyes had glassed over, her chest still.

'Please! Please!' Elias was still screaming.

Anna looked to him, and saw the guards pointing their guns at him – warning him. She stood, ready to run to him, to tell him to stop, that it was all too late – and then a gun fired.

Anna did not want to remember any more. She did not want to remember how her brother's body fell, crumpled to the ground after the shot rang out. She did not want to remember how she ran to him, seeing his face still contorted with anguish, save for the small bullet hole in his forehead, so neat and round that she could not take her eyes from it, expecting it to be messy, bigger.

The doctor who had tried to help her mother pulled at her arm, trying to get her away, but she had resisted – lifting his head with her hand, feeling the warm, wet, bloody mess at the back of his skull.

She drew her hand away, looking at the crimson that covered it, the blood dripping into the dust.

'Come, get up, come with me.' The doctor had his hands under her armpits, pulling her, then dragging her away as she kicked and screamed and cried.

People were moving; a gate had opened. They were getting on the boxcars.

'You have to come now,' the doctor said.

Anna didn't know how that doctor had got her into the train, how he had helped her to stand and walk. All she knew was that the train began to move, clacking its way away from her home, from her family, her head resting on the doctor's shoulder as she stared at her brother's blood on her hands.

Suddenly, Anna felt Nina's hand on her head, stroking it to soothe her.

'You're crying,' she whispered.

Anna turned to her friend. 'I remembered – I remembered it all.'

CHAPTER TEN

Friedrich

Friedrich stood in his mother's bedroom, staring at his reflection in the mirror. He looked at his gangly frame, his brown trousers and green knitted jumper, and tried to see what Anna had been so sad about.

He had liked his mother's dress on her – it was the same colour as the cap she wore – and he had been about to talk to her, to tell her that she was beautiful, but that was when she had got angry and started to cry, and then he hadn't known what to say.

'What are you doing in here?' His mother was in the doorway, her face flushed, her hands full of bags.

'I had something in my eye,' Friedrich said. 'I was trying to see it.'

She shook her head at him and came into the bedroom. She sat down on the edge of the bed and said, 'Come here, come see what I bought.'

His mother was happy, her eyes bright. She pulled dress after dress from the bags to show him. Friedrich tried to find nice things to say about them, and each thing he did say made her smile.

'You are a good boy,' she said, as she stood and kissed the top of his head.

He wondered whether he should tell her about Anna – whether it would make her happy that he had been a good boy and told her what people had been doing when she was away. 'Mother, I—'

'Go now.' She looked at him. 'I'm tired. You know how tired I get, and your presence will not help.' Her voice had become stern again; that angry crease between her eyebrows was back.

He wandered downstairs, not really knowing what he was planning to do. Perhaps, if he was quiet, and only put the volume low, he could listen to the radio or the gramophone.

With quick steps he entered the living room, and there sat Schmidt once more.

'You again.' Schmidt turned to him. 'You're not allowed in here.'

'I am.' Friedrich stood tall, his hands balled into fists at his side as if he were at school and the dormitory bully was in front of him once more, teasing him for his height, his hair, his baby toys.

Schmidt smiled at him and Friedrich was not sure what to do.

'Come here, Friedrich,' Schmidt said silkily.

Friedrich did not move.

'I said, come here!' Schmidt demanded.

Friedrich walked slowly towards him, his stomach turning over. He stood in front of Schmidt, who sat perched on the edge of the sofa.

Schmidt suddenly grabbed Friedrich's shoulders, and hissed, 'I am the boss in this house when your father is not here – do you understand me?'

Schmidt's eyes were narrowed, his voice different – harsh and guttural – and Friedrich felt like crying.

Suddenly Schmidt began to laugh and sat back into the thick cushions of the sofa. 'Go and play with your toys now, boy. And do as I say – you hear me?'

Friedrich did not answer, did not look behind him, and ran up the stairs to his room where he shut and latched the door.

He lay on his bed until his breathing calmed and the tears had stopped. He wiped his nose with the cuff of his jumper. He wished he could tell his mother what Schmidt had said, but she would either not believe him or she would say that it had been Friedrich's fault.

He had thought that Schmidt would have to be nice to him because of his father, but Friedrich realised that his presence in the house was unwelcome for everyone, including Schmidt – no one wanted him here and they were all happy to make that clear to him.

He looked at the spider cracks in the ceiling, then heard his mother cry out downstairs for Greta – she was hungry, she said, and she would like some whiskey. She had had an exhausting day – she'd take it in the living room; Schmidt was hungry too.

Friedrich wondered how it could be so exhausting, buying things. Whenever he had been taken to a bookshop or a toy shop, he had been full of excitement and when he got home, he couldn't wait to play or read. He wasn't exhausted.

Downstairs the telephone trilled out and his mother's quick footsteps ran to answer it, her voice tinkling as she realised his father had called to say goodnight from Munich.

The telephone. It was fixed – Isaac had done it. Friedrich felt his stomach turn with shame at the way he had spoken to the old man. He had seen how sad his eyes had become, as Friedrich had said those words; the same disappointment he had seen when one day he had kicked a dog in the street for a dare – a look that dug deep into him and made him feel ill.

When he had fallen out with Otto in the past, he had always given him a present to make it all OK again. He could do the same for Isaac. He could give him something – but what?

Friedrich sat on the edge of his bed and looked about his room. There was nothing much here that Isaac would want – schoolbooks, postcards, a few toys. He looked out of the window and saw that it was snowing again, bulbous flakes that promised to change the landscape overnight, whitewashing the grey.

Then, he knew. He knew exactly what Isaac would want.

CHAPTER ELEVEN

Isaac

Elijah was unwell. All night he tossed and turned, the fever grabbing him and making him hot then cold. Isaac did not sleep. He watched Elijah, feeling helpless – he could not even get him water, a cool cloth to calm his forehead.

'He'll be dead before morning,' Jan muttered in the bunk beneath him. 'If he's lucky, that is.'

'Should we tell someone?' Isaac whispered. 'Maybe he should go to the infirmary?'

Isaac heard Jan sigh, then there was a scuffle as he got out of bed. Suddenly Jan's face was in front of Isaac's. 'He's your friend, isn't he?'

'Yes.'

'If you want to help him then I wouldn't bother asking for anything. The infirmary will kill him quicker than if he stays here the night.'

'So there's nothing we can do?'

'You'll be the death of me, Isaac, I can tell,' Jan said, then turned from him and walked quietly down the aisle of sleeping men on their bunks towards the rear of the bunkhouse. Within minutes he was back, and he placed something on Elijah's forehead, so that he immediately fell silent.

'What have you done?' Isaac made to get out of bed.

'Shhh, stay where you are.' Jan turned to glare at him, then went back to concentrating on Elijah.

'What are you doing?'

'There's a secret I have at the back – a hiding place under a loose floorboard. I've been keeping clean snow in there, in cups, so we have a little extra water. All I've done is place some on his head – it is taking the fever down.'

Jan soon climbed back into bed and Isaac lay on his side, his eyes fixed on his friend.

'Thank you,' Isaac said.

'We'll see if it helps. I gave him a small remedy too.'

'A remedy?'

'My father was a chemist. I know plants, what their properties can do. When I am at work each day, I take bits of flowers, weeds, anything that I can make into a salve or a painkiller, anything that may help us. What I've given him will either break the fever, or it is too late. We will see how he is in the morning.'

Come morning, Elijah's face was still pale, but his breathing had become softer. Isaac placed his palm on his forehead, the cool skin underneath signalling that Jan's remedy had been effective.

'It worked!' He turned to smile at Jan who was lacing his shoes.

Jan stood and leaned over the sleeping Elijah, pulling back his eyelids, then placing two fingers on the side of his neck to check his pulse. 'I'm not surprised. I'm good at what I do, you know.'

'You were a chemist like your father?'

Jan shook his head. 'I was studying to become a doctor. But then, things changed.'

Isaac thought of Jan and the hollow-cheeked man – how they had branded him like Adam the Kapo, how he had felt unnerved by them, scared even, and yet now he saw Jan caring for Elijah as if he were a newborn baby, stroking back his lank hair still laden with sweat, how he dipped his finger into the water and ran it over his cracked lips.

'I'm not what you think I am,' Isaac said.

Jan looked at him, his large forehead creasing as he thought of his response.

'They just have me fix things,' Isaac continued. 'Watches mostly.' He held his hands open, palms facing up, as if lifting a prayer or a promise to God.

The crease deepened in Jan's brow, then disappeared as he relaxed. 'I believe you, Isaac, I do. The others are suspicious – of course they are. But I believe you.'

'Is it morning?' Elijah suddenly croaked. He looked at Isaac and managed a weak grin.

'It is indeed.' Isaac returned the smile.

'You'll feel weak for a day or so. We're on the same work detail, building a road. I'll help you today.' Jan patted Elijah on his arm. 'You'll be fine.'

'Thank you, Jan,' Isaac said.

'We have to look after each other here,' Jan said.

'We do,' Isaac agreed.

Isaac backed away and allowed Jan to take care of Elijah, a knot in his stomach as he thought of the things the others had been saying about him. All of a sudden, it felt as though everyone's eyes in the bunkhouse were on him, tracking the way he moved, questioning who he really was.

The sun made a rare appearance that afternoon, lightening the chill in the air, the snow yielding to its warmth, its crystals winking in the glow as they melted away.

'Spring's not far away,' Levi said, as he rummaged in the shed to find the shears.

Isaac was glad of Levi's company. It was his third visit to the house, seemingly only brought here when one of the Bechers noticed something in the garden that was amiss. He liked the way Levi spoke – always about a bird he saw, or the bud of a flower in the ground, trying to push its head out. He made Isaac feel almost normal again – as though he were simply in his own workshop and a friend had dropped in for a quick chat.

Isaac watched Levi fumble about, his hands near the jerry can that marked the spot of the loose floorboard and the bundle hidden beneath. *Was it Levi?* Isaac thought, thinking of the initials J. A. L. written in the corner.

'You know, I love spring – the way it all seems new again,' Levi said.

'It's still the middle of winter,' Isaac replied.

'February tomorrow. A nice short month, and then we'll be into spring.'

'February?'

'You have lost track of time, haven't you? That's what happens here. You've been here a week or more.'

Isaac looked at the typewriter in front of him that he had been asked to fix, three others on the floor near his feet. First the train engine, the grandfather clock, the bags of watches that belonged to others, the telephone. *A week. A week or more.* 'It feels longer, and yet at the same time, it feels as though it has been only a day or so.' Isaac shook his head.

'Like I said, you've lost track of time. You will. It's normal. Ah, here!' Levi held up the shears and stood. 'What do you think they would do if I escaped, a pair of shears in my hand, ready to attack?'

'You'd get shot,' Isaac said ruefully.

'Really? I think I'd have a fighting chance. I've thought about it, you know, escaping. Especially from here – we've got the chance to, they forget we are here.'

'Apart from the guards at the gate, and then the guards further down the track, and the fact that you are so tired and weak you wouldn't get far.'

Levi grinned. 'You're right. I'll think of a different way. Shame we are not here overnight. That's when we could make a break for it!'

'You talk as if you are a child. As if this is some sort of adventure,' he scolded, yet he could feel the tug of a smile on his lips.

'I talk as if I am a man who is trying to survive; you talk like a man who has given up.'

'I am surviving,' Isaac responded, then looked at his hands which were dry and chapped, the spidery blue of his veins pulsing against his pale skin.

'At least we have work to do – good work. You know, when they ask me to come here, I am so happy. Otherwise I do nothing all day.' Levi set about sharpening the dull blades of the shears whilst Isaac watched.

'Nothing? I see the others going to work each day.' Isaac thought of poorly Elijah having to dig a new road near the camp, which led through a clump of trees out into the middle of nowhere.

'Nothing. There was work to begin with – so much. They worked us day and night. But you've heard what's happening? The Americans are coming, and the guards know it. All they'll do now is work the sickest until they drop dead doing something mundane. Like I said, I'm glad I have this job.'

Elijah's pale face accosted Isaac – his friend would be worked to death.

'You all right?' Levi was looking at Isaac, his brows creased together as they did whenever he was being serious.

Isaac nodded.

'All right. Well, I've branches to prune.' Levi doffed his cap as was his custom. 'You have yourself a nice day. And, Isaac? Smile and think of good things.'

He left Isaac alone with just the faint tune of him whistling as he worked in the garden. Isaac fiddled with the tool in his hand, trying to do as Levi told him, imagining the Americans arriving, taking him home, where he would sit in his armchair by the fireplace and sink into dreamless sleeps.

'I hope I'm not interrupting you?' Becher's voice came from outside the shed. Isaac quickly stood and opened the door. Becher smiled and waved him outside. 'Come and enjoy some sun for a moment.'

Isaac did as he was told, and stood with Becher as he watched Anna hang some sheets on the laundry line. Isaac noticed that her stripy camp uniform was gone, and in its place she wore a plain brown dress, the cornflower-blue cap still on her head.

'It's a beautiful day, is it not?' Becher said, his eyes not straying from Anna.

'It is.'

'It is a shame,' Becher turned to face Isaac, 'that God would give certain women attributes that would be better on others. Take Anna, for example; a beautiful face, a body that is light and yet womanly. But she is stuck here, and throughout the city there are plump, ugly German women, gems around their necks, who would do better to have this beauty so that it would benefit the Reich.'

Isaac did not know how to reply. His fingers balled into his palms, his nails biting into the skin, the pain stopping his brain from understanding what Becher was really trying to say.

'Now, I have another bag for you. These are a few watches – special pocket watches, in fact – that I was given on one of my trips to Munich. I'd like to gift them to some comrades, yet they need any engravings removed, a polish, a service, before they are ready.'

He handed Isaac the bag, the weight of the watches inside substantially heavier than before.

'I must be going,' Becher said, his eyes once more trailing Anna as she pegged the last sheet. 'I've told the maid to bring you coffee and food each day – I cannot have you wasting away, can I?' He laughed.

Isaac forced a smile, realising that Becher had no idea about Greta's small gifts of food. Perhaps he could save some, take it back to the camp for Elijah?

'Work your magic,' Becher said, walking away, following Anna into the house.

Isaac watched him. He touched Anna's shoulder just before she reached the kitchen door. She turned and Becher said something to her. She smiled, but Isaac could see from her body language that she was terrified.

Becher laughed, then pushed past Anna so that his arm brushed against her chest. When he had gone, Anna looked to her chest, then smoothed her brown dress in place and walked inside after him.

Isaac turned away and spilled the bag of watches onto the table – gold pocket watches, silver, and heavy men's wristwatches, all of good quality. A few were engraved with messages from a wife to a husband, from children to their fathers, birthday wishes and all with love.

Isaac imagined Becher sitting in a smoky bar in Munich, his colleagues next to him, all of them bartering each other's treasures whilst they drank and talked of women, of their rich lives, of the new world they were making for their own children.

'What did Father give you?' Isaac turned to see the boy at the door of the shed, holding something in his hands.

'Watches. More watches.' He turned away from Friedrich, from the meanness of the boy's tongue that could whip him again.

'I brought you these.' Friedrich stepped forward and gave him what had been in his hands. Isaac sat down and looked at the gift – a pair of black woollen gloves, the fingertips cut away.

'My hands are smaller than yours, so I thought if I cut the fingertips out then they would fit you and you could still mend things.'

'Thank you,' Isaac turned the gloves over and then held them out to the boy, 'but I can't take them.'

'Please. It's from me, to say I am sorry for what I said the other day. I wanted to bring them to you sooner, but Mother has been home, and Father. They've gone out now – he's taking her to an opera, they won't be back until late.'

'If they see me with them, they will take them away. It's pointless that I keep them.'

Friedrich sat on an upturned bucket. 'Then hide them in here and just wear them when you're working. They'll keep you warm. If anyone finds them, I'll say I put them in here when I was playing and forgot them.'

Isaac smiled at the boy and pulled the gloves on.

'Are you magic?' the boy asked, his elbows on his knees, his palms upturned to hold his chin.

'Excuse me?'

'I heard Father say that you had to work your magic. Are you then? Magic?'

'I don't know magic, no.'

'That's a shame. If I were a magician, I would make myself disappear from here.'

'And where would you go?'

'I'd go to see my friend Otto. His father lets him build tree-houses. My father won't let me.'

'That sounds like a nice idea.' Isaac picked up a wristwatch, its glass face smashed, the tiny clock face scratched and scarred. He doubted he could mend this one.

'Where would you go?' The boy stood and peered at the watches, and reached out his finger to trace the engravings of birds, ships and flowers etched into the pocket watch cases.

'What do you mean?'

'If you were magic, where would you make yourself go? Would you stay in the town with the others or would you leave?'

'I would go home.'

'Where is that?'

Isaac leaned back in his chair and watched the boy for a moment. Could he really talk to him, share something with him?

Before Isaac could answer, Greta's voice rang out, shouting for Friedrich to come for lunch.

Friedrich looked towards the voice, then at Isaac. The boy grinned and said, 'See you later!' and ran from the shed, his jacket flapping out behind him as if he were really going to take flight, lift from the ground and disappear to Otto's home.

For the third time that day, Isaac found himself smiling.

That afternoon, Anna came to the shed and stood before him, a cup of coffee in one hand and a plate with bread and cheese in the other.

'I was told to bring you something every day. Herr Becher wants to make sure you are fed,' she said.

Isaac cleared a space on his little desk, and Anna placed the cup and plate down.

'You have a new dress,' Isaac said.

'It was Greta's idea, to make me blend in a little better.'

'You need to blend in?'

'Frau Becher doesn't like me being in the house. Maybe this way she won't notice me so much.'

Isaac nodded and thought of the way Becher had noticed her instead.

'I'll bring coffee again this afternoon.' Anna made to leave, then she suddenly reached out her hand to touch the broken wristwatch on the table. She picked it up and placed it on her tiny wrist.

'I've never had a watch,' she said. 'This one... this is so like Father's.'

Isaac leaned over and helped her with the clasp. It was far too large, and drooped over her hand. Anna laughed. 'I look like a child playing with adult things.'

'It can't be fixed, I don't think.' Isaac watched her.

'It can't? Whose is it?'

Isaac shrugged.

'Never mind.' Anna took the watch off her wrist and placed it on the desk. 'At least you have something to keep your mind occupied.'

'You don't?' Isaac held the watch she had removed, noticing that the links of the strap had smaller links between the larger ones.

'Cleaning and cooking doesn't engage your mind. It makes it worse – it wanders free from itself, imagining things, trying to understand things. When I was younger, I had diaries, I would write in them when I couldn't sleep – anything I was scared of, I would write down and then, in the morning, it was as if it had disappeared into the night.'

She smiled weakly at Isaac. 'Silly, I know. I wish I could write my diaries now.'

Anna shrugged then went to the door, leaving Isaac alone to his meal. Her eyes, so much like Hannah's, made him feel protective of her, as though he wanted to wrap her in a blanket and let her tell him all the things she was scared of so he could make them disappear into the night.

Ignoring his coffee and food, he thought of the secret bundle of papers underneath the floorboard, and wondered whether there was perhaps a spare sheet, just one page that he could give to Anna so she could write once more.

He scrabbled around on the dusty floor and prised the board away, taking out the bundle. He did not intend to read anything; he merely wanted to find a gift for Anna. But the first page caught his eye, the sentences calling out to him to be read:

> *Today I remembered the time that Father took me fishing. It was a day much like today, when the blossom buds unfurled on branches, finally covering their nakedness with the most delicate and colourful of clothing...*

CHAPTER TWELVE

J. A. L.

May 1944

Today I remembered the time that Father took me fishing. It was a day much like today, when the blossom buds unfurled on branches, finally covering their nakedness with the most delicate and colourful of clothing. Everywhere you looked, life was beginning again – newborn lambs and calves that suckled at their mothers, and played and ran with their little friends in fields that were a thick carpet of green.

The birds were the first to alert me to the change of today, that change of hopefulness. A nest in the tree behind me has finally come to life, the squeaks and squawks of hungry mouths keeping their blackbird mother busy most of the day. It is nice to hear the birds sing once more. In the camp there are only crows, hawking and screaming as if they too realise what is happening on the ground below them.

But today is for remembering. Father and I went fishing for the first time. I was perhaps five or six, yet I felt like a grown man with my fishing rod slung over my shoulder, Father's cap on my head too large and slipping constantly. I walked with him, three or four steps to keep up with his own long stride, and as we walked through the city, people waved at him, said hello, and I felt so proud to be by his side.

Father did not usually fish. He was not a man for the outdoors, preferring to stay inside and read his books, write a new lecture for his students, or make his children sit at his feet as he told us stories from his research, or sometimes from his own mind.

I cannot remember why he took me fishing that day, other than when I woke, he was there at the dining room table, a small fishing rod bought just for me propped on the wall, waiting for me.

I am sure we must have talked during our walk through the busy city streets, past the flower market that lit up the grey, gothic buildings around it with reds, yellows and purples. Past the university where students sat on the grass, reading, enjoying the spring sunshine, and waved at my father. Soon we reached the river that was held captive by bridges and pavements in the city, and followed it until we reached the outskirts, where buildings were fewer, and human traffic had quietened.

The cathedral's dome, mottled green, sat behind a stretch of river which Father had deemed perfect for our outing, telling me that we would hear the bells chime the hours and we could listen to a simple, beautiful sound that we perhaps did not listen to very often.

'What's a cathedral?' I asked him as I settled onto the bank, careful not to let my feet get too close to the thick mud that slopped into the water; the thought of being stuck in there forever was on my mind.

'It's where people go to pray and to talk to God,' my father said. He sat a little way behind me on a blanket he had brought from home, and emptied his bag which he had filled with a picnic and a jar of worms for me to hook onto my rod.

'Like a synagogue?' I asked.

'Exactly so.'

'So why don't we call the synagogue a cathedral?' I took a wiggly worm from him and impaled him on the hook as I'd seen my friends do.

'Very good.' Father nodded his approval at my handiwork. 'We don't call it a cathedral, because we are Jewish and people who go to a cathedral are not Jewish.'

'But you said they talk to God?' I was confused and struggling to get the line in the water.

Father stood and took the rod from me, casting it out into the dappled water until it plopped with a satisfying noise into the depths. We sat back then and waited, the rod in my hand, Father pouring two cups of fresh orange juice. Then, he lit his pipe.

'There are a lot of people who will tell you I am wrong, but all I can tell you is what I believe. I believe that they too are talking to our God, that we Jews and they Christians are not so different after all.'

'So it doesn't matter then, where you talk to God?' I moved the rod into my left hand and gulped down some juice.

'It doesn't matter one bit. Why, you can talk to Him here if you like!'

'Right here?' I looked out across the river, the line of the city not far away.

'Right here. He's everywhere, so whenever you feel like talking to Him, just talk, He'll hear you. All of this, He created. Look around at all the new life that spring brings – that's where you can see God most at work.'

I nodded. I liked to think that I could just have a quick talk with God wherever I was, and vowed to do so.

Perhaps the memory came to me today, not because of spring, or even those baby birds, but to remind me that I can still talk to God, that He is still here, even though it does not feel like it at all.

It is hard to believe that God is here when all around me I see my friends, my camp mates, starving to death, dying of diseases that wreck their bodies, see them shot, beaten and then disappear.

The blackbird has returned to the nest and her babies are now giving a quiet chirrup of satisfaction at their meal. Perhaps, if I close my eyes and listen to the birds and pretend I am on the riverbank with my father once more, I can remember how to talk to God, I can remember how to pray, I can remember how to feel hope.

A parcel arrived today that caused much excitement in the house. Her Majesty, Liesl Becher, was awake before dawn as I worked in the garden, raking the last of the dead leaves and heaping them ready for a fire.

She surprised me. I have never seen her awake so early before, but her face was at each window every few minutes, staring out onto the driveway in anticipation. I knew it must be important as I was told to leave clearing the driveway and return to the shed, lest anyone see me – she hated the thought of visitors seeing a prisoner on the grounds of her home. When they hide me away in this dank shed, I am glad of it. I get to sit, to write, to stretch my body out.

I keep a keen ear out for any movement so I can always look as though I am working. Around me are

scattered old pots and a few packets of seeds, to seem as
though I am planting, if anyone ever bothered to check,
but I doubt they will.

I heard the crunch of tyres on the driveway and
crouched down to look out of the window. All I could
make out was the side of a van, and then two men
coming round towards the kitchen door. Neither had
anything in their arms to begin with, but then they
returned to the van and brought out a package which
they carried together carefully.

There was a cry from Liesl inside, annoyed that
they had used the kitchen entrance, but then a hush
descended, and I realised that Herr Becher must be at
home – he is the only one who can silence her.

I desperately wanted to know what was in that
parcel. Deliveries occur every day here – dresses she
orders, or food, even furniture. It is as though they
cannot live one day without something new arriving.
But this was different; it woke her before dawn and that
meant it was something important.

I must have dozed off for perhaps an hour, but not
more, and it was the parcel that woke me.

At first, I could not understand the noise – scratching, then a woman singing, loud, then quiet, then
silence. Finally, I understood they had taken receipt of a
gramophone. Sure enough, Beethoven was soon heard,
blasting through the house and sailing out to me in the
garden. Then the music changed to something lighter.
I imagined both Herr Becher and his wife arguing over
which music to play – their tastes so different. They are
so different from one another; it is only to be expected.
Herr Becher is ramrod straight in everything he does;
his orders, the way he moves. He seems kind but can

then turn, quick as a flash. He reminds me of the old cat my grandmother had for catching mice. One moment you could stroke him and hear his purr, then the next, he would bite you or swipe at you, leaving a trail of blood, then simply walk away. That's how Herr Becher is – you cannot trust the smile, the random thanks he sometimes bestows on my work in the garden. You cannot trust it at all.

Liesl is more transparent. She must be forty, yet she has not aged from being a spoilt child. She does nothing all day but eat and sleep. She will entertain guests now and then, but mostly she is surly and distant until her husband comes home, and then she transforms herself. She dresses for dinner with her husband as if they are going to the opera – ball gowns of silk and velvet, her hair shining and pinned back with mother of pearl pins, her lips rouged and her eyes bright and eager.

I see her, but she rarely sees me. She cannot help but look at her reflection in the window glass. If her husband is late, she stands fingering the pearls at her neck, as if he is away fighting in some foreign land and not simply down the rutted track that leads to the camp.

I tried to leave the shed a while ago, but was told to stay inside by the cook. Guests will be arriving soon and I cannot be seen. I asked when I was to leave to return to the camp, but the cook shook her head and has now locked me in here for the night. I cannot say I mind; I have a small torch, a bundle of food, and some water the kindly cook has given me to see me through the night, and I have made myself a bed from the old sacks and bit of rubbish stashed away in here. Besides, when I lie back, there are cracks in the shed roof, and from here I can see the stars and listen to the music that streams out from the dining room, and pretend I am somewhere else altogether.

I should talk to God tonight; I am sure He will hear me here.

CHAPTER THIRTEEN

Anna

February 1944

A wave of typhus hit the camp, reminding Anna of those violent winds of summer storms that struck trees, leaving little in their wake. It seemed as though it was located in just one bunkhouse, where each morning Anna, Joanna and Nina were made to check sleeping bodies for a pulse, a breath, and those that expired were to be carried out to a pit at the rear of the bunkhouses where they were thrown in, one on top of the other, then their bodies set alight, the smell of burning flesh and hair clinging on to Anna's clothes and skin.

Nina had fashioned them masks from pieces of material she had sneaked out of the laundry, which they wore when moving the bodies and then again when the pyres were lit.

Anna was moving the first body of the day, a woman from another bunkhouse who had died in the night, the others too weak to help. She carried the woman by her arms, Nina carrying her by the ankles. She looked to Anna the same as the others had – her mouth open, the skin on her body stretched so thin that it looked as though it would rip, her ribs pronounced like the carcasses of cows Anna had seen hanging in butcher shop windows.

At first, Anna had vomited when she had moved three bodies during those first days, her retching bringing up yellow bile that stung her throat and made her eyes water. She had cried too at night, silently into her pillow, mumbling a prayer for each of them. Yet now, after two weeks, the vomiting had stopped, the crying stilled to a few tears, but she still prayed for each of them.

Nina would not speak to Anna of the death that surrounded them. Instead she would talk of her birthdays she had spent with her family when she was small, of her father who she had adored, of the books she had read – anything but what was in front of her each day.

They threw the woman into the pit, her limbs tangled and bent at odd angles as she lay on top of another, and Anna felt a wave of nausea rise from her stomach, reaching her throat. She was glad of it – glad to know that she had not become so indifferent, so immune to the horror – she wanted to feel it.

'I was just remembering the day my father bought us a dog.' Nina walked a few steps in front of Anna towards the bunkhouse. 'I loved that dog – did you ever have a pet, Anna?'

Anna shook her head – did the woman she had just thrown into that pit have a pet? Did she have a cat, perhaps, pure white and silky, that sat on a windowsill somewhere, waiting for her to come home?

'You in?' Joanna asked as soon as they both entered the bunkhouse, waving a deck of cards at them, fashioned from some cardboard she had bartered for with a lump of bread.

Nina sat down on the dusty floorboards, an upturned box featuring as a playing table. Anna stood watching Joanna count out the cards; for herself, Nina, a woman called Ami and for Anna. She sat next to Nina and crossed her legs, then removed her mask, breathing in the damp air. Around her women slept on their bunks, their blankets covering their whole bodies so that you could only see the scruff of hair on a pillow. Others sat together, talking – one had a book she had been gifted by a male camp guard. Joanna had told Anna and Nina not to ask what she had done to be given it.

As Anna looked at the scruffy designs Joanna had drawn, she recalled playing a game with Piotr, who had tried to cheat the entire time so that they had eventually fallen about, laughing like children.

'What are you smiling at?' Joanna asked, raising her dark eyes from her hand.

'A memory,' she answered, then rearranged her cards to try and find a sequence to get rid of some of them. She couldn't, and picked up a card from the deck.

'That's all we have now,' Joanna said. 'Speaking of which…' She rummaged around in her pocket and drew out four cigarettes, laying them down next to the cards.

'Where did you get these?' Nina picked one up, staring at it as if she had never seen one before.

'A guard,' Joanna said out of the side of her mouth, as she tried to light it with a thin match from a tiny box. 'Got these too.' She blew out the smoke and chucked the matches towards Nina.

'But how?' Anna asked, placing her own cards down to pick up the cigarette.

'That fat guard, what's her name – Elsa? Something like that. Anyway, she's bringing in a few things as long as we give her some petrol and scraps of metal from the sheds and munitions store. She says she's getting a fair price for them on the outside. So she pays me in these.' Joanna blew out a long stream of smoke, closed her eyes and smiled, savouring the tobacco.

Anna did not smoke, not really. She had sometimes had a puff of Piotr's, and now and again when she had drunk wine, and had once begged a cigarette from her brother.

'You don't want it?' Joanna asked, nodding towards the cigarette Anna held in her hand.

'I do.' Anna placed it in her mouth and allowed Nina to light it for her. The first drag made her cough and splutter, which made the others laugh. But after a few drags, she felt lightheaded and decided she liked the feeling. 'Won't you get in trouble?' Anna asked.

'Maybe. I say it's worth the risk. Besides, I doubt a guard is going to let everyone know what she is doing.'

Anna played three eights, then Nina two fours.

'You know, the typhus is gone,' Joanna said, as she took the last drag of her smoke where it fizzled and crackled against the filter. 'It's pure starvation that's killing people now.'

Anna shook her head – she had seen how weak these women were, how they coughed and sweated.

'I'm telling you. There's no food. They know it. Easier to control us if they keep us locked up – no food, let all the weakest go.'

At the mention of food, Anna's stomach rumbled in response. She placed a hand on her abdomen, feeling how it had shrunk even more, flat, full of air and nothing else.

'Lange!' someone shouted, running into the bunkhouse.

Joanna quickly grabbed the cards and shoved them down her dress; Anna, Nina and Ami extinguished their cigarettes.

'You!' Lange boomed as she entered, pointing at Anna. 'Come with me.'

Frightened, Anna turned to Joanna and Nina – what had she done? Had Lange seen the cards, the cigarettes? Did she think Anna was behind it?

Anna walked towards Lange, then out into the open.

'You're needed at the house,' Lange sneered. 'Seems they can't do without you.'

'But I thought we were in quarantine?' As soon as the question had left Anna's mouth, she wished she could shove it back inside.

'Are you questioning me?' Lange narrowed her eyes at her, her hand already on her baton.

'No. No. I just don't want to make them sick.'

Lange slapped the side of Anna's face, then looked at her hand and grinned. 'You feel fine to me,' she laughed, leaving Anna with a red handprint on her cheek.

As they walked towards the gate, she thought of what Joanna had said – there was no typhus anymore. They were keeping them locked away, starving them until there would be no one left.

'It is so good to see you.' Greta enveloped her in an embrace as soon as she entered, her body warm and comforting.

'And you,' Anna said as she pulled away.

'You'd better change. Your dress is in the drawer over there.'

Anna dressed quickly, almost happy to be wearing the brown dress once more, feeling as though she were something more than just an inmate in a camp – she was almost human again.

'Take this to Isaac, will you?' Greta handed her a mug of coffee. 'And tell him that Herr Becher wants the typewriters fixed by tomorrow at the latest.'

Anna nodded and walked towards the shed, the glow of the lamp welcoming her.

'You're back.' Isaac looked up at her as she entered, his hands already reaching for the warm drink.

'I am.' She smiled at him. 'I'm glad you are well.'

'I was not quarantined; it seems to have missed the men's camp somehow.'

'Well, I am glad to see you are all right,' she said, and she turned to leave him to his work.

'You are?'

She looked back at him, his face thinner than the last time she had seen him, his hands trembling as they held the weight of the mug. 'Of course.'

'Will you…'

'Will I…?'

He shook his head. 'Sorry... I am being foolish.'

'What were you going to ask me?'

'Will you sit a while? Whilst I drink this?'

She nodded and sat on the upturned bucket that seemed to serve as the guest's seat.

'I have so few people to speak to during the day,' he began in between sips.

'But you have friends in the camp?'

Isaac nodded. 'One. Elijah. He was sick for some time, and then he became quite close with a few of the others.'

'But you are not close to them too?'

'This work,' Isaac looked at the tiny screws on his desk, the ribbon from the typewriters, the small can of oil he used to lubricate the cogs and wheels, 'it makes them think I'm different from them. As though I am friends somehow with Herr Becher, or I am receiving a privilege.'

Anna nodded. She knew how he felt. Apart from Nina and Joanna, she too had felt excluded – noticed the looks the other women gave her, the whispers as she walked past – and had often wondered what the others really thought of her.

'You think I am a silly old man, I'm sure,' Isaac said, interrupting her thoughts.

'I think I understand. And you're not old.'

Isaac placed his coffee cup down, the quiver of his hand making the coffee spill onto the wood. He wiped it with his sleeve. He glanced up and saw Anna watching. 'They are getting worse,' he said, looking down at his hands as if they did not belong to him.

'It's the hunger and the tiredness,' she said. 'I find that my legs shiver when I stand too long, as if they are going to collapse under me at any moment.'

'It is my age, my dear. I have aged more in these past weeks. It is as though I have added ten years to myself.'

'It will be better when you can leave, when you can go home.'

'Where is your home, Anna?'

'A small town, north of Baden-Baden.'

'Near the forest?'

Anna nodded and smiled widely at the thought of the Scots pines, beeches and elms that covered miles of countryside – the memory of home. The words rushed out of her, welcome as a cool stream in summer. 'We played in the forest when the wind would not play with us – when we could not fly our kites. The ground there is always carpeted with dead leaves and twigs, so that when you walk it crunches and crackles. I loved that sound. Then,' she leaned forward, 'then you would hear the screech of a raven or the char-char of a woodpecker before the drumming as it made a new hole. One day we came across a wild boar who was giving birth. We sat in a thicket of ferns, and waited and watched whilst she grunted with the strain, her belly rippling as the babies tried to find a way out. It started to rain, but under the canopy of leaves we were mostly dry, with just the sound of the patter as the drops hit the leaves above us.

'My brother asked me if the pig would die. It seemed as though she must do. She could not move, could barely breathe. He wanted to go home and fetch Father's old shotgun, to end her misery, he said. But before I could chastise him, there was a new sound, a squeak, and there on the leafy carpet was a tiny pink boar. It must've been less than a minute before another one arrived, and then another. Then the mother wriggled herself to her feet to meet her babies. She cleaned them and nudged each one, until she lay down again and they each found a teat and began to suckle.'

Anna stopped, then felt herself redden. 'I'm sorry,' she said. 'I don't know why I told you that. You must think me the silly one.'

'Not at all. It sounds magical to me.'

'It was. Before all this,' Anna opened her palms and raised her arms, 'it was sort of perfect, even when it wasn't, even when bad things happened. It was still magical – but then, that is memory. To look back and make things brighter, bigger and better than they really were.'

'When I look back, things are hazy for me. But then, that is my elderly mind.' Isaac grinned at her then finished the rest of his coffee.

'You're hardly old, Isaac. It really is just this place. Here, I should get back.' Anna stood and picked up the cup. 'They are so beautiful.' She looked at the watches Isaac had laid out in a box behind him in neat rows.

'They're almost fixed. Almost. But first the typewriters, and then I will finish them.'

'I'll see you tomorrow.' Anna left Isaac hunched once more over his tools, the light flickering on the walls of the shed as if he were not alone, as if ghosts of the past were watching over him.

Anna shuddered at the thought as she walked back to the house. She had never believed in ghosts before – they were made up in tales told by friends or to siblings on a dark winter's night, when the wind howled and trees tapped their spindly fingers against the windows, all designed to scare the listeners to squeals and laughter.

She looked back at the shed before she opened the kitchen door, leaving the crouching watchmaker to his work, yet watching everything he did.

'Do you believe in ghosts?' Anna asked Greta, as soon as she was inside the warmth of the kitchen.

'I do.'

'Are they evil, do you think, like the tales you tell as children?'

'No, not evil. They are restless, trying to find their way home again. Why, have you seen something?' Greta looked up at Anna, ignoring the bubbling pot on the stove which was threatening to boil over.

'No. I don't think so, no.'

'If you do, say a prayer and wish it on its way, it'll leave you be then.' Greta nodded at her.

Anna smiled and left Greta to her cooking, making her way to clear the dining table after the family's breakfast.

Yet when she reached the dining room, the table was not empty of the family. Liesl Becher sat at her end of the table, the fireplace an open mouth behind her.

'I'm sorry,' Anna said, unsure of whether to leave or to stay.

Liesl looked up, her eyes red and puffy as if she had been crying all night. She waved a hand at the table. 'Clear it.'

Anna nodded and began to stack the plates, one on top of the other, watching her every movement so as not to spill any crumbs from the bread plate, or allow a smear of egg yolk to drop onto the table and stain it.

'Do you know what I miss?'

Anna looked at Liesl, shocked. Liesl's red eyes were trained on her, her pink dressing gown wrapped around her, her enormous bosom escaping through a gap. Anna shook her head.

'I miss dancing. And restaurants. That is what I miss. Not that *you* would know what I'm talking about.' Liesl sighed, then stirred her coffee so that the spoon tinkled at the side of the china.

Anna made to leave, but Liesl continued to talk so she stood, dumbly holding the dirty plates in her hands, her eyes focusing on the fireplace behind Liesl.

'I don't like the heat. Well, I do, when we holiday, and I can cool off in the sea or a swimming pool. But the heat, all day every day…'

Anna's hands were cold, her feet frozen. What was she talking about?

'You wouldn't know anything about it.' Liesl stood and walked towards her. 'But in a strange way, it's all your fault, isn't it? That

I should perish in the heat. That I should miss dancing. It is, isn't it, your fault?'

'I don't know,' Anna muttered, the plates knocking against each other as her hands shook.

Liesl, standing directly in front of Anna now, laughed, and then Anna felt the sting of her palm across her face, and dropped the plates in shock.

As Anna bent down to pick up the crockery, Liesl laughed once more as she walked out of the room. 'Clean it up,' she said, her cackle continuing as she climbed the stairs.

'What happened?' Greta was by Anna's side, trying to help her with the dishes.

'I don't know. I really don't. She was talking about the heat. But it's cold. And then she said it was my fault.'

'Go and put some cool water on your cheek, I can see her handprint.'

Anna gingerly touched her face, then returned to the kitchen and splashed cool water on her skin, soothing the sting of the second slap of the day.

CHAPTER FOURTEEN

Isaac

That evening, Isaac was glad to see that Anna would be walking back to the camp with him. As soon as he saw her, he smiled, then wished that Levi were there to see him doing as he wished – trying to find some happiness.

Then, he saw her – really saw her – a young woman, and he an ageing man, and his smile faltered for a moment until he saw her return the gesture, allowing it to reach her eyes.

They fell into a matching stride, their shoulders touching, Schmidt a few steps behind, humming his annoying tune and smoking his cigar, not realising that Isaac was glad he was making them walk slowly, glad of the extra moments with Anna.

'How was your day?' he asked her, his tone the same as if he were asking Hannah when he returned from the workshop.

She looked at him, then bit her lower lip as if she were about to cry.

'What is it?'

'I just want to go home,' she said, a tear tracing down her cheek.

Without thinking, he took her hand in his, briefly, and gave it a squeeze as if he were hugging her with all his might.

Shocked, she looked down at her hand.

'I'm sorry,' Isaac whispered, then moved away from her.

They walked in silence, only the crunch of their footsteps on the ground, and the rustle of leaves and undergrowth as night-time visitors sought food.

Then, her arm was back against his and a slight brush of her fingers on his fingertips, so fleeting that he wondered if he had imagined it.

As they reached the gates, quietly she said, 'Thank you,' and disappeared towards the women's block, the spotlights from the watchtower illuminating her as she walked.

Three bunks were empty in the bunkhouse when Isaac reached them. All three belonged to brothers, aged between eighteen and twenty-two.

'Where are they?' Isaac asked Jan as he washed his face.

'Where do you think?' Jan said, then pushed past to his own bunk.

Isaac followed, the coughing and quiet murmurs echoing around the bunkhouse.

'Where?'

'Are you really going to ask me that? Do you not see the chimneys, not smell the burning?'

'I'm at the house,' Isaac said dumbly.

'Ah yes, that you are. At the house. Lucky you.'

'I didn't ask for it. They asked for me.'

'Well, whilst you are at the house, at the pleasure of our guards, men are taken away every day to the buildings with chimneys. Do you know what happens in those rooms? They are gassed, all together in one room, and then their bodies are burned.'

'How do you know?' Isaac's throat was dry.

'How can I not know? They make us burn the bodies. They make some of us march them to the room in which they will die. We tell them they are going for a shower.'

A chill ran down Isaac's spine as he remembered the shower room from his first day, the iced water running over his body, the men pushed together, frightened. Was that how it was?

'I – I didn't know.'

'Like I said, you are lucky.' Jan lay down and turned his back on Isaac. Then, his head turned briefly. 'You said before, to Elijah, that you would get out of here, that the Americans and British would save us. I didn't believe you, but I do now. They are coming, you can see it in the guards' faces. They are forgetting things; they talk amongst themselves more. But more of us are dying – so I'd say you've got a fifty-fifty chance of getting through this. Maybe more so because you're at the house.'

'You think we will survive?'

'I'm telling you this so that you make sure you do. Keep your head down, don't get into trouble.'

'Thank you,' Isaac said.

'Don't thank me yet.'

The following morning, Isaac worked quickly. He took the tiny face from the woman's watch, leaving just the leather strap which was worn and ripped. The hands were still, yet the design on the face was nothing like he had seen before. Where each number should be was a tiny design. There were birds at twelve, as if they were kissing, made to look like the number itself. The number one was a tiny weeping willow, two a swan, then three a squirrel eating. It was something he would have thought suitable for a child, yet the tiny pictures were almost miniature works of art that only an adult could appreciate. When he had seen the watch face in amongst the others, he had thought at once of Anna, of her tale of the forest and the trees and animals that dwelled there. It was made for her, he knew, and he would make it even more exquisite.

He knelt down and placed it in the hole where the bundle of papers lay, along with the tiny clasps he had taken from the man's wristwatch weeks before. Bit by bit, he would make something new, something beautiful that would work and live again – something for Anna so he could see her face when he gave her his creation. He wanted to see her eyes smile, just as Hannah's had done.

'I'm alive!' Levi's voice was behind him, and Isaac got to his feet as quickly as he could.

'So you are! Where have you been? Have you been sick?' Isaac said, shaking Levi's hand, both of them grinning at each other as if they were long lost friends.

Levi sat on the upturned bucket, his long legs in front of him, thinner than before, his face almost skeletal. 'I was. A bit of a bad chest, that's all. Took a while but I made it. I knew I would.'

'How did you know?'

'I didn't smell lemons,' Levi said, then began to tie up a shoelace that had come undone.

'Lemons?'

'Yes, lemons.'

'Levi, you will have to elucidate.'

Levi sat up straight. 'Lemons. It's what you smell when you are dying.'

'Who told you that?'

'My grandfather and grandmother smelled lemons,' Levi counted on his fingers, 'my cousin, and probably my dog – he couldn't actually tell me, but I knew.'

'So that's what I need to remember: if I smell lemons, I am near death.'

'Well,' Levi considered. 'I mean, if you are perhaps near a lemon tree then you can logically conclude that it is not death you are smelling but an actual lemon.'

'Thank you for explaining.' Isaac sat down and added some oil to his lamp.

'To work I must go.' Levi stood. 'Promise me if you smell lemons whilst I am gone, you will resist.'

'I promise. What have they got you doing today?'

'They want a brick wall instead of a fence around the back of the garden.'

'Perhaps they are worried you will finally find a way to escape?' Isaac grinned.

'Perhaps. I think it is more likely they are worried who may want to get in.'

Levi pretended to doff his cap, then left Isaac alone.

He looked down at his work, at the watches staring silently at him, waiting for him to make time pass once more.

Each watch told a story to Isaac as he mended them. The way they were worn, the way they broke, gave clues to him like a detective at a crime scene – a crack in the glass coupled with a missing link spoke to him of a busy, distracted husband, perhaps wealthy, who did not care what happened to his timepiece. Isaac imagined that he would come home each day and undo his watch, throwing it in the general direction of a table, yet missing, not even noticing when it fell on the floor with a thud.

A thin gold chain that was attached to a pocket watch caught his eye. There was no cover, simply the watch face that ticked the seconds by. It was not broken. He lifted it and held it to his ear, listening to the soft tick-tock as it counted the seconds. There was nothing remarkable about the watch; it was simple, with no decoration or engraving, yet the thought of the gear train stopping to allow for the sound, the balance wheel oscillating back and forth to keep the time, was magical to Isaac, and he found himself laughing with joy.

'Why are you laughing?' Anna appeared in front of him – how long had she been standing there?

'It's this. Here.' He held the watch out to her.

She placed the mug of coffee she was carrying onto his desk and held the watch.

'It's very nice,' she said, and raised her eyebrow at him in question.

'No, no, hold it to your ear.'

Anna did as she was told and Isaac watched her, waiting. Within a few seconds, she closed her eyes as if she were going to fall asleep on the spot.

He said, 'It's so soft, the ticking. Almost as if it wants to remain secret. In some, you can almost feel the pulse as it tells the time. Whoever made this did so with such care, the insides work beautifully together.'

She opened her eyes. 'The insides? You speak of them as if they are people!'

Isaac's smile faltered and he held his hand out for her to give the watch back.

'I'm sorry,' she said as she sat down. 'I didn't mean to poke fun. I like the way you are so passionate about them.'

'It's all I have,' he said, brushing his thumb over the clear glass.

'Were you always a watchmaker, Isaac?' Anna asked, her elbows on her knees, her hands cupping her chin like a small child. Isaac warmed at the picture of her – it was the same way he had sat as a child when his father would tell stories of his day.

'I was.'

'You did not have a family?'

'I did, once.' Isaac sipped at his coffee. 'I was married. She was twenty and I twenty-two, but I had known her most of my life. Her parents ran a farm and I first saw her on the day the puppies were born.'

'The puppies?'

'It is a childish story – are you sure you want to hear it?'

'Absolutely.'

'Very well.' Isaac sat back, holding the coffee mug in both hands. 'There was a farm dog, a bitch. She was black and white all over with a black patch over one eye, so I called her Pirate. She was not a great farm dog, and instead of rounding up sheep or chasing away strangers, she would befriend them, laying her head in the soft wool of the sheep or licking a stranger's palm. Every day she wandered into the village, and that was where I met her, on a street corner when I was twelve and sitting on the side of the road, trying to throw a stone to the other side in one go.

'I'd had an accident the year before, falling through a frozen lake when I was playing with friends. I sliced my thigh open on the ice, tearing through the tendons and muscles, leaving me with a permanent scar, limp and pain. The throwing of stones was all I could do a year after my injury, and it was nice to have company from Pirate, who would nuzzle me and lick my face when I got mad that my game was not going well.

'It must have been a week or more, and I had not seen her. I asked my father, who told me to take the walk to the farm – it would do my leg good, he said. I didn't want to go. I knew how I looked and saw the glances from those on the street, their sympathy at the poor crippled boy. But my father, he was a man who could convince anyone to do something if he thought it was good for you, and after a few kind words of encouragement, he sent me on my way.

'When I reached the farm track, I walked slower, my leg already aching. Cows munched on grass by the fence, their doleful brown eyes following me, and the sun warmed my back. I liked the farm track, the way the wildflowers bobbed their heads in the breeze and how the fields all around were dotted with sheep, cows and horses – it reminded me of the small figurines I would play with at home.

'I was perhaps halfway to the farmhouse, the large barns looming in the distance, when a girl came running past me, screaming that they were coming.

'I of course had no idea what she meant and called out to her, but instead of answering me, she stopped and asked me what was wrong with my leg.

'"I hurt it," I told her stupidly.

'She looked at the barn, the farmhouse and then back at me, as if deciding something. "I'll walk with you," she said, then traced her running steps back to me.

'We walked together towards the farm, she explaining excitedly to me how her dog, the one I had called Pirate, was in fact a bitch and was about to have puppies.

'I told her to run on ahead so she wouldn't miss the birth, and she made a deal with me that if she ran on and left me alone, we would always be friends. We shook on it, and that was the deal sealed – from that day on until the day she died, we were each other's best friend.'

Isaac finished his story and looked to Anna whose eyes were closed.

'That's beautiful,' she said. 'The way you describe it, it is as if I was there, as if I met her.'

'I rarely think of that day, but now I have, it is as if it happened yesterday,' Isaac said.

Anna opened her eyes. 'I tried to imagine what you would have looked like as a boy, and a young man on your wedding day.'

'I certainly looked better than this!' Isaac laughed, then ran a hand over the grey beard that now covered his chin and upper lip.

'I can still see you – as you were,' Anna said, then blushed.

Isaac looked at his coffee cup, and drank some back. 'You said you had a fiancé?' he ventured.

Anna was silent, and he looked to her, to see that she was crying.

'I'm sorry, I didn't mean to make you cry.'

'It's all right. How can we not cry?' She gave a weak smile.

Isaac finished his coffee, not pushing the subject of her fiancé anymore. 'Tomorrow?' he asked her.

She stood and took the mug away from him. 'Tomorrow,' she agreed.

Isaac placed the quietly ticking watch inside the bundle he was keeping below the shed. He would tell Becher there were a few he could not fix. He was desperate to take a look at the quietly working mechanisms of the watch, using them in the one he was building for Anna.

As he tucked it away, his hand found the bundle of papers. He pulled them out and shuffled backwards so his back leaned against the wall of the shed, then straightened his legs out in front of him. Slowly he found where he had read up to the day before, desperate to hear the voice from within, desperate to hear someone else's story to take his mind away from the memory of Hannah.

CHAPTER FIFTEEN

J. A. L.

June 1944

Dearest,

Do you remember when I said I would write to you?

I kept my promise and here I am, in a dank shed, finding words to say.

It is strange to me that when I see you, I can think of so many things to tell you, yet now as my pen scratches words on this paper, my mind has gone blank. Perhaps it is too full of everything I want to say and now I am faced with it, I am not sure what should come first.

Today it has rained all day, from the moment I woke before dawn until now, mid-afternoon. It is the kind of rain that sheets down, so that you can barely see in front of you. Liesl left the house a few hours ago to visit her son, who is at a school in Munich. Becher did not go with her, and I could sense her reluctance to go, as she kept returning to the house to fetch something else she may need for the trip.

Again, they think I do not see them, do not know of their comings and goings, but because I am a ghost, a nothing, they do not see me, and I find that I can wander around their garden and grounds with little interruption.

The cook sent me to the shed as soon as they left and brought me some food. She told me to stay inside for a while and said she will fetch me if she hears a car. She is a nice woman, and it is she, in fact, who has given me the means by which to write to you – something to do, she told me when she passed me some sheets of paper and a leaking pen, something to keep your mind busy.

She is right, of course; my mind seems so slow and jumbled. The days roll into one large chunk of time that is mostly misery and despair. The bodies – so many of them. Piled high, awaiting burial, or, as someone told me, a fire, where a pit is dug into the ground and the dead thrown in, allowing the flames to eat away at what is left of them.

This is not the letter I wished to write you.

Let me begin again, my love.

I always thought that at this age, I would be a professor of mathematics, or perhaps history, like my father. It was he who taught me about logic, about fact, about looking at what is presented to you and finding the truth within. I wonder now, what would he think of this?

When I was thirteen, I sneaked into one of his lectures, where he spoke of the Roman Empire, of the developments they made and the atrocities they committed. It was afterwards, when I sneaked back out again and set off, walking quickly home in the weak winter light, that I felt a tap on my shoulder as I rounded the corner by the bookshop, and there he was. I expected him to scold me for sneaking out of the house, but all he did was smile and walk the rest of the way home with me.

At the time, I remember being confused by his behaviour, but now I realise he was happy that I was like him – that I had a mind that could not settle, that had to know everything.

My mother used to call my father's mind a rubbish bin – one that collected every morsel of information, every scrap that no one else wanted. Yet he turned those pieces of knowledge into something more, something beautiful and useful.

I wish now I could make you something beautiful. I wish I could take all of this nonsense and make some sense of it for you, and give you hope. Yet all I can give you is the words I know, to tell you I love you, and that you have made all this bearable; it is you who have given me something beautiful and hopeful.

One day I picture us together. I can hear you laughing as I write this! Yes, together. I see us in a farmhouse, out in the countryside where I used to spend summer holidays, near the lakes of Zakopane. We could have a life together there, me studying and researching, you tending our garden and making the flowers grow. If it were not for you, and your knowledge of the earth, I think I would not still be alive. It is your mind I use to do the work they ask of me, and when I plant, I imagine it is your hands in the dirt, pushing down seeds, carefully patting the soil on top, smiling to yourself as you think of what will push out of the ground come spring and summer.

We will have a dog, perhaps a cat for mousing, but it must be a friendly cat – not like that scrap of fur that was my grandmother's. We will walk every afternoon, hike into the hills and mountains and stop to look at the view, holding hands and laughing.

In the evening we will rest by the fire in winter, and in the summer, we will sit in our garden, sipping at drinks, eating our supper and planning our days ahead.

Can you imagine it? Are you lying down, your eyes closed, seeing the vision of our life together?

The rain has stopped now, and I see a break in the clouds and hope that the sun will shine – although it will take me from you – for a short time at least.

I will go now, and write soon.

I love you.

*

July 1944

In summer my mother cleaned the house, from top to bottom. She would say that most people do it in spring, ready for the summer months, yet she wanted the warmth that the season provided.

She would fling open every door and window, allowing the cool breeze to seep into our home, take out rugs and, with our help, beat the dust out of them with a wooden beater.

The dust would fly up in the air and I would wonder where it went. Did it just rain back down and cling once more to the threads of the carpets? Did it cling to me?

Father said that dust was particles of us – of our life – our skin, our hair, the outside that we brought in with us on our shoes. When I told Mother this, she would frown with distaste and say, 'All the more reason to clean them then.'

I didn't like that she was getting rid of us, our past year. In my child's mind I would imagine that the dust was me, playing with my friends as we fought battles down by the river, the dirt and soot I brought home with me forever clinging to the life around us.

There is dust in the air today.

It began just after I arrived at the house, and I can hear the crackle, smell the burning, see the clouds of smoke that filter into the sky and block out the sun. Dust – that is what we all are and what we become, filtered back into the sky and back into the world once more.

It is macabre that I think this way. But it gives me some sort of joy to think that those bodies burning in the pyre today are finding their way back to their loved ones, where they will cling onto their clothes, their hair, the furniture in their homes, reluctant to leave.

I have promised myself that if I ever leave here I will never beat a carpet again, I will not move the dust that settles around me; I will let it sit, and let it live next to me, allowing those who have died to come back once more.

*

August 1944

The mood in the camp is changing.

It is as though the guards are emboldened by the heat. It reminds me of Shakespeare: *For now, these hot days, is the mad blood stirring.*

The blood is boiling in their veins and I can see it as they count us in the morning, the sun already high and burning, their faces red and sweating. Their nostrils flare as if they are bulls ready to charge us at any moment, for any mistake they think we have made.

This morning a young inmate fell. The heat, the exhaustion of digging ditches and the lack of food and water overcame him, and his legs fell from under him as if the bones had been removed. A guard pounced on him, kicking him as he lay unconscious, until another joined in, and then another. The thuds of their boots striking his body were sickening. He leapt off the ground with each strike, like a fish flapping out of water, yet he did not make a sound.

Eventually they stopped, and he lay still. Someone was asked to take his body to the morgue. No one checked if he was dead – I just hoped that he was, as the pyres have been burning for days now and the thought that he might be awake, his body enveloped in flames, is too much to bear.

Word has spread amongst us that the war may soon be over. The Americans are coming, so they say, getting closer each day. Indeed, the planes that have been flying overhead have increased, the drone of their engines a constant hum in the air, and sometimes we hear as bombs drop and crash into the ground.

Will they come?

Why are the pyres burning so much? Why are the guards more sadistic than usual? Why are they agitated when the planes fly overhead, each of them looking upwards, their eyes showing the fear that we have all felt for so long? Can it be true?

My days are as long as the sun deigns to shine now. I am to dig a new flower bed for Liesl, to uproot young trees that she does not like. I am to chop firewood for their fires in the winter, I am to work until I cannot move. And yet I cannot complain, for it would be worse to be digging and building on the camp, or on the roads; it would be worse to be stuck in the cramped hot factory making munitions; it would be worse.

*

My dearest,

Another letter to you. I dreamt of you last night, a frantic dream that seemed so real, so that when I woke, I was not sure where I was.

We were visiting my family, and I was nervous. I stood at the front door, your hand in mine, and you kissed me and told me it was going to be all right.

My father opened the door, and looked at us, and smiled.

That smile was all I needed from him – that smile said that he approved and that our lives would now be blessed. But then you disappeared, and I looked to my hand and yours was gone. Instead I stood alone in the street and the front door was now closed, my father hiding inside.

What do you think that means? Do you think dreams mean anything at all?

You told me once that dreams were where we could be free, where our lives could intertwine. I felt bereft after this dream, though, as if we were lost to each other forever. I wish I could dream of happier things, of life away from here. Yet I feel as though my mind is slowly catching up with reality and that my night-time escape is no longer that – there is no escape.

This sounds like madness, I know; I am slowly going mad. The heat, the hunger, the nightmare we are living in… at times I find myself closing my eyes during the day and willing myself to wake up.

I wish I could write the letters to you that I want to – the letters full of happiness, of memories of us – yet today there are none. There is only my madness to keep me company and such words to fill a page.

CHAPTER SIXTEEN

Friedrich

The arguments between his parents continued. After the phone had been thrown, things had settled for a day or two, until one day his father came home from work and would not speak to anyone at dinner, taking his meal into his study and locking the door. When Friedrich had gone to bed, he had heard the tired screams from his mother, his father's voice low and dangerous.

It was towards the end of February when his father spoke to him for the first time in weeks.

'It is almost spring,' his father said, turning to him with surprise in his eyes, as if he had just noticed the warmer air, the buds swelling on tree branches.

The slice of toast was halfway to Friedrich's mouth and he froze, unsure whether to continue his breakfast on the rest of its journey or answer his father.

'Speak!' His mother's voice was unusually high. 'Speak! Are you deaf *and* dumb?'

Friedrich placed his toast back on the china plate, which had twirls and swirls of roses on the rim.

'It is,' he stuttered.

'You like the sun, don't you, Fried?' His father's eyes were large as he looked at him, and it scared him. When he called him Fried, his nickname, it made him anxious.

'Remember when we went away to the coast? You played in the sand. Do you remember that?'

Friedrich shook his head.

'No, no, maybe not. You were young. But you loved it. Being outdoors all day, swimming.'

'Peter!' his mother shouted. 'Stop it.'

'Stop what? Friedrich likes the sun, don't you, the heat?'

'I suppose,' he said. He looked down at his toast, which had grown cold.

'Let the boy speak!' His father turned on his mother. 'This constant barrage from you is exhausting! Don't you know what I have to do each day? Don't you know what is facing us?'

His mother began to cry, proper tears this time, which made her shoulders heave up and down.

Friedrich waited for his father to calm her, but he did not. Instead his teeth tore into his toast, ripping it then chewing silently, a little muscle in his cheek moving up and down with each bite.

'May I be excused?' Friedrich asked.

No one answered. No one looked at him, so he scraped his chair back, waiting for someone to shout at him for doing so, and when neither did, he walked from the room to his bedroom.

He sat on the edge of his bed and tried to understand what had happened, why his father had asked about the heat, or why it had made his mother cry.

His hands were cold. He tucked them under his armpits then thought of the gloves he had given Isaac. Isaac – was he still there? He must be. Anna was back, and the gardener.

He had tried to sneak out many times, but had always been caught by Schmidt, whose presence was forever felt in the house; either he sat in the living room, entertaining his mother whilst his father was at work – and not in the study as he should be –

or he was prowling the hallways, looking for something amiss, something to scold Greta or Friedrich about.

He hated Schmidt. He hated the way he stank of tobacco from the cigarettes he rolled himself, and how he dropped ash all over the house and the furniture as if it were his own home. He hated the way he made his mother laugh, or would dine with her when his father was busy or away.

Schmidt had found it easy to lock him inside – literally by locking the kitchen and front doors – but Friedrich decided that today would be the day he outwitted the lazy fat Schmidt. He would go and talk to Isaac and maybe Anna, and they would make him feel a little better.

With his decision made, he waited for the slam of the front door signalling his father's departure for work, and then the slow footsteps of his mother to her bedroom.

He heard her door shut, and Friedrich climbed off his bed and went into his parents' bathroom where a cabinet was hung on the wall by the mirror – he knew what was inside.

He had to jump up to retrieve the bottle he was looking for, the tiny white pills rattling inside the brown glass. He shook out two, then three, then thought of Schmidt's rotund body – maybe he needed four? He thought for a minute. His mother would take one and sleep all day, and if she had fought with his father, perhaps two, and then come to dinner in the evening, groggy and strange.

Two. That would be enough. He tipped the other two back into the bottle, then made his way downstairs to the kitchen.

'May I have some hot chocolate?' he asked Anna who stood washing dishes, her eyes looking out of the window. She jumped as he spoke, then turned to him.

'Can I? Please?' he asked, giving her the sweetest smile he could muster.

'Greta should make it for you.' Anna looked to the kitchen door, as if someone else would walk through.

'Where is she?' Friedrich asked.

'She's gone to the market for your mother.'

'Well then, you'll have to do it. Please?'

'I'm not supposed to,' she whispered to him, and he saw that her eyes were filling with tears.

'Don't be upset.' He walked towards her then, just as he would have done if his mother let him. He wrapped his arms around her waist and gave her a quick hug. 'Why are you upset? Don't you know how to make it? I do – I can show you if you like?'

He pulled away and saw that she was smiling at him now. 'I know how to make it. Wait in the living room and I will bring it to you.'

'It's all right.' He sat at the kitchen table. 'I'll wait here.'

He watched as she poured the cold milk into a pan and set it on the heat, then slowly spooned in the chocolate powder and gently stirred.

'I haven't seen you for ages,' Friedrich said. 'Where did you go?'

Anna looked hesitant. 'There were some sick people, and your mother thought it best I didn't come back to the house in case I made you unwell.'

'I heard Father say that people were dying. Is it in the same town that Isaac lives in?'

She nodded.

'Is Isaac all right?'

'He is.'

'I knew you were here. I could hear your footsteps, they're not like Mother's – they're really light, like a tiny mouse or a ghost. But when I'd try and find you, you always disappeared!'

'Perhaps I am a ghost.' She poured the chocolate milk into a green mug, then handed it to him.

'I haven't been able to look outside for Isaac though, so I'm glad to know he is back too.'

'Do you want me to blow on it for you?' She nodded at the mug, which he hadn't touched yet.

He wanted to sit longer in the warm kitchen with the smell of fresh vegetable soup on the stove, the rich yeasty scent of bread baking in the oven, but he knew his job awaited him.

'It's all right, I'll blow on it. I'll take it into the living room. Have you seen Schmidt yet this morning?'

'Herr Schmidt was carrying two boxes of papers into your father's study the last I saw of him. I expect that is where he is. Do you want me to call him for you?'

'No! I'll find him if I need him.' Friedrich smiled at her. 'Thank you, Anna.'

In the hallway, Friedrich held the mug carefully in one hand whilst he knocked on the study door with the other.

'Who is it?' Schmidt's voice rang out, making Friedrich angry – it was his house, his father's study; how dare he ask?

He swallowed his anger and instead replied, 'Friedrich. I've brought you a hot chocolate.'

The door clicked open and Schmidt's face appeared, redder than usual, sweat on his brow, his piggy eyes staring at the mug.

'What are you doing?' Friedrich could see the flames in the fire-place leaping behind Schmidt, the smell of burning paper in the air.

'None of your business. Give it to me then.' Schmidt's hand was already out, reaching for the drink. Friedrich stifled a grin; he knew Schmidt wouldn't be able to resist. 'I should be asking you what *you* are doing,' Schmidt said as he finished swallowing his first gulp, a line of chocolate milk on his top lip that he did not rub away.

'Nothing. Playing with my train set.'

'Good. Good boy.' Schmidt patted him on the head. 'Stay in your room. Your mother is unwell, and I have a lot of work to do, so keep quiet.'

'Yes, sir.' Friedrich walked away, hearing the click of the latch as the study door closed and the lock was turned.

He waited in the living room for an hour, to make sure that the tablets he had placed in Schmidt's drink had taken effect.

He was rarely allowed in the living room; it was his parents' domain after dinner, or perhaps in the afternoon, to sit and listen to the gramophone or read a book.

The gramophone was of interest to Friedrich. He loved the way the speaker fluted out like a strange bronze shell. He looked inside it, then said, 'Hello!', listening as his voice echoed in the cylinder. He wished he could add a record to the turning table, and place the needle on the grooves as he had seen his parents do, waiting as it scratched and buzzed to find the notes. But he knew what would happen if he woke his mother, so he backed away from it, resisting the temptation.

As soon as the grandfather clock in the hallway chimed that an hour had duly passed, Friedrich raced to the study and knocked loudly. There was no answer. He tried again, then again and waited. Then, sure that Schmidt was now fast asleep, he tiptoed to the kitchen, listening at the door for anyone inside. It was quiet.

Quickly he ran through the kitchen to the back door and opened it, running out towards the shed, feeling the cool air on his skin.

'Hello!' Friedrich flung open the shed door. Isaac, taken by surprise, dropped something on the floor, then scrabbled around trying to pick it up.

'Sorry.' Friedrich moved towards him to help, but Isaac waved him away, and folded some papers that had fallen on the floor and placed them in his pocket.

'I haven't seen you for some time,' Isaac said.

'I know. They made me stay in the house, even locked the doors!'

'But they opened them for you today.'

Friedrich shuffled one foot to the other. 'Sort of.'

The old man raised his eyebrows at him. 'Are you supposed to be outside?'

'Well, in a way no one knows, so I am.' Isaac laughed, taking Friedrich by surprise now. 'Is it funny?'

'It is, it is! I'm not sure why. Perhaps because you are being young, perhaps because you are making your own rules.'

'Can I sit for a while, whilst you work? I promise I will be quiet; I just don't want to be on my own anymore.'

'You can,' Isaac said, and pointed at the upturned bucket.

Friedrich went over to it and sat down. 'It's spring, Father said.'

'Almost.'

He watched Isaac prise the back off a watch and peer inside.

'I like spring. I like it when the sun goes to bed later, and the birds wake up earlier. If I had my way, I'd build a treehouse ready for summer when Otto comes to visit.'

'So your friend is coming to visit?'

Friedrich shook his head. 'Maybe. If Father says it's all right, but he's not around much lately and Mother is hysterical all the time. I don't understand it.'

'What do you mean?' Isaac stopped what he was doing and peered at him.

'I don't know. It's all a bit strange. There are phone calls late at night, and Father was asking me if I like hot weather and Mother got upset about it. And they are always fighting. She wants to go and see her friends, but he says she is not allowed to and that makes her angry. It's like – I don't know – like we are locked up in a prison.'

'A prison, eh? But you get fed nice food, have a bed, can play with your toys?' Isaac raised his eyebrows at him, willing him to find the correct answer as his teachers did.

'I suppose.'

'So not like a prison then. In a prison, you have to work, you cannot play with toys, and you get little food or warmth.'

'Have you been in a prison?' Friedrich asked. 'Are you really a jewel thief?'

Isaac grinned at him. 'No. I am not a jewel thief, although I wish I were. But I have been in prison.'

'What did you do? Are you a murderer?'

Isaac shook his head. 'There's no need to be afraid. I didn't do anything.'

Friedrich was confused yet again. His whole day was confusing. Why would Isaac have to go to prison if he had done nothing wrong?

Then Friedrich looked at Isaac's striped clothing, his hollowed cheeks, his skin so thin you could see the blue veins beneath.

'The town isn't a town, is it?' Friedrich asked finally.

Isaac shook his head.

'Did Father put you there, in the prison?'

Isaac nodded. 'It is bigger than that. It's the war. It's everyone. Not just your father.'

Friedrich felt stupid. Like a silly little boy who played with trains and believed stories that fell from his parents' lips. A town where they were happy. A place where they could stay to keep him and his parents safe. He wasn't supposed to like the Jews, he knew. He wasn't supposed to like foreign people, or black people, or gypsies. He had sworn his allegiance to his Führer every morning at school, he had read about what all the Jews and foreign people were doing to his country, and yet he did not feel hate for them, and why would he – he rarely met any of them.

Now here was a Jew, and he was nice to him, even though he shouldn't be. He did not know what he was supposed to think.

'Do you want to help me with the watch?' Isaac's voice was soft and broke through his complicated musings.

Friedrich stood. 'I do,' he said, and he pulled the bucket close to the desk and listened as Isaac told him about the magic of time.

CHAPTER SEVENTEEN

Anna

It was late. The clock in the hallway struck eleven as Anna sat in the kitchen, checking on the plate of food still sitting in the oven, waiting for its master.

Greta had gone home early, the raspy cough she had been trying to conceal finally drawing phlegm and bending her double with painful hacks.

Anna was to stay until Herr Becher returned home, give him his dinner, and then a guard would return her to the camp. If they did not, she was to sleep on the cold tiles of the kitchen floor.

She finally heard the rumble of the car on the driveway and stood, then sat back down again – should she go to the door to greet him? Should she wait?

His footsteps echoed on the lacquered wood as he walked down the hallway, his boots making a heavy thump with each step. She heard him shout out for Schmidt, and then she heard the slam of his study door. Schmidt was still here? She hadn't seen him all day. Liesl had not left her room and the boy had played quietly by himself, only appearing for dinner which he took to his room.

The study door opened, then slammed closed once more. There was the thump of footsteps, then they stopped and there was quiet. She heard the music next, soft, inviting – he was in the living room. She stood and, using a rag, pulled the warm plate from the oven and placed it on a silver tray along with cutlery and a napkin.

After a quick knock on the living room door, she heard him bid her enter.

'Anna,' he said, surprised perhaps.

She set the tray down on the low coffee table in front of him. He relaxed back in the stuffed sofa, his top shirt buttons open, a glass in his hand and the crystal whiskey decanter half empty on the side table.

'Greta was ill,' she apologised. 'She will be back tomorrow.'

His eyes were red, watery already from the alcohol. 'She will, will she?'

'I should go. Should I ask Schmidt to take me?'

'Ah, Schmidt.' He poured another measure of whiskey into his glass and drank it back in one go, then repeated the exercise once more. 'Schmidt. Schmidt is asleep, Anna. Fast asleep on the couch in my study. The work I asked him to do, not completed. My wife, she's asleep. My son – asleep? Who knows?'

Anna was unsure of what she should say or do. Her eyes moved about the room, settling on the portrait of Liesl that hung above the fireplace.

'She was a beauty, wasn't she?' He nodded towards the oil painting of his wife.

'She is very beautiful.'

'Not so much anymore,' he whispered, then laughed. 'Sit down, Anna.' He patted the sofa cushion next to him.

She pulled at a ragged nail and looked at the sofa. He patted it again. She willed her legs to move but they would not.

'Anna?' He patted the sofa with more force, causing a dancing of dust motes to spiral into the air under the lamplight.

She stepped forward, her legs shaking, then sat and placed her hands on her lap as if she were at school, afraid to do the wrong thing.

'Do you like the music, Anna?'

'It's very nice.'

'It's Chopin. Do you know Chopin, Anna?'

She shook her head.

He leaned back on the sofa and conducted an imaginary orchestra with his hand, sloshing the whiskey in the glass. 'It's old. So very old.' Then he suddenly sat upright and faced Anna, who looked at him even though she didn't want to.

'Isn't it funny how the past catches up with you, Anna? Isn't it funny that no matter what, it will come back to you, whether you want it to or not?'

'I – I'm not sure what you mean, Herr Becher,' she said.

'Of course you don't understand,' he sighed. 'You couldn't.'

'I think I should probably go.'

'Yes. Yes, you're probably right. I'll ask one of the guards at the gate to take you to the camp.'

Anna stood, then felt something on her leg. She looked down and saw Becher's hand stroking her knee, creeping up below the hem of her dress.

'It's a nice dress on you, Anna. Very nice.' He smiled at her, showing his teeth which were moist from his drink.

Anna nodded and walked away, feeling goose-pimples on her skin from where he had touched her. As she closed the door, she saw he was conducting his orchestra once more, his smile gone, his face set like stone.

'Nina,' Anna whispered. 'Nina, are you awake?' Anna stood with her feet on her bottom bunk, her face close to Nina's, who was deep in sleep, her eyelids flickering with dreams.

'Nina,' she tried again.

Nina's eyes opened. 'What's wrong?'

'Shhh.' Anna climbed into the bunk and curled in next to Nina.

'What's wrong?' Nina asked again.

'Tonight. I don't know. Something strange happened.'

'What was it?'

'It was Herr Becher. He...' She tried to find the words. 'I don't know. He wanted to talk to me, and he put his hand on my leg as I left.'

'Did he...?' Nina trailed off.

'No. Nothing like that. But I'm scared. I don't want to go back. How can I make it so I don't have to go back?'

Nina stroked Anna's head, just as Anna did for her when she was scared, worried about Kuba. 'It'll be all right,' she soothed. 'You don't want to work here. It'll be fine. Just stay out of his way – it'll be fine.'

Anna allowed Nina to soothe her to sleep, her hand stroking her head, reminding her of her father doing the same when she was small.

Isaac welcomed her the next morning with a broad grin, his hands outstretched, ready to take the coffee from her like a child who is being given a present for the first time.

'You look worried,' he said between sips.

'It's nothing. I just didn't sleep so well.'

'You're lying,' he said.

She shook her head, then sat on the bucket and waited for him to drink his coffee. 'How are the watches coming along?'

'Don't try and change the subject – what's wrong?'

'Nothing, really. I was just thinking about my family and it upset me, that's all, I promise you.'

'Tell me a happy memory of your family,' Isaac said. 'Trust me, it will make you feel better, just as the story I told you of Hannah has lightened my heart.'

'I'm not sure I can think of anything.' She tried, but couldn't think past the buzzing in her ears from the sleepless night.

'Tell me again about playing with your brother. You said you would fly kites when the wind picked up – tell me about that.'

She sat for a minute, then closed her eyes trying to summon up the picture of her running in the wind, laughing as the kites caught a gust and flapped into the sky.

'I was nine years old when my father died,' she began. 'He was rarely at home so when he died, I felt guilty that I did not miss him more. My brother, he missed him, but I think he missed the thought of him – the thought of having a father like his friends had. My brother was younger than me by two years, but we were close as we only really had each other.'

'What about your mother?'

'She was never the same after Father died. It was as though we reminded her too much of him, or perhaps the life we used to have. It was easier for her to spend time with friends, or organising events – anything to keep her mind away from us. But I did not mind. When she was home, she loved us, of course she did, but I could see the sadness in her all the time, so I was almost glad when she would tell us to amuse ourselves for the day, or that an aunt was coming to visit.

'The kites. My brother loved them so we made three or four, all different colours, and would sit by the window each day, waiting for the wind to pick up so we could run in the park, my brother in front with the kite trying to catch a gust, and me behind holding onto the string. There was always something so thrilling, almost dangerous, about flying kites. They were attached by just that thin piece of string and anything could tear them away. If I didn't give enough, it would not fly properly and crash into a tree where it would tear. If I gave too much, it would fly too high, catch a stronger gust, and the string would burn my hand as the kite tried to make its escape.'

She opened her eyes, seeing Isaac, his elbows on the table in front of him, the mug in his hands, listening as if she were telling him how to magically disappear, and not a simple story of childhood.

'I can see it,' he said. 'I can see you running, trying to control your kite. Your brother with you. It is as though it is my own memory.'

'You did not have children?'

'I did,' he said. 'A son, Haim – meaning "life". We had tried for so long that when he came, he was a complete blessing.'

'Where is he now?' she asked, not really wanting to know the answer.

Isaac smiled weakly at her, his eyes watery. 'He died. On his tenth birthday. He was a sickly child… On that day, on his birthday, I had done this for him – come here, look.' Isaac waved her over to him.

She stood and walked the few steps to where he sat. One by one he pulled the tools from his pouch, then handed her something that looked like a tiny knife.

'See there, at the end, underneath my own,' he said.

She brought the tool towards the thin light, but she felt the engraving under her thumb before she saw it – H. S.

Silently, she handed the tool back, then returned to the upturned bucket, not knowing what to say.

'It was Hannah who told me. She ran to me just like she had as a child, kicking dust up in her wake. But it was not a cry that I'd heard before – not one of joy, of pure excitement – it was like an animal that had been caught in a trap, in pain, unable to find its way out. I knew what had happened as soon as I saw her, as soon as I heard it. I knew my son was dead.'

Isaac cried without making any noise. He sat staring at her, letting the tears fall freely from his eyes. She felt a lump in her throat, the sadness not just for Isaac but of knowing the noise that his wife had made – she had made it once herself.

'You asked me before about my fiancé,' she said. 'The day I found out he had died, I made the same noise as your wife. I remember that I fell to the floor, pulling at the skirt of my dress, then I put it over my head as if I could make it all go away – make myself go away.'

Isaac stood and walked towards her. He took her hands in his and squeezed them gently, as he had done when they had walked back to the camp one evening.

Then he turned from her, got down on all fours and scrambled around near an old jerry can.

'What are you doing?' she asked, wiping her face with the back of her hand.

'Wait. Just wait there.'

A minute passed as Isaac looked under a floorboard, and then he stood upright, a bundle of papers in his hands.

'What is it?' She stood and looked at the papers in his hands, all covered with curly, neat writing.

'I found them,' he said proudly.

'Where?'

'Here, in the shed, underneath the floorboard.'

'What are they?'

'Letters, diaries, look here – drawings even.' He pointed to a beautiful picture of a bumblebee that sniffed at a rose.

'Sit. Sit.' He waved his hand towards the upturned bucket. 'I've been reading them. Not many. Perhaps we can read together? That way we don't have to dwell on our own memories; we can read someone else's.'

Anna sat, her heart pounding as if they had both found the secret way out of the camp, and waited for Isaac to begin.

CHAPTER EIGHTEEN

J. A. L.

August 1944

Love's not Time's fool, though rosy lips and cheeks
Within his bending sickle's compass come;
Love alters not with his brief hours and weeks,
But bears it out even to the edge of doom.

I begin my writing today with Shakespeare once more. This time with words of love as I cannot find my own.

Love endures. Is that what Shakespeare meant? I hope that is correct; I hope that love can endure, even in the doom we now find ourselves in.

Love.

I learned the word when I was little: first the love for my parents and my siblings, and then for a pet dog. Each love was different though – the love for my parents stupidly taken advantage of, as if they would always love me and me them. The love for my siblings was similar, yet I was aware that at times we could hate each other for any slight that we assumed one had committed.

The love I had for my dog, for Bernard, was different again. This was a love for a best friend, and something that I had to care for. It made me wonder sometimes if it was how my parents felt about me.

Bernard was truly my best friend in the whole world. My sister was jealous of him, of the bond I had with him, yet I know she loved him too and would find her napping with him, her arms wrapped around his neck, afraid to let him go.

I did not have many friends as a child; I didn't like playing the games the boys at school enjoyed. Instead I was happier with my nose in a book, trying to imagine the worlds that were described to me, trying to imagine what it would be like to live that life.

No one wrote anything about this life, though. No one said that this could be a possibility. Even when it began, when friends and family disappeared into the night, when my father lost his job and we were made to wear the yellow stars – it still seemed impossible that this could be where we ended up.

We moved as the German army marched into our town on the Polish-German border, first to an aunt in the countryside and then to a friend of my father's, another academic who told us he could hide us and keep us safe.

The fact that we spoke both German and Polish helped somewhat. It meant that we were not confined to one country, and could pass ourselves off as someone else.

'We'll head to France,' my father said one evening, as we sat in his friend's basement, our home for over a year.

He was feverish after catching a cold from the damp that lived on the walls, the mould that grew in between the cracks of the bricks, and the drips of water that ran down in summer and froze in winter.

'Hush now,' my mother told him, and placed a cool washcloth on his head.

He did not stop, however. He sat in the bed he shared with Mother, bent over papers on which he drew maps, added dates and times of trains that his friend gave him.

I sat with my sister and younger brother, all three of us huddled on a single bed that we had learned to sleep in together – not one of us daring to move in our sleep so it was as if we were mummies in their sarcophagi; their arms across their chests, perfectly still.

I watched Father as he scribbled, his beard now long and white, his eyes squinting behind his wire-rimmed glasses. He had grown old this past year. There were more creases in his brow, more wrinkles around his thinning face.

'Do you think he has gone mad?' my brother, Szymon, asked me. He was eating as usual, popping small pieces of bread in his mouth and chewing them slowly.

'Why can't you eat it all in one go?' My sister's arm flung out and hit him.

'Because it gives me something to do,' he said and grinned.

The pair of them loved to fight; my sister Katharina, almost nineteen, Szymon sixteen, and me the eldest, always trying to settle their disputes.

'Don't fight,' I told them. 'You're always playing. It's as though you don't realise where we are.'

'I do,' Szymon said. 'But I also have a theory.'

'A theory? Your brain is the size of a pea; I doubt you have any theory in there.' Katharina laughed.

'I'll have you know that it's not just you two who have brains. I might not understand mathematics, or philosophy—'

'Or anything,' Katharina interjected.

'But,' Szymon pressed on, 'I have a theory that if you act happy, even when things are bad, and if you find some humour, then you can survive. If we are serious and scared all the time, then where will that get us?' He popped another tiny crumb of bread in his mouth, acting as if he were tasting fine chocolates.

'You two are mad,' I said, shaking my head, then looking at Father again, who mumbled something to Mother and made her smile.

'We'll go to England!' Suddenly Father sat up straight, then tried to get out of bed, his thin legs like pencils inside his trousers. He stood, wobbly, his dressing gown over his shirt, cardigan and trousers, his kippah on his head.

Szymon elbowed me in the ribs and giggled. 'Told you – mad,' he whispered.

'Listen, listen to me now. We get to France and then we get to England. I have it all worked out. All of it.' He flapped the papers at us.

I took one of the sheets from him and saw a large circle with lines coming in and out of it, random scribbles by the side. I looked to Mother, whose eyes were filling with tears.

Szymon took the paper next, and he did not joke, but looked to me and Katharina with wide scared eyes.

'Yes, Papa, that's exactly what we will do,' I said. I climbed off the bed and led him back to his, laying him down and covering him with blankets. I placed the damp washcloth on his head, and nodded at his feverish murmurings.

Soon he fell asleep.

Mother sat on one of the two wooden chairs next to him, and sang prayers to him, allowing the weak tears to fall down her face as he slept.

'It's bad, isn't it.' Katharina had huddled herself into a ball on one corner of our bed; Szymon had stopped pecking at his bread.

I nodded.

'So we're not going to France?' Szymon asked.

'No.'

'We will be safe here.' Katharina shunted over to him and wrapped her arm around his shoulders. 'We have been safe so far and we will stay safe.'

I remember sitting on the other chair, my eyes darting from my brother to my sister and then to my parents. I had to figure a way out for us, I had to get us to safety.

But how?

CHAPTER NINETEEN

Isaac

Isaac stopped reading. Anna's face showed the emotions he felt – fear, sadness.

'What happened next?' Anna asked.

'We can continue tomorrow,' Isaac said.

'Is it wrong that I want to read more? It's as though the voice, the words – I don't know.'

Isaac nodded. 'I know what you mean. It is as though it is our story, all the things we wished to say.'

Anna picked up the empty mug from Isaac's desk. 'Tomorrow?'

'Tomorrow,' he said, watching her leave and walk down the path towards the house where lights began to illuminate the darkened interior, where the Bechers awaited their breakfast and coffee, the fires to be lit.

He placed the papers back into their hiding place and took out the pieces of watches he had hidden for his masterpiece.

Ignoring the bag that held the jewellery he was to work on – removing engravings, fixing bracelets and earrings – he continued to work on the watch for Anna, wanting her to have something beautiful in her life that would always be hers.

That evening Isaac returned to the camp, somewhat satisfied with his work for the day. The watch was coming together nicely, especially the strap, which he was joining together with gemstones and gold links so that whichever way the wrist moved, it would catch the light.

He sat with Elijah in the bunkhouse, where tired yet eager faces awaited their evening meal. Tonight, it was soup again. Watery with vegetables that tasted rotten – one ladle each into a tin bowl, one lump of bread to be halved and kept for breakfast the following day, and a weak cup of coffee or a cup of water.

'I cannot bear it.' Elijah was crying over his soup. 'I cannot bear even eating it.'

'You're sick?' Isaac asked.

Elijah shook his head. 'I want to eat it, but then as soon as I do, it is gone, and I am hungry, and I cannot bear it being gone.'

Isaac looked at his own bowl. He had eaten some bread that day, brought to him by Greta, who looked as thin and gaunt as he did now, her chest rattling with her cough.

'Eat yours, then you will eat mine,' Isaac said.

'Really?' Elijah wiped his face with his sleeve. 'You really mean it?'

'I do. Now eat.'

Isaac watched his friend gulp the first bowl of soup down, then, taking Isaac's, he ate slower, as if he were at home eating dinner with a family, his spoon politely dipped in and out of the liquid.

'Where's Jan?' Isaac asked, looking around and not seeing his stern face.

'He was taken from work this afternoon – he had to do a job or something,' Elijah said between sips. 'But he didn't come back.'

Isaac's mouth was suddenly dry. 'Were others taken with him?'

Elijah nodded. 'A few. They said they had a special job for them.'

Jan's bunk was still empty over an hour after dinner. Isaac looked around as if he would find him on another, as if Jan were playing a game with him.

'He's gone,' he said quietly.

Elijah, too tired to respond, climbed into his bed and fell asleep within seconds. Isaac did not know what to do. He asked the others if they had seen Jan, seen where he had gone, but all of them were unconcerned with his questions. Instead, they had heard a rumour – someone had overheard the guards talking about the Americans, how they were close, how bombs were falling all over Germany and they would soon be set free.

Despite the fear he had in his belly, Isaac was drawn to listen to them as they eagerly discussed their freedom.

'It's true, it has to be. You know that guard, the one with the scar over his eyebrow?' someone said.

'I know him,' someone chimed in. 'He's the angel of death. He likes to take prisoners and torture them. Trust me, I know.' He raised his jacket to show his bare skin where thick, puckered scars stared angrily at them.

'Anyway, he stank of alcohol, I could smell it. He was swaying and his eyes were glassy, and he didn't even notice me when I walked past. He was talking to another guard – the young one with blond hair – he was saying how it was time, that it was going to happen soon and what would become of them? Other camps have been liberated. It is going to happen – I swear to you it is!'

'If they don't kill us first,' a voice from the back said, silencing them all. It was Jan.

Slowly, Jan appeared, like a ghost with sockets that were black where his eyes should be, his face paler than freshly fallen snow.

'They can't burn the bodies quickly enough. The trains we came in on, they're full,' Jan said.

'Full with what?' someone asked.

'Bodies. The boxcars are full. We moved some today. All day. Carting them there. There's no food left either. No food.'

Jan came closer, sweat on his brow, and Isaac sat him down and rubbed his back as though he was a child.

'They said there was little time. The Americans are coming. But I don't know if we will meet them alive.'

The men were silent, all of them looking at their hands which were not much more than bone. 'What else did they say?' someone whispered. 'Maybe we can escape?'

Jan shook his head. 'We could try. But how far could we get like this? We are almost dead. We may as well let them end it for us.' Jan stood and allowed Isaac to lead him to his bed. He lay down, staring at Isaac's bunk above him.

'I have to do it again tomorrow. There's so many of them, Isaac. So many. All one on top of the other so you cannot tell which part belongs to whom. A tangled mess of bodies, Isaac.'

Isaac sat on the edge of Jan's bunk. Words failed him. There was nothing to say, nothing to take that memory away.

So he sat until Jan fell asleep, then he sat and waited until morning, his mind tumbling over his own memories – of his son, of Hannah – and then the imagining of future memories that he hoped one day to make, if he could survive just a little longer.

Over the next few weeks, more died. From hunger, from torture, from gunshots when they tried to escape. Bodies were piled high in the camp grounds, the buzz of flies a constant hum over them. They were not asked to move them; they were not told anything. It was as though it had always been this way and they had to accept it.

Isaac had not returned to the house – no guard had come to collect him, and no word had come to him that he should have a different role. Instead, work details ceased and they were left to roam the camp, day in and day out, waiting for something to happen, whilst food was thrown at them from carts. If you were lucky and caught something, then you ate; if you did not, then you would starve.

The guards roamed too. Like a pack of hungry lost wolves. Their fingers were trigger happy, their arms filled with random strength to beat anyone who took their fancy.

Isaac stayed in the bunkhouse as much as possible. He spoke to Elijah, to Jan. They made up games to keep their minds active, and counted the time and days as they slowly crept by. He thought often of Anna and wondered if she was at the house or whether she too had been confined to the camp. When there was no game to play, no stories to tell, Isaac lay on his bunk and daydreamed of a life outside the camp. In his daydream he was a little younger, and Anna was by his side, and by his other, a small boy – an age similar to Friedrich – who wanted to mend watches, who wanted to run and play with kites when the wind whipped up.

Then he would shake the silliness from his mind, settling on real memories of his life before – of the person he used to be, of the days spent with his son in his arms, and when he was well enough, their short walks in the meadows, teaching him how to talk, the names of the trees and the birds.

If Isaac was honest with himself, he had always known his son was not for this world. He was fragile from birth, with weak spindly limbs and a cry that was so feeble, it sounded like a newborn kitten.

But his son had been full of life – full of questions, his eyes roaming over everything, wanting to know more, see more. When he had met Friedrich and the boy had asked questions, his keenness to have someone to talk to, his desire to know what else was happening in the world, had reminded Isaac of his son. And with that, a part of him, the part of loving someone, caring for someone, which he had shut down after both his son and Hannah had died, woke up.

Although the memory of the shed, of the watches, of the Bechers, was becoming ever more distant with each day that passed, he still thought of Friedrich. He worried for him, and wished he could talk to him and tell him that everything would be all right.

One afternoon, Isaac sat on a patch of grass, watching the trees rustle in the wind just beyond the fences of the camp. They were so near, so near and yet so far from him. He coughed, feeling it swell in his chest, his ribs hurting with each movement. It was getting worse.

'Schüller?' A guard stood before him. 'I need you to come with me.'

Isaac stood, then had to wait a moment for blood to find its way around his body, air into his lungs. He shuffled after the guard who walked him to the Bechers' home, his gun trained on Isaac's back as if he could run away at any moment.

On the driveway were two cars, one a black town car, the other an older model that was a deep burgundy.

'Ah, Isaac.' Becher walked towards him and dismissed the guard with a flick of his wrist. 'I am sorry I have not needed you for a while, but I need you now. You once told me you could fix anything, is that not so?'

'I did, I think I did.'

'Good, well, here are two cars. I bought them myself, and I need them to work perfectly. They are not new, from a friend. And I need you to look at the engines, check everything, make sure that they can go for miles and miles without anything happening to them.'

Isaac looked at the cars and then at Becher, whose smile was set firmly in place, the top button of his shirt undone, the tie askew.

'So you'll do it then?' Becher slapped him on the back, which made Isaac start a coughing fit.

Becher took a step away from him, lit a cigarette and blew the smoke directly in Isaac's face. 'You won't let me down, will you?

The mechanic I had, well, he isn't here anymore, and I need this to stay between us, you understand? The other guards would be jealous if they knew I had bought cars – they'd wonder why they weren't getting paid more!' Becher forced a laugh.

Isaac recovered himself, wiping away the tears that had filled his eyes as he coughed. 'I'm not a mechanic,' he said simply.

'But you can fix things.' Becher took a step towards him, pointing at him with his cigarette. 'You said you could fix things.'

Isaac nodded. 'But I've rarely fixed cars.'

'Rarely? So you have done it before?'

Isaac remembered a tractor he had fixed, and he'd helped a neighbour with his car when the fuel pipe had been clogged. 'Only a couple.'

'Well, that'll have to do then. Like I said, take a look. Tell me what you need. Take the pieces back to the shed, clean them, fix them.' Becher waved his hand in the air. 'Do whatever you need to do with them. Just make sure I can trust them, is that clear?'

Isaac nodded and Becher grinned at him. 'I knew I could rely on you. Now, here, I'll open the bonnets for you. Take a look and then get to work – quickly, now, as quickly as you can.'

Becher switched on the engines and Isaac watched as they sprang to life. The black car seemed to clink and clang every thirty seconds, as if something were knocking against it. He counted and waited for each clang – yes, thirty seconds.

The burgundy car ran quieter, yet there was a churning noise, as if something were rubbing against another part.

Becher turned off the engines. 'So?'

'I need to look at them for a while.'

'Yes. I'll leave you to it,' Becher said, but did not move. Isaac saw that Becher's eyes could not stay still; they roamed the fence, the gate, then settled back on the cars once more. 'Yes. I'll leave you to it,' Becher repeated, then walked back to the house.

*

Isaac spent a few hours looking at the engines, trying to under-stand how they worked. His mind was tired, clouded with hunger, and it took him longer than normal to see the basic workings. What was he supposed to do? Clear the carburettor? Clear the fuel pipes, check the oil? That was all he could see to do. He wiped his oil-smeared hands on his coat, then made his way towards the shed. He needed to think.

'Where are you going? What do you need?' Becher was bounding towards him.

'I need to think about the engines,' Isaac told him calmly. 'Like I did with the grandfather clock. I need to think.'

'Yes! Quite right. I will bring you some paper and a pencil like before, and you can do your diagrams and work it all out, yes?'

Before Isaac could answer, Becher was gone, then returned a minute later, the paper in his hands. 'Remember, you come to me, only to me, and tell me what you need, all right?'

Isaac nodded, took the paper and pencil, and headed towards the shed he'd not seen in weeks.

He was in the shed barely a moment before Anna burst in and took him in an embrace.

'I thought you were dead,' she said, her bottom lip trembling.

'I'm still here.' Isaac began to cough again, and Anna helped him to sit.

'Wait here, I'll be back.' Anna ran from the shed, leaving Isaac to find his breath.

'Here.' Anna was back, the hot mug of coffee in one hand, a lump of bread and cheese in the other. 'Take it, eat, drink. You look so weak.'

Isaac ate without tasting the bread and then sat sipping at the coffee, allowing himself to savour it.

'You're sick,' Anna said, a crease in her brow.

'And you look even thinner,' Isaac remarked.

Anna nodded. 'Things are changing though; the Americans are coming,' she said excitedly. Although dark circles were beneath Anna's eyes, she was brighter than before, as if the thought of the Americans was bringing her hope.

Isaac wanted to tell her that they would be lucky to see them, that maybe by the time they arrived they would all be dead from hunger, but he could not take that hope from her. 'They are,' he said simply.

'Just think, Isaac, that soon we will be out of this place! We can find our family; we can go wherever we want to go.'

'And where will you go, Anna?'

'Away from Germany. Maybe America. I'd take my friend Nina, and her brother and anyone else I can find. We can live in the sun, near a coast, and everything will be bright and colourful.'

Anna's dream lifted a weight from him, and he allowed himself a moment to imagine her laughing, wearing a bright red dress, her cheeks plump and belly full.

'I have to get back.' Anna looked at the house. 'Frau Becher is hysterical at the moment, demanding things every minute of the day and then screaming at everyone. I'll come back later?'

Isaac nodded and let her leave. He looked at the blank pages in front of him and realised they were not the papers he wanted to see.

It took him over five minutes to get down on all fours and find the bundle of J. A. L.'s musings. He had to sit and catch his breath before he started to read, and as soon as he'd finished the first page, he wished he had never started.

CHAPTER TWENTY

J. A. L.

August 1944

Things have changed yet again. It is strange to think that things do change here – it surprised even me, whose days are spent working and nights sleeping.

I was asked yesterday to help at the morgue. This was unusual, and I felt a shiver of fear as soon as my number was called for the work detail. I wanted to tell the guard that this was not where I was supposed to be, that I was meant to be in Herr Becher's garden, pruning, mowing their lawn.

I and two others were led to the rear of the morgue, where on the grass lay the naked body of a teenaged boy who was over six feet tall, and another smaller boy, perhaps only three feet.

'Freaks,' the guard said, and kicked the foot of the taller boy. 'You know, they are both fifteen – can you imagine, a fifteen-year-old who keeps growing to the sky, and then a boy the same age shunted towards the ground?'

The guard lit a cigarette and blew a plume of smoke so that for a second the bodies were in a haze, almost as if it were all a dream, or a nightmare.

'See those barrels over there?' The guard pointed to two large vats with steam pouring out of them. 'Put them in there, then sit and wait until all the flesh is off them. Then bring them out and lay them on the ground. Keep the water boiling – stoke the coals underneath, don't let them go out. You've no idea how long it took me this morning to get them going.'

I felt vomit rise in my throat, the coffee and bread from the morning stuck there as I tried to swallow it down.

One of the others did vomit, covering his shoes. The guard spat on the floor in distaste.

'They're coming to collect the skeletons tomorrow, so we need it done today.'

'Where are they going?' I asked, surprising myself and waiting for the inevitable blow that was to come from either his fist or baton.

The guard seemed happy to talk though, his eyes excited. 'The Führer's museum, of course! He will have skeletons of all the strange shapes you Jews grow into. Can you imagine it? A whole museum showing the truth! It will be a sight to see when it is finished.'

With that, the guard dropped the rest of his cigarette on the ground, his black boot scuffing it until it died.

'I'll be over there,' he indicated a watchtower, 'and if I'm not, someone else will be.'

We nodded at him – we knew. There was always someone watching, always someone with a gun in their hands, desperate to pull the trigger for any reason.

'Is he serious?' the man who didn't vomit asked me.

'I don't see how this can be a joke,' I said. My eye caught the naked bodies of the boys once more, flies already buzzing around the taut skin across their ribs, their pubic bones jutting out.

'I can't,' the vomiting man said.

'We've no choice,' I replied.

Between the three of us, we picked up the tall boy and carried his body towards the hot water. We laid him there and did the same with his smaller friend, who weighed so little, I think I could have carried him in my arms alone.

'We should give them names,' I said.

'That's disgusting. What on earth are you saying that for?' the vomiting man said.

'They deserve a name before we do this. They deserve to be thought of as people.'

'Fine,' the non-vomiting man said. 'The tall one, he can have my name, Alexander.'

'And he, the small one, he can have mine,' the vomiting man said, 'Jeremiah.'

I nodded and said a small prayer for them both. Then together we placed each one in the vats of boiling water.

'They're not going in all the way,' Alexander said. I looked and saw his dead counterpart's head bobbing on top of the water.

'We need to weigh them down,' I said.

We took them out once more, feeling the warmth that came from their skin as if the water were making them alive again. With effort, we secured some rocks to their feet and tried again, this time seeing them sink under the water.

'What do we do now?' Jeremiah asked. 'Watch them cook?'

'I think so.' I sat near the vat and prodded at the coals with a stick that had been left for us, along with a heap of coal and a few bits of firewood.

I tried not to think of the boys in the water. I tried not to think of their parents who would wonder what had happened to them.

'How do you think they died?' Alexander asked.

'I don't even want to guess,' I said.

'They were experimented on.' Jeremiah sat the furthest away from the vats, his eyes searching the camp grounds for something to look at.

'Experimented?' Alexander asked.

'There's a doctor. Well, he was a doctor. He was asked to work in one of the buildings here. He said that they experiment on women, men and children. They like twins, he said, when they are identical. He said he saw twin girls have injections given to them every day that made them cry out for their mother. He could not sleep after seeing that. He wanted to save them – but what could he do, what can any of us do?'

'I didn't know,' I said. I felt foolish, useless – how could I not know? Had I been blind, or did I just not want to see?

'I hear you work at the house?' Alexander tried to change the subject.

I nodded. 'Gardener.'

'Is that who you were before?'

'I was a student. I will be again.' Then I looked at the vats and realised that I probably would never be the same person again.

We were allowed lunch. A thin soup in the mess hall whilst two others watched over the boiling bodies.

For the first time in months, I could not eat. Neither could Jeremiah or Alexander. My stomach growled and moaned with hunger; even my saliva was not upset by what I had seen and filled my mouth at the scent of food. Yet, there was a block between my hunger and my heart. I could not, would not eat today. The boys in the water deserved that much from me.

When we returned to the vats…

I don't think I can write it.

I know I must. I must write it. I must explain what is happening here but the sight, my Lord, the sight that awaited us.

The two men who had been asked to watch the water and keep it boiling had not been told what was in the vats. I wish now I had said something – I wish I hadn't tried to save them from the knowledge.

They were eating. They were eating the pieces of flesh that had come away from the bones and were floating on top of the water.

This time I vomited. Alexander ran towards them, waving his arms in the air. I did not hear what he said to them – perhaps he told them they would get in trouble. Either way, the two men walked right past me, neither looking as though they knew what they had done, leaving us with the memory instead.

It is a week since I last wrote. It feels like longer.

I could not raise a word, either by my hand or mouth, after what happened last week. It was as though I was struck dumb with the images that swirled in my brain.

I have slept weakly. My dreams merging all the time with water, and sometimes a doctor who looks over me and tries to give me an injection.

Alexander and Jeremiah have slept badly too. I see them walking around the camp as if they are dead, as if all three of us died a little bit that day.

One thing I cannot understand is that the hum of bees, the singing of birds and the colours of flowers still exist. How can things carry on as if nothing so horrific is happening around us?

CHAPTER TWENTY-ONE

Anna

March 1945

She felt lighter than she had done in weeks. Seeing Isaac again, hearing the rumours of the Americans coming closer – all of it filled her with a happiness that she could not contain. Greta was a little better and returned to work for half-days, once again mothering her, making sure she ate and drank.

She did not fear Liesl's screaming demands, did not care that Herr Becher was home more often, locked in his study, always smelling of alcohol, the fires always burning as if someone were adding fuel to them that she never saw.

The arrival of the cars surprised her. Neither was new and shiny like the ones they had had before – both were a little worn, beaten and average.

But they had brought Isaac back to her; he was to fix them, he told her. He was to make it so that they worked perfectly. So now, instead of watches, he had engine parts in front of him, his trembling hands constantly smeared with oil, his fingernails blackened with it.

Anna made coffee for Liesl and took it to her room. She knocked gently on the door, expecting not to receive an answer and to leave it outside. Yet Anna heard her voice from within, weak, pleading, 'Come in.'

She turned the doorknob, and instead of finding Liesl in bed, she was in her silk shift, her breasts straining against the material, her hair uncombed, falling in knotted tendrils down her back.

Liesl did not turn to look at Anna but stared at herself in the mirror, surrounded by a puddle of dresses and skirts, as if she had tried on everything in her wardrobe and found them all wanting.

'I brought you coffee.' Anna placed the cup on her bedside table and made to leave.

'Look at me.' Liesl turned, her eyes red and puffy, a smear of lipstick on her cheek where she had attempted to wipe it away with the back of her hand.

Anna did. She looked at her. Her arms were thick at the top, tapering until her wrists met her childlike hands. Her thighs were dimpled and there was a bruise on one of her knees.

'What am I to do?' she asked. 'Look at me. Is this a woman who can survive this?'

'I think we can survive many things,' Anna ventured.

'You have,' Liesl spat, then looked at herself again.

'I'll leave you to dress.' Anna tried to walk backwards, her hand feeling for the doorknob behind her.

'When I was younger – wait, how old are you?'

'Twenty-nine,' Anna answered.

'Yes, when I was about your age, I had everything. Men wanted me – all of them, and I took my time choosing. It's not like choosing a dress, or a lipstick, or even a piece of jewellery, it's more than that – you have to be sure. I can't deny I liked the courting, however.' Liesl smiled to herself, then sat on her dressing chair and opened a small gold cigarette case, taking from it a long thin cigarette which she lit with shaking fingers.

Anna had never seen her smoke before, and the surprise must have shown in her face.

'Oh, this,' Liesl waved the cigarette, 'I used to smoke, when I was young. But then I stopped because my husband said that it was common.' She grinned again, showing some lipstick on her teeth, then took a deep drag and blew out a plume.

'Would you like something to eat?' Anna tried, her hand on the brass doorknob now, waiting to turn it and leave.

'They all wanted me.' Liesl looked through the smoke as if she were looking back on a memory contained there. 'All of them. Lawyers, nobles, wealthy, powerful men. But then, I fell in love. Have you been in love?'

Anna didn't answer.

'Well, look at you!' Liesl tipped her head back and laughed. 'Those arms like spindles, your chest flat as a child. But me, I was the stunning one. I was the one who was slim, but not too slim.' Liesl tapped the ash on the floor, then smudged it with a big toe that had chipped red nail polish. 'He loved that about me – couldn't get enough. Thank God the Führer came to power when he did – made him a rising star! Before that, he was plain, but soon he grew in confidence, and I grew towards that as a sunflower seeks out the sun. But then, all things good must change. Friedrich changed it. He… didn't see me as before anymore, he dare not touch me for a year after the birth. I was a mother, you see – I had ceased to be the new bride. I was just a mother.'

'Friedrich loves you,' Anna said, sure that she needed to say something about the boy.

'Does he?' Liesl looked surprised now, and ground out her cigarette on her dressing table. 'He looks at me with those sad eyes, and I can't bear it. It's as if he wants something from me all the time. I carried him in my body, gave him life – is that not enough?'

Liesl stood and walked to the mirror once more, running her hands over her hips, tilting her head to the side. 'I must find something to wear,' she muttered to herself.

Anna took this as a signal to leave and quickly departed, her breath coming quick as soon as she was out of that room. She decided that Greta should take the coffee to Liesl next – she could not do it again.

That afternoon, Anna found her thoughts turning towards Piotr, but in her mind's eye his features were mingled with Isaac's, his voice Isaac's too. She tried to concentrate on polishing the windows in the dining room, now and then allowing herself to look out into the garden. As she did, she saw a robin that flitted from branch to branch, singing a song, his red breast thrust out proudly. She swallowed, then opened the window a crack and called to the bird. He flew closer to her, sitting on the edge of a stone planter, his wings twitching as his tiny black eyes looked at her.

'Piotr?' she whispered.

The bird twitched once more, then let out a quick trill before flying off into a thicket of trees.

Closing the window, she sat on the window seat, feeling foolish for talking to the bird – Piotr's favourite. If her mother were here, she would tell her that it was a sign – that Piotr had come to let her know he was all right, that it was good she was replacing his face in her mind with someone else's.

A small ball of anger surged in Anna's chest – something she could not quell completely. He had left her to work with the resistance and by doing so had been shot in a raid, leaving her without him, without anyone. Then, she saw a figure move in the garden – Isaac – who walked slowly around the shed, stopping at a sprig of daffodils to touch their petals. Then he walked back to the shed, and Anna did not feel completely alone.

That evening, the camp was unusually quiet. Anna was led to her bunkhouse in the dark, some of the floodlights switched off. She tripped on what she thought was a stone or twig, but when she looked down, she saw that it was a foot protruding in all its whiteness from a heap of bodies that had been dumped.

Nina had stayed awake for her, and climbed into her bunk as soon as she could.

'They're coming.' Anna could see her grin, even in the gloom. 'That's why the lights are out – we've been hearing the bombs drop all day. They're really coming, Anna.'

Anna felt some of her hopefulness fall away as the reality of their present thrust itself into her mind – the bodies outside, the fact that they were still here, the hunger and the tiredness that plagued them all.

'Just think, we can plan now – what it will be like when we leave. Remember we used to talk about how I would be a dancer?' Nina continued.

Anna nodded, remembering. That's all they had done. Remember their past, try to ignore it, try to get through each day. But now, Anna felt fear instead of the hope that oozed through Nina's every pore.

'What is that saying?' Anna mumbled. 'The calm before the storm.'

'What do you mean?'

'I mean it may get worse before it gets better.'

'How can it get worse? We didn't even get counted tonight – imagine that! They're giving up, Anna, I can tell. Then soon we can find Kuba, and you …' Nina tailed off.

'I will find someone,' Anna said, thinking of Isaac.

'Not someone.' Nina hugged her, held her close. 'You will have me; we will have each other.'

CHAPTER TWENTY-TWO

Friedrich

Mother was acting strangely – this Friedrich knew. At first it had scared him, seeing her half dressed for dinner, or wandering about the hallways with a cigarette in her hand, her nightdress askew. But now, it had become almost comforting. She did not shout at him when she was like this – she barely even noticed that he was there.

So on the day he asked her to open the bedroom doors opposite his own, the ones that had windows looking out into the garden, she simply handed him the key, her eyes glassy and uninterested.

He looked at the key in his palm and could not believe his luck. Finally, he could see the place where Isaac was taken back to each night – finally, he could see what his parents had been trying to hide from him.

He did not waste time and hurried to the first door, which would not yield. The lock in the second, however, gave way to his key and he pushed open the door, revealing a bare room, the long windows grimy with dust and dirt.

He spat on the sleeve of his jumper, then pulled it over his hand and wiped a pane clear, smearing the grey muck as he did.

At first, he saw Isaac's shed. The light wasn't burning in the window; instead the door was open, and he could see Isaac just inside, sitting on a stool cleaning something in his hands.

His eyes focused next on the row of trees behind the shed. Then beyond, where wire fences could be seen. He ran back into his bedroom and found the binoculars his father had given him for Christmas two years ago. At the window he held them up to his eyes and corrected the focus, so he could see what lay inside the wire.

There were people moving slowly, all wearing the same striped uniform as Isaac and Anna. He could see the guards' watchtower and saw that they held guns.

He scanned left, then right, where he could see children sitting playing in the dirt, all of them thin, skeletal, their faces indistinguishable from each other.

Friedrich lowered the binoculars.

He ran from the room, down the stairs and out into the back garden. He passed Isaac, who looked at him with surprise as he ran to the trees at the edge of the garden and tried to find his way through. He didn't think about what he would do when he got there – all he knew was that he had to see it up close, had to see what was really there.

But the undergrowth was too thick, and his jumper snagged on a branch. He tried to pull himself free while scratching himself all over, his tears hot and thick running down his cheeks.

Suddenly there were hands on him, hands that tugged him free and drew him into an embrace.

He sobbed into Isaac's chest. Isaac did not speak, did not ask what he was doing. He just let him cry until the sobs became fewer, shorter, and he found his breath again through sorrowful hiccups.

Isaac wrapped his arm around Friedrich's shoulder and led him away from the trees back to the garden, towards the shed, then sat him down in his chair and placed a blanket on his lap.

Friedrich did not know what to say. There were questions swirling in his brain as he tried to piece it all together, but again,

Isaac did not prompt him – did not ask what was wrong – he simply waited.

'I saw,' Friedrich finally said, gazing upwards at Isaac.

'I know.'

'There are children. Like me.'

'I know.'

'Father – he put them there. He said they were evil – that you were all evil – that you were dangerous.'

Isaac smiled at the boy. 'But you see we are not.'

Friedrich nodded then wiped his nose on his sleeve. 'My parents are wrong. I need to tell them they are wrong.' Friedrich stood, but then felt Isaac's hands on his shoulders pushing him back into the seat.

'You cannot. It would not matter, not one bit. It's not just your parents, Friedrich, it's so many people. If you tell them, and you tell them that we are friends, then that will be dangerous for me.'

'We are friends?' Friedrich asked.

'Of course we are!'

Friedrich smiled then. 'I only had one friend, Otto. But now I have two.'

'You do. You have two friends.'

From the house, a murmur of music lifted out and carried towards them. 'Father keeps playing music,' Friedrich said. 'All the time. He locks himself away and plays music. Greta leaves bottles of whiskey for him outside the door, and when I go back a few minutes later, they are gone.'

'Things are changing,' Isaac said.

'What does that mean?'

'I don't really know. Perhaps it means I can go home soon. Perhaps it means that your father will need to find a new job.'

'You will leave? But I thought we were friends?'

'We are.' Isaac knelt down and took Friedrich's hands in his. 'We are friends. And one day, when you are old enough, you will come to my workshop and I will show you how to mend watches, just like me, and we will walk in the fields together and look at the wildflowers, and sit in my garden in the evening.'

'And we can listen to music – but different music to Father's,' Friedrich added.

'I would have to get myself a gramophone, but yes, we could listen to music.'

Friedrich watched as Isaac stood slowly, holding his thigh as he did, his face a picture of pain. Isaac sat on the bucket, stretching his leg in front of him.

'It's nothing,' Isaac told him. 'Just my age.'

'Does it hurt all the time?'

'Most of the time, yes.'

'It's just that, I was thinking… I was thinking about the music and when I was at school, sometimes there was a song on the radio and Otto and I would dance around the room, and it was really fun. I thought you may want to dance to music too?'

'I cannot dance.' Isaac shook his head.

'Because of your leg?'

'Because I've never really tried.'

'Not even with a lady?'

'Only once, at my wedding. And I was no good.'

Friedrich thought for a moment, a seed of an idea forming in his brain.

'Do you think Anna can dance?' Friedrich asked.

'I have no idea. I would imagine so – you should ask her,' Isaac said.

'She is your friend, isn't she?'

'She is.'

'So do you think she will be mine too? Then when you teach me about watches maybe Anna can come too?'

Isaac looked at his hands and did not speak.

'Is that not a good idea?' Friedrich asked.

Isaac looked at him. 'It is the best idea I have heard for a very long time.'

Friedrich stood. 'I have something important to do,' he said. 'I'll come back soon.'

'Where are you going?' Isaac called after him, as he ran back towards the house.

Friedrich turned and smiled and waved, his plan in motion.

Friedrich knew his father and mother would be out that evening – it was just a matter of dealing with Schmidt. He had done it before and would do it again.

Friedrich found Anna in the kitchen that afternoon, interrupting her as she chopped vegetables for dinner whilst Greta stirred at something on the stove. 'Anna, can you dance?'

'Should you be in here?' Greta warned, looking behind him as if his parents were there.

'Oh, Greta, Father said can you please go and see him in the study – he has something to say to you about this evening.'

Greta slowly walked towards him, her face showing the same pain Isaac's had when he had moved his leg.

Friedrich waited until Greta had shuffled from the room and asked again, 'Can you dance, Anna?'

'I used to be able to.'

'Like the dancing with a man, when he spins you around a room? Like that sort of dancing?'

Anna laughed. 'Yes. I suppose so. Why do you ask?'

'No reason!' Friedrich ran out of the kitchen and bounded up the stairs to his parents' bathroom – he had to act quickly.

When he returned, Greta was talking to Anna and he stood at the kitchen door whilst they spoke.

'To Munich, tonight?' Anna asked.

'That's what he said. Him and the wife. Back tomorrow.'

'What about Friedrich?'

'Schmidt will be staying over to mind him.'

'He makes me feel really strange. He's always looking at me and things in the house as if he is weighing up whether he wants them or not,' Anna said.

'Oh, Friedrich.' Greta caught a glimpse of him. 'What do you want?'

'I'm hungry,' he said. 'Can I please have one of those cakes you made yesterday?'

'Now?' Greta glanced at the clock. 'It'll be time for tea soon enough.'

'But if Mother and Father are going out, maybe they won't take tea, so maybe I could have my cake now?'

Greta shook her head and Friedrich held his breath – he needed that cake. 'Fine, here.' She cut a slice of stodgy fruit cake and handed it to him on a small plate.

He scurried from the kitchen and sat waiting in the living room. He would pounce as soon as his parents left.

By four, his parents stood at the doorway of the living room, explaining that they would be back tomorrow.

'Don't misbehave for Schmidt,' his father said.

His mother barely glanced at him, her eyes on the front door, waiting to make her escape. She had managed to dress herself properly, Friedrich noted, her dress perfectly fitted, though it was at odds with her wild hair and pained expression.

'Yes. Yes, be good. Come now, Peter, let's go.'

He watched their chauffeured car disappear down the drive and turn onto the road. Then he jumped up.

He knew where Schmidt was, where he always was, in his father's study. He knocked on the door, but this time did not wait for Schmidt and simply left the cake outside the door, hoping that he would think Greta or Anna had left it for him, just in case he had connected his previous tiredness with the unexpected gift from Friedrich.

He waited in the living room once more, hearing the study door open then close. He tiptoed back – the plate was gone.

Greta brought him a sandwich which he ate at the dining room table, as though he were king of the house.

'Greta,' Friedrich said to her retreating back, 'Father said to tell you that you can go home because you have been poorly; he said Anna could give me my supper and Schmidt will take her back to the camp.'

'He did, did he?' She raised her eyebrow at him. 'Are you sure that's what he said?'

'Completely sure. He said to tell you just before he left. He said he didn't have time to be giving orders about me, so I was to tell you instead.'

Greta seemed to believe him, nodding her head and returning to the kitchen. Soon, he saw her walking past the dining room window, her coat buttoned up, her hat placed firmly on her head.

The gramophone was heavy, and it took him a while to get it from the living room into the dining room, which overlooked the garden and was close to the kitchen. Once he had it in position, he ran back, his hands sweaty, and chose the record that had a picture of a woman on the sleeve cover, the music he remembered as something his mother had played years before.

Just as he was threading the hole of the shiny black vinyl onto the spoke, he heard the study door open.

He held his breath, the record hovering above the player. There were no footsteps, there was no voice shouting out.

He heard a grunt, then the study door closed again.

He hadn't eaten the cake yet.

Friedrich placed the record down. He had to get rid of Schmidt – but how? He was sure he would eat the cake; he was sure that the sleeping tablets would work again. He just had to wait.

Suddenly there was a crashing in the study, as if a heavy tome had fallen off a shelf.

Anna came running from the kitchen and saw Friedrich. 'What's going on?'

Friedrich shrugged. 'It came from the study.'

Anna's eyes glanced at the gramophone, then she walked quickly away, Friedrich at her heels.

At the study door she knocked once, twice, three times, and there was no answer.

'Maybe we should go in?' Friedrich suggested. 'Just to check.'

Anna's hand went to the doorknob, then pulled back again.

'Here, I'll do it. I'll go in first – that way, if he shouts then he can shout at me. He does it all the time anyway.'

Anna nodded at him, and with confidence he opened the door to find Schmidt face-down on the rug in front of his father's desk, drool spilling out of his mouth as he snored.

'Oh!' Anna gasped behind him. 'He's hurt.'

'No! Not hurt.' Friedrich pushed her out of the room, closed the door and stood in front of it, barring her entrance. 'He's just sleeping. He does that all the time, especially when Father goes out.'

'Sleeping – on the floor?' Anna's hands were on her hips.

'Yes. Father said he could not sleep on the couch as it was not his, so I saw him lie down the other day and go to sleep.' Friedrich wanted to laugh at how easily the lies rolled off his tongue. He wished Otto were here so he could witness his prowess.

'Are you sure – maybe we should call a doctor to be safe?'

Although Anna looked concerned, she did not move to go to the telephone and Friedrich realised that she wanted to believe him.

'Really, Anna.' He took her hand in his, leading her away. 'Better let him sleep. You know how grumpy he is. Imagine if we make a fuss and wake him, imagine then how angry he will be.'

Anna left him in the hallway and returned to the kitchen, and he noticed that she walked with her head a little higher now his parents were gone and Schmidt was no longer a threat.

He went back to the gramophone and finished setting it up. Then, he lit some candles around the room, closed the drapes, and pushed the large table out of the centre of the room as much as he could, leaving some space on the floor.

He stood back and looked at his handiwork – it was magical, he decided, fit for a king and queen.

Isaac was still tinkering with a piece of rubber piping when Friedrich opened the door to the shed, blowing into it and then cleaning it with a black rag.

'Come with me,' Friedrich said, making Isaac look up.

'Where?'

'It's a surprise. Please, come with me.'

'I can't, I have to finish this for your father.' He held up the rubber piping. 'It's for the car, for the fuel. It had a hole in it.'

'Father and Mother have gone to Munich. They won't be back tonight. Please, Isaac. If you do this for me, I promise in my whole life whilst we are friends, I will never ask for anything else. Please!'

Friedrich had come so close – so very close. He had not thought that Isaac might not do as he wanted.

'It's Anna!' he suddenly blurted out. 'She needs you.'

'Anna?' Isaac stood and looked to the house. 'I thought you said it was a surprise?'

'It is. Sort of. I was in a rush and my words got all jumbled. Anyway, please, it's Anna, she needs you.'

Slowly Isaac nodded and he followed Friedrich to the house, through the kitchen door where Anna was washing sheets in a large sink, water creeping up the arms of her brown work dress, causing it to darken.

'What's going on?' Anna spun round, water dripping onto the tiled floor.

'Come with me.' Friedrich held out his hands to the two of them and dumbly they took them, allowing him to lead them into the dining room.

Anna gasped when she entered. 'This is what you've been doing?'

Friedrich dropped their hands and placed the needle on the record, the smooth melody of a saxophone ringing out, then accompanied by the tinkle of light keys on the piano.

'It's for you both. To dance. It made Mother happy when Father would dance with her. And when Otto and I would dance at school. I thought you would like it.'

They both stood as still as statues, staring at him.

He had got it wrong; he had got it all so wrong. They didn't want to dance – they didn't like his surprise.

He felt tears prick at his eyes, then Anna stepped forward, crouched down and put her arms around him.

'Thank you,' she whispered in his ear, her voice breaking. 'Thank you. It's perfect.'

A woman's voice began to sing – deep, rich with English words that Friedrich did not know.

Isaac still stood motionless, and Friedrich watched as Anna moved towards him and took his hands in hers. 'May I have this dance?' she asked him.

Slowly, ever so slowly, Isaac put his arm around Anna and the two began to sway to the music, moving silently, carefully. Friedrich sat on a chair and watched them, the flicker of the candles in the darkened room causing shadows to jump on the walls, so that their shadows danced too, as if there were more people in the room, all of them dancing whilst the voice of the woman, who his mother had said was named Billie Holiday, sang out, making Anna cry.

CHAPTER TWENTY-THREE

Isaac

April 1945

Isaac dreamt that he was with Hannah. They danced in the spring meadows, the music filtering from the heavens, a woman's voice, rich and deep, the tinkle of piano keys helping her to hold the melody.

There was someone else with them too – a child, a boy, who clung to them both – who had Hannah's eyes. In that moment he felt a rush of warmth, of happiness swelling in his body.

Hannah did not speak to him as they danced. They held each other close.

When he woke, he felt bereft. His body was cold, his fingers numb, and he realised where he really was.

'You were muttering in your sleep,' Elijah told him as he climbed out of his bunk.

'What did I say?'

'I don't know – just mutterings. We all do it, I suppose. But I haven't heard you do it before.'

Isaac tried to talk but a wave of coughing overtook him, and he felt Elijah's hand patting him gently on the back.

'You're getting worse,' he said.

Jan's face appeared, his hand on Isaac's forehead. 'He is. You are.'

'I'll be fine.' Isaac made to get out of bed. 'It's just a cold. Nothing more.'

He allowed Elijah and Jan to help him up, get him dressed, and walk him to the roll-call square.

As they walked, Isaac saw three men carrying a body, the figure somehow familiar, adding it to the pile beside the morgue – the overflow of death all around them, dotted in heaps as if they were mounds of manure, waiting to be spread in a garden.

A garden. Levi.

Isaac pulled away from his friends and hobbled as quickly as he could towards the men, towards the body. It lay on top of the pile, the face contorted, the mouth wide open, a fly settling inside.

'Died a few days ago,' one of the prisoners who had carried the body told him. 'Knew him, did you?'

Isaac stroked Levi's forehead, then tried to push his eyelids down to cover the dark staring eyes. He felt the rise of a moan but swallowed it down, where it lodged like a piece of stale bread in his throat.

'Won't work. Rigor has set in.'

'You can't leave him here, like this,' he croaked, willing himself not to cry.

'No choice. We can't leave any of them here, but where are we meant to put them? The guards won't let us bury them.'

'He always smiled,' Isaac said. 'He always smiled and told jokes. He was going to get out – I knew he was.'

Elijah was now by his side. 'Who knows who is going to survive, Isaac? Come. We have to be counted.'

He did not hear his number called; he did not care. Levi's face haunted him. The grin gone, the humour and light disappeared.

When he sat in his shed later that morning, he could not remember getting there. It was the same feeling he had had when

Hannah had died – one minute he would be in his workshop tinkering with a broken clock, the next he would find himself at home, sitting in front of the empty fireplace, wood in his hands as if ready to light it, yet with no memory of how he'd got to this point in time.

He coughed, a tightness in his chest, wishing it would overcome him, forcing his heart to stop right there and then so he could go to Hannah and dance in the field, just like in his dream.

When he had calmed his breathing, he managed to extract his gift for Anna from underneath the loose floorboard. This was something he could do – something his brain could concentrate on. He laid it out in front of him, the watch face with the tiny designs, the strap that linked together gold clasps, the tiny rubies and sapphires he had taken from the bracelet straps of some of the finer ladies' watches. The only thing left to do was to empty the insides of the quiet watch she had so admired and transplant them into this one.

With shaking hands and wheezing breath, he spent hours picking up cogs and springs with his delicate tweezers, fitting them together in a puzzle only he knew how to solve.

'Isaac?' He was dreaming again. It was Anna's voice in the dream. Where was the music?

'Isaac?' she said again, this time releasing the anchor of sleep, leading him into the cold reality that made him feel nauseous as he surfaced.

'You were sleeping,' she said, as she placed a mug of hot water in front of him. 'You are still so unwell. I thought hot water with some lemon juice, sugar and honey would help more than coffee.'

He took the drink, still dopey with sleep, and sipped at it, tasting the sweetness, feeling the warmth seep to his belly.

'Thank you,' he managed to croak, his voice becoming hoarser with each coughing fit.

'Let me find you something to eat.' She turned to hurry back to the kitchen.

'No.' He stopped her, waving the suggestion away. 'I'm not hungry.'

'You must eat, Isaac. You must.'

'I cannot. Not today. Please.'

Anna hesitated, then sat and faced him, her brow crinkled with concern.

'You shouldn't worry like that,' he said. 'Your face may stay that way.'

She grinned at him. 'I knew you had it in you to make a joke.'

'A wise man once told me that I should smile more and try to find the humour, even here. I thought he was mad. But I have come to realise that he was right. It is the only thing they can't take away from us – the part of us that makes us completely ourselves, completely unique.'

'When we danced,' Anna said, 'that's when I felt myself again. As if the music and the movement brought me out once more. I have a friend, Nina, and she loves to dance. I haven't told her yet that I danced in Sturmbannführer Becher's dining room, but when I do, I can't wait to see the surprise and delight in her eyes.' Anna paused, looking thoughtful, and then she nodded towards the hiding place.

'Will you read me some more?' she asked.

Isaac thought of the last time he had read – the bodies in the vats of water.

'I'm not sure,' he said.

'Please. It will fill our minds with something else.'

Before he could protest, Anna went to the loose floorboard and lifted it, pulling out the pages.

'Here.' She handed it to him.

He was glad that he had kept the watch in his pocket, ready to give it to her, but now she sat there, he wanted to wait, wanted it to be a special moment, like the dancing, something that would bring them both joy. He looked at the pages in his hands. He wasn't sure that J. A. L.'s writings would achieve that goal.

The last entry he had read alone, he discarded.

'All right, let's see,' he said, and began.

CHAPTER TWENTY-FOUR

J. A. L.

September 1944

My love, I have not written you for some time. It is not that I did not want to, rather my words were not of love, not of beautiful things or drawings that I think will amuse and delight you.

Today though, my mind is clearer. Autumn has set in, and as I raked leaves today, I marvelled at the colours before me. The yellows, golds, reds and browns, all mingled together, all different and yet the same.

I picked up a leaf, deep red, its skeleton coming through a sparkling gold. I have it here with me and have placed it within the pages to show you. Can you see the way its edges are frayed, not by man, but by design? Little tiny nicks along the sides. It made me think that I am like this leaf, as are you. We are frayed, tattered, of course, by what has been done to us, and yet it will become a part of us, so much so that we will seem as though we are frayed by design and not by circumstance.

One day I will be able to see you, all of you. I will wake early every morning, not to wake you but just to see you. Will you do the same for me?

Liesl Becher is getting fat. I noticed it today. She left the house for the first time in months and snipped back the last few flowers that were holding on, the tops of her arms straining underneath the sleeves of her dress, her cleavage spilling out. I envied her. That is odd to say, but I do. I envy the weight she carries and imagine the food she eats to get that way. I can hear you now, telling me you should never call a woman fat, and I do agree – but what does it matter? She is so surly, so mean, that I can't apologise. I actually laughed to myself as I wrote it – a slight against her, one she will never hear, but still it is my small revenge.

I try to remember the last good meal I ate. I think it was in that basement of my father's friend, on the day Father died – a last meal with the family all together – chicken and potatoes; hardly a feast, but something I wish for now.

He had held on, trying to fight against the fever that rose with each hour. We tried to calm him in those deluded moments, and it was Szymon's idea to tell him that we were already in England – we were safe.

As soon as I told him, he let out a long sigh and a smile touched his lips. He was gone.

Mother screamed and tore at her dress, her hair, and now it was her we had to calm. Katharina knocked on the hatch that led to the basement and waited. Soon, my father's friend, Max, descended the stairs.

He did not know where to look, I think. There was my mother on the floor in a ball, me trying to get her to be quiet, my father still on the bed, Szymon wide-eyed and quiet in the corner, and Katharina behind him, as if she did not want to return into the room.

'Is he…?' Max asked.

'Yes,' I said. 'But Mother, she won't calm down, I don't know what to do.'

Max left, his short legs stomping up the basement stairs then clattering above us. He returned quickly, a glass vial in his hands, a pipette already half full of potent liquid.

I had to hold my mother's head whilst Max placed the drops on her tongue, then I held her to me as she sobbed, soon growing quiet.

Between us we moved her to the other bed and let her sleep.

'What's going to happen to Papa?' Katharina asked quietly.

Max scratched at his beard, lost in thought. 'It'll have to wait until tonight,' he finally said. 'You'll come with me.' He nodded at me.

'I should come too,' Katharina said.

'No. You stay here, watch your mother and brother,' Max told her.

She stepped forward, confident now. 'I must. I have to say the *Kel Maleh Rachamim* for him. Mother would have done it. It is for me to do it now.'

Max looked at me – it was my decision now; I was the eldest. I looked to Szymon, waiting for him to say he would go in Katharina's place, but his earlier bravado had left him, and he looked younger than his sixteen years.

'I'll stay with Mother,' he said, and sat by her on the bed.

I knew I shouldn't have let her, I knew at the time it was a bad idea, yet I also knew that Father would want his daughter, with her soft, childish voice, to say the prayer for him.

'Fine,' I said reluctantly. 'But you do as Max says. You must stay quiet at all times.'

Katharina nodded; she was ready.

It was past midnight when Max came to the basement once more, and gave both Katharina and me black coats and hats to wear.

Szymon was curled up next to Mother, his arm around her, seeking comfort as he had done when he was very small.

'If she wakes, give her a few more drops – no more than half the pipette, understand?' Max asked him.

Szymon nodded.

'Do you want to say goodbye?' I asked.

Szymon stood and walked to Father, tears already spilling down his face. He kissed Father's forehead then returned to Mother, curling himself around her once more.

Katharina and I wrapped Father in a clean white sheet that Max had given us, then a dark blue blanket. Between the three of us, we clambered up the basement stairs to Max's living room. Max promptly closed the hatch and shifted the dresser back on top of it.

I hadn't been outside for months – a year perhaps, or more – and it was strange at first to breathe the clean air. It was almost thick, like soup, and I could not get enough of it.

Max had procured a small horse and cart from a neighbour, and we placed the body on the cart, Max setting off quickly down the dark cobbled streets of his village, the horse's hooves too loud, echoing and bouncing off the buildings so I was sure at any moment someone would appear.

But luck was on our side. The night was clear, so clear that Katharina and I did not speak for some time. Instead we looked to the sky, which seemed so big now, dotted with stars that winked at us.

'Have they always done that?' Katharina asked. 'The stars, have they always looked that way?'

I knew what she meant. It was as though we were seeing the sky, a road, a tree, for the first time. As if we had been blind and someone had given us back our sight.

Max drove up a slight hill and stopped at a thick wood, the town below us.

'I think this is the best place,' he said, getting down from the cart. 'When we can, we will bury him properly, but for now, this will have to do.'

We chose a pine tree to bury him under, close to the grassy slope of a field that ran down into the valley. 'That way, he'll still be able to see the stars,' Katharina said.

Max suddenly realised the time. 'I'll have to get the cart back now – they need it for deliveries come dawn.' He looked at our hole, Father not yet buried, the prayers not yet said.

'You go,' I told him. He had done so much for us; I did not want him to worry more than he needed to.

'Are you sure?'

'There's no one about. We'll be quick as we can, then we'll walk back to the house. We'll be an hour or so at most.'

Max bit his lip. 'It's risky.'

'Probably less risky than the empty cart going back into town?' Katharina added.

'You're right, yes, you're right.' Max climbed aboard the cart and guided the horses back down the hill, leaving Katharina and me to say our final farewells to Papa.

We were placing the last clod of earth over him when it happened. Katharina was ready to say the prayer, tears streaming down her face, when a car turned in the valley below, its headlights now shining up the hill.

We backed our way into the wood, the spades dropping from our hands as we stepped further and further into the darkness.

'It'll just go past,' I whispered, feeling my heart beating in my throat, my temples.

She gripped my hand tightly and I hers, hearing the engine strain as it reached the crest of the hill and then it slowed, the gears quieter.

It did drive past – slowly, ever so slowly, and I exhaled with relief, but it was too soon. The car stopped, the red beams of the rear lights shining like menacing eyes through the branches.

'We should run.' Katharina began to move, but I pulled her to me.

'It's safer if we just stay still, just stay still and be quiet.'

Someone got out of the car and began to whistle. I could not see them completely, but I could hear them as they pissed on the dank earth of the wood, hitting twigs and leaves.

'How much further?' the voice rang out.

Another car door opened, then slammed shut. The smell of cigarette smoke. 'Not far. An hour.'

'Did you eat before we left?' the first man asked. 'I'm starving.'

'No time. You know what it's like when we get a fresh batch of them in – you don't have a minute to think, let alone eat.'

'Did you get anything good at least?'

'One rat fell off the train, half dead he was. Had a pocket full of rare gold coins though. They spilled out and I got them before anyone else saw.'

'Good work. Bastard Jews don't deserve all that money.'

'Well, it's back where it belongs now.' The man laughed.

'You need to piss?'

'Take the rest of my cigarette, I'll try.'

The other man began to urinate, the stream slower. Katharina sneezed.

That's all it was. A sneeze. A stupid sneeze.

The man stopped pissing. They went quiet. Katharina began to cry.

'Shhh,' I told her. If she would just stay quiet, then perhaps they would leave.

But she could not. She sobbed louder, her hand still gripping mine.

'Run!' I told her.

We ran, tripping on fallen logs, our hands flailing through the air, pushing ourselves back up again. There was a shot in the darkness, then shouting for us to stop.

I felt as though I was in a dream where I was trying to run but my legs would not work. I knew they could, must, go faster.

'Oh God, oh God!' I said aloud. It was over. I knew it was over.

They reached Katharina first, and I think perhaps I could have got away, but I could hear her screaming and crying, and I had to go back for her – I could not leave her alone.

Leaves were stuck to my clothing. Leaves not like the one I have found and kept for you here. These leaves were rotten and damp. These leaves were dying.

*

My father would always tell me that you should try to find the positive in a negative event.

'When you have two negative numbers, you can add them together to make a positive, just as you can translate this into your life. Take a negative, or two negative events, and you will surely find a positive.'

'That can't be, not in life,' I had said to him.

'Well, let's find some examples.' He relaxed into his wingback chair that he sat on in the evenings, either by the fireplace in winter or near the open windows in summer, the breeze causing the papers on his desk to flap as if they were wings about to take flight. 'Let's take my experiences as your first example. Your grandparents – my parents – died when I was still a young man. I had only your uncle for company and I felt completely at sea without my parents. Now, that was a negative experience in my life, and it did not end there. Soon, your uncle became sick, a disease of the brain, they say. In my opinion, it was pure grief. He was stricken with it, as you are when you have a fever, when you cannot move, feed yourself or dress yourself.

'It was getting worse and I couldn't manage him. A friend suggested a sanatorium at the lakes – a place where we could both rest, breathe in the fresh air and walk the gardens, marvelling at nature. I of course leapt at the chance – why, I had no other choice but to try, so your uncle and I travelled to the lakes. They were nestled deep in a valley, so that when we happened upon the house itself where we were to stay, it seemed at odds with all the nature surrounding it, as though we humans were not welcome and had built a structure to drain the earth of its beauty. I believe that I too, at that time, perhaps had a slight sickness in my brain, for I could only see the ugliness in the world, the sadness that came with loving, and I was unsure whether this world was really for me.

'The sanatorium offered a quiet respite from the world. We had a room each, painted white with small watercolour paintings hanging on the walls – a boat at sea, a landscape. No doubt to bring some modicum of calm, yet they frightened me in a way I could not describe, and to this day still do not fully understand.

'We spent our days walking, swimming, sitting on majestic lawns and reading books of fiction, not an academic argument in sight! I read voraciously, classical novels of wars and romance, adventures of pirates and Arabian nights. I read trying to fill my mind, and I told the stories to my brother in the evenings, who, bit by bit, was beginning to speak again and engage with me.

'You can see that the two negatives were almost catastrophic to my life. There was little cheer in my soul and even my academic books, the promise of a lecturing job when I returned, were not enough to give me hope that things would ever be any different.

'I had been there for perhaps three weeks when I admitted that I would always feel this way, and that perhaps I would just have to move through life a shadow of myself, until it was time for me to expire.

'It was a Monday when things abruptly changed. It was, as it had been on most days, a clear day. The skies were bright blue, almost achingly so, with wisps of clouds streaking across. The birds sang, as birds do, the bumblebees buzzed, the leaves rustled in trees as a light wind blew through them – in a word, it was perfect and as it should be.

'I sat on the lawn alone, for my brother had found a friend in another resident, who had convinced him to try his hand at painting. I was loath to join them with my silly fear of the paintings that hung in my room, so instead I sat in a deckchair, my sun hat tipped forward to avoid the glare, and read a story about a man who wanted to climb mountains to find if he could one day reach the heavens and touch the hand of God.

'I can't remember the name of the man in my book, but I was at a chapter where he was trying to convince an elderly relative to loan him the money he needed to go on his quest. It irked me, this chapter, the way the man was going to take all of his elderly relative's money and spend it on something so foolish.

'I threw the book down on the grass in temper, and must have proclaimed out loud, "Selfish, that's all you are, selfish!"

'A voice answered my outburst: "Well, that's a fine thing to say when you don't even know me."

'I tipped the brow of my hat back to take a look at the speaker, and there she sat, a few feet away from me on her own deckchair, wearing a cream summer dress, her hat on her lap, tendrils of hair escaping from the bun at the back of her head so that for a moment, to me at least, she wasn't real but an image of a woman that I might dream about.

'"I'm sorry," I told her, my voice clumsy so that I internally scolded myself for sounding so childish.

'She laughed at me then, a nice laugh, not mocking me, but delighting in my tantrum and my pathetic apology. "I forgive you," she said.

'She told me her name – Eve – and held out her hand so I had to stand and take it in mine in greeting. I must have bowed slightly, for she laughed again.

'"Eve, the first woman," I said.

'"Well, I'm not quite the first, but I can say one thing." She crooked her finger so I would come closer, then whispered, "I don't like apples at all."

'I laughed then, a laugh that filled my belly, rose up, covered my face and reached my eyes – a laugh I had not known I was capable of.

'When I sat once more, she told me her story, of how she was visiting her aunt and how she did not like the journey here, as she had had to come alone.

'"When do you return home?" I asked.

'"The day after next," she said.

'I was not meant to leave for another week or more, yet I found myself eager to leave now. "I will escort you home."

'"My home is Posen," she said. "Where do you come from?"

'"Gdansk."

'"Well, it is on your way, I suppose."

'"It is."

'"Then I accept your offer. You may escort me home."

'Her home became my own very quickly, and when my brother was well, he joined us and celebrated our marriage.'

'Mother…' I said to him, interrupting his story, realising it was the story of how they had met.

'Indeed, your mother. She was the positive out of my negatives, and since then, she had given me three more positives which have filled my life up so much that no negative experience can ever diminish them.'

*

I write this story of my parents mostly for you, because, you see, you are my positive out of the two negatives – losing my father and being sent here. If it were not for those two circumstances, I would never have met you, and I would never have fallen in love.

So, you see, my life will be defined by this positive experience and it will grow into a life of more great things, the negatives soon overshadowed and forgotten like a bad dream. This I carry with me now, this message, because it's all we can do. It's the only thing that they cannot take from us.

CHAPTER TWENTY-FIVE

Anna

It was Herr Becher's turn to be frantic. His wife had quietened since her evening in Munich, and Greta had told Anna that she suspected he had given her some laudanum. 'She's got that same ghostly stare my grandmother had when she had taken it. Mark my words, he's drugged her to keep her quiet.'

Now though, Becher roamed the hallways like a hungry bear, kicking at things that he deemed in his way, screaming at his son if he dared to leave his room. Greta and Anna tried to stay away from him as much as possible.

'Greta!' Becher screamed one evening from the living room, his voice contending with the music that ripped out of the gramophone. Never had Anna heard classical music sound so menacing, so utterly consuming.

'He wants you to serve him his dinner,' Greta said when she returned to the kitchen, shaken and pale.

Anna remembered the last time she had been alone with Becher and wished that she could refuse.

'Now, girl. Go and give it to him before he screams the house down.'

Anna took the tray, the rare meat he had asked for swimming in its own blood, staining the white, fluffy potatoes pink.

She set it as carefully as she could in front of him in the living room.

'Do you know who touched the gramophone?' he asked her, cutting into the meat with force so that the knife scraped and squealed against the plate.

'No, sir,' she answered.

'It's just that I noticed a week or so ago that it had been used and moved slightly from its home. I wondered whether you would know something about that?'

She shook her head and tried to stay still, not shift, not look guilty.

Then he laughed. 'As if you would even know how to work one!'

He shoved another chunk of meat into his mouth and settled back against the couch cushions to chew it. 'Probably my darling wife. She would know that it would irk me.'

Suddenly he stood and licked the juice from the meat off his lips, missing some that dripped down his chin. He moved towards her, smiling, and she stood as still as possible, wishing that she could suddenly become completely invisible.

He stood a head or so taller than her, but he bent his knees slightly so that his nose was tip to tip with hers, and she felt his hand find its way underneath her dress to roughly grab her inner thigh and begin to work its way upwards. She pulled back, but his other hand seized her waist and pulled her to him. 'Now, now, Anna, you're mine – you know that, don't you? I own all of you *Juden*. Whatever I say, you must do.'

She felt his fingers near her underwear and she closed her eyes, smelling the alcohol and meat breath as his lips settled on her cheek, her neck.

He groaned with the pleasure of touching her and it made her open her eyes. She stared beyond him at the oil painting of his wife.

'Father?' Friedrich's voice came from behind her, and suddenly Becher set her free.

She ran from the room, leaving the boy to be shouted at for disturbing his father, for ruining his evening.

Greta took one look at Anna's face as she ran back into the kitchen and hurried her outside. 'Go to the shed. Go now to Isaac, and I will fetch Schmidt and tell him to take you both back to the camp as soon as he can.'

'But they have not said we can go yet.' Anna began to cry.

'You leave him to me, all right? You go now.'

Anna did as she was told and ran across the garden to the shed. She found Isaac hunched over another piece of the car engine, his hands shaking as he tried to clean it.

He looked at her as she came in, concern on his face. 'What happened?'

'When do you think they will come, Isaac?' she beseeched him. 'Please tell me the Americans will be here soon – please tell me this will all be over?'

'Come here.' Isaac opened his arms to her.

She went to him, perched on his knee and let him hold her, soothing her until she found some peace.

'Better now?' he asked.

She sniffed and nodded, then climbed off his lap and sat on the upturned bucket, her arms wrapped around herself, suddenly feeling cold.

Isaac gave her a blanket, then said, 'Anna, close your eyes.'

She wiped her face with a corner of the blanket, then did as she was told.

Isaac's voice was soft, soothing. He began to sing the English words to the music Friedrich had played for them on the gramophone. His voice was surprisingly good and she opened her eyes to look at him. 'No, close them and listen.'

Anna did as she was told. 'Now, as I sing, imagine something wonderful, Anna, imagine a happier place.' Isaac's voice lifted and fell, his hand tapping the time and beat on the desk.

She imagined herself in the summer. She was in a large house with patio doors in the living room leading out onto a luscious lawn which ran all the way to a lake at the bottom.

The gramophone played Billie Holiday to her as she drank a cocktail standing at the open doors, looking out into the garden. Suddenly there were people on the lawn, small people, children. A boy with a sailor hat on his head being chased by an older sister who wore the blue dress from Liesl's wardrobe – the dress so like her mother's. The girl caught up with the boy and grabbed him – they tumbled and fell onto the grass, laughing and rolling over and over.

A man strode towards the pair and lifted the girl high into the air, then did the same with the boy. She knew they were hers; she knew she could join them and spin around on the grass, but something held her back.

Behind her there was someone else.

She turned and saw it was two people, Isaac and her brother, Elias, both sitting on a sofa stuffed with pillows.

'Come outside,' she said to them. 'Come outside where it is warm. See, the sun is shining. Let's go outside.'

Elias and Isaac shook their heads, and then they were gone. The music had stopped.

Anna opened her eyes, and saw Isaac doubled up coughing.

She went to him, helped him to sip some water until he rested, and some colour returned to his cheeks.

'Isaac, I'm worried about you.'

He waved his hand in dismissal. 'Whatever for?'

'You're not eating, your cough is getting worse, you have a slight fever.' Her hand touched his forehead.

'I haven't smelled lemons, so I am not dying just yet.'

Anna narrowed her eyes at him – was he delusional?

He laughed at her, and then was gripped by another fit of coughing. When he settled, he sipped at the water. 'I think I had that expression on my face when Levi said it to me. He said that when you die, you smell lemons in the air, and you know it is time to go.'

'I think I'd quite like that,' Anna said. 'Lemons. Fresh and clean.'

Isaac nodded. 'Get the papers, will you?' he asked. 'Let us see if we can ask our mysterious friend to provide us with some comfort.'

Anna retrieved the papers, this time holding them to herself, then flicking through the pages. 'Here – this one talks of hope, of love. I shall read this.'

Anna began. '*Of all the years to have been in love, this is the one – a joke, surely?*

CHAPTER TWENTY-SIX

J. A. L.

September 1944

Of all the years to have been in love, this is the one – a joke, surely?

Of all the years I have lived, which are so few, in this one my heart is both full and broken at the same time.

I imagined that I would find wonderful things in my life that would remind me of you – the smell of a flower, perhaps, one you had tended to with your own hands, or perhaps the warmth of summer heat on my back, bringing me the memory of when we spent a summer at the beach. All of these things I had hoped for my first love, for my first reminiscences of love.

Yet the things that remind me of you are foolish and lack poetry, lack the depth of what I actually feel.

Take this morning, for example. I stubbed my toe on the bunk, and was reminded of the time I did that in front of you, and how you had checked on me, looking at my toe, patting it and then smacking the wood that hurt it, telling it that it was a naughty piece of wood. It had made me laugh and I quickly forgot about my toe.

It is a sweet memory, of course, but not the one I wished to carry with me. I wanted this year to be full

of memories we made together, travelling, eating at
restaurants, laughing with friends. Instead I am here,
and everything is grey and muddled. Although I know
the war is changing, my future outside here still seems
so far away, as if I could reach out and touch it but then
it inches away from my grasp each time.

I have been thinking of Katharina too, lately. Not
that I ever really stop thinking about her; she is always
there, a part of me. Yet these past days, the violence
has increased and I heard that a group of children were
gassed – all alone, without their mothers – and I could
not help but think of my younger sister and wish with
all my heart that she is still alive.

I picture both Mother and Szymon waiting out
the days in Max's basement – oh God, I hope they are
still there, I hope that we were not traced back to Max
somehow. Not that Katharina and I ever said anything
to those SS who took us, but I have no way of knowing
what became of them.

I have this idea that one day, you, Katharina and I
will go to Max's. We will lift the hatch above the basement and take my mother and Szymon out, show them
the outside world once more, and visit my father who
lies under the pines on the hill. I always thought that
we would re-bury him and give him the funeral he so
deserved, but the more I have pondered this, the more
I have come to think that he would have liked the spot
we chose for him far more than a cemetery.

I have a friend in my bunkhouse. His name is Levi
and he makes jokes all the time. If the guards were to
hear him, I think they would shoot him on the spot
as most of the jokes are about Hitler, but I admire his

spirit – he will not let it be broken. This is his second camp and he says it is not as bad as the last one.

At first, I thought he was joking and laughed at him. But he did not smile, and I stopped.

'Auschwitz is worse, believe me,' he said. 'My wife and children are still there. When I was first relocated, I was worried for myself – I thought that whatever they had in store for me next would be far worse than what I had already endured. But when I arrived, the beatings were fewer, the guards less sadistic. And then I worried for them – left behind.'

Auschwitz. A place I know. A town we once drove through on our way to Zakopane for a holiday. It was a pretty little town, and I could not imagine such a place being redesigned to suit the desires of these mad men. A place that perhaps held Katharina.

Levi told me, 'Deaths there were more frequent, the chambers and ovens working at all hours – it was as if they couldn't get rid of us quickly enough. *Lice*, they called us. Lice. Indeed, we had them – I still do!' He laughed then. 'Imagine thinking that another human being is like a louse? Or a rat. Indeed, I often wondered whether they had drunk some form of potion that sent their minds crazy, as I could figure no other reason for man to view man this way.'

I agreed with Levi, waiting for him to tell me more. But he did not. Instead he stood in the bunkhouse and did a funny walk, telling jokes, trying to get everyone to smile. Does he hide behind the humour? I do not know. But I am glad that he is my friend.

CHAPTER TWENTY-SEVEN

Isaac

'He knew Levi!' Isaac said, interrupting Anna. 'How I wish I had asked him more questions when he was still alive. J. A. L. could have been the gardener before Levi. I wonder if Levi knew about his writing too?'

Footsteps could be heard coming towards them and Anna hurriedly placed the papers back, then sat, awaiting the visitor.

It was Schmidt.

'Come to take you back to the camp,' he said.

Isaac stood at the same time as Anna.

'No. Not you,' Schmidt told Isaac. 'Herr Becher wants you to keep working. He wants the cars ready in a few days.'

Unsteadily, Isaac sat back down. 'They are almost finished.'

'Well, almost is not complete, is it?' Schmidt said. 'Come on, I haven't got all night.'

Anna followed Schmidt from the shed, giving Isaac a little wave as she closed the door behind her.

Bewildered, Isaac looked at the car parts. The engines would work – they would be fine, possibly by tomorrow. Yet he was to spend a night in the shed, just as J. A. L. had done.

He was suddenly filled with despair. Not at the thought of being away from the bunkhouse, but what it would mean when the cars were ready. The family were clearly leaving for a long journey – Isaac was not stupid; he could see the fear in Becher, he had heard about the Americans coming. Then he thought of the bodies piled around the camp grounds, and imagined that his would soon be added to the twisted heap of arms and legs, no longer Isaac, instead a collection of jumbled parts, another victim of their hate.

He hated the thought of lying in death in one of the pits that they threw the bodies into – with everyone, but with no one at the same time.

A chill caught on the back of his neck as if someone were in the room with him. He looked about but nothing was there – no ghosts to speak of.

Then he saw the flash of a shadow outside the window – was Anna back?

The door creaked open ever so slightly, then another inch and another, and Isaac felt as though Death himself were here to collect him. Instead, it was Friedrich.

'It's really late,' Friedrich whispered, even though his voice could not carry to the house. 'I saw the lamp burning and Anna leaving, and I wondered if you were still here.'

'As you can see, I am. You should not be here though, Friedrich, you will get in trouble, as will I – your parents are home.'

'They are, but they really aren't,' he said, almost philosophically. 'Mother is asleep, and the dead could not wake her. I saw Father in the living room, an empty bottle of whiskey on the floor – he will not wake either and, even if he did, he would not come looking for me.'

Despite the danger, Isaac wanted the company and did not insist that Friedrich leave as he should.

A rumble in the sky made both Isaac and Friedrich look to the ceiling of the shed.

'Planes,' Friedrich announced.

Isaac turned off the gas lamp, pitching them into darkness. They listened as the planes flew low, the engines whirring, Isaac's ears ringing with the vibrations.

Soon, the rumble became a distant hum and Isaac waited, counted the seconds and minutes, and when no crash of bombs came, he turned the light back on, keeping it low.

'Will they come back, do you think?' Friedrich's voice was barely a whisper.

'I don't know,' Isaac said.

'Do they know about the prison?'

'Yes. I think they know about the camp.'

'Will they take Father away for what he has done?'

Isaac was unsure whether Friedrich's voice betrayed worry for his father or an eagerness to rid himself of his parent. 'I really don't know, Friedrich. I can't tell you what will happen.'

'Tell me what the camp is like.'

Isaac shook his head. 'There is no good that can come of you knowing. You are too young.'

'But there are children in there – I saw them – they know what it is like,' his childish logic concluded.

'Quite. But they will have to carry that knowledge with them the rest of their lives, and it will not be easy for them.'

Friedrich was not to be dissuaded. 'I can tell people, Isaac. I can tell people what it was like. Otto, I bet he doesn't know that children have to be sent away, and if he doesn't know, he will grow up and maybe he won't believe them. But if I tell the story, if I tell it, maybe he will.'

The boy was wearing on him. It was late, and he was hungry and sick, the fever chilling his skin rather than heating it. 'I don't think I can, Friedrich. I'm sorry. But one day, perhaps I will.'

CHAPTER TWENTY-EIGHT

Friedrich

Last spring Friedrich had foraged in the woods with Otto. They had found a bird's nest, high up in one of the trees they had been looking at, hoping that it would prove a suitable spot for a treehouse.

The eggs were tiny, a pale blue with mottled brown spots. Otto had wanted to touch them, his podgy hand reaching out as he steadied himself on the branch.

'Don't!' Friedrich warned him. 'If you touch them, the mother bird will leave them as you'll have left your smell on them.'

'Says who?' Otto asked.

'I can't remember who said it, but it's true – don't touch them.'

Otto withdrew his hand, and Friedrich, who had been about to join his friend, slithered down the tree trunk, scraping his palms and legs on the bark.

Otto soon followed and dusted off his hands when he reached the ground. 'I didn't touch them. Can't have the treehouse here anymore – we'll have to find somewhere else.'

Friedrich looked at the thick long arms of the oak. 'It's perfect though – absolutely perfect.'

'They won't be there forever, will they?' Otto mused. 'If we come back in a week or so, maybe they will have hatched and flown away?'

Carly Schabowski

Friedrich agreed; as soon as the birds had gone, they could begin building their secret hiding place.

The following week the boys returned to find tiny pink chicks in the nest, their mouths wide and screaming for food.

At first, Friedrich recoiled from the sight and moved away from them on the branch. Their naked bodies and black unseeing eyes were not what he had been expecting a baby bird to look like.

'They are so strange,' Otto said. 'Really strange, like they aren't really birds at all.'

They had left the nest alone, sitting with their backs against another tree, their hands randomly picking up dead leaves and twigs as they spoke.

'If we wait here long enough, we can see the mother bring them some food.' Otto looked to the canopy above them and Friedrich did the same.

'Will you go home in the holidays?' Friedrich suddenly asked.

'Probably. I'd say so. Mother wrote and said something about going to Grandmother's house in the countryside. I'd rather not go there though. She's always a bit mean and slaps my hands when I try to reach for cakes or sweets.'

'I'd happily go to your grandmother's,' Friedrich said.

'You not going home then?'

'I don't even know where home is at the moment. They've moved to a new place – Father got a promotion.'

'If you could go anywhere, though, anywhere in the world, where would you go?'

Friedrich thought for a moment, ripping a leaf to shreds in his hands, then watched as the breeze took them.

'I guess I'd be here with you.' Friedrich grinned at Otto. 'At least when you're around we have fun and I have someone to talk to.'

'Look!' Otto raised his hand and pointed to the sky where a blackbird had shot past, then landed on the branch with the nest of baby birds. 'She's a good mother, flying off to find food then bringing it all the way back for them. That's a lot to do. I think if I had been born a baby bird and my mother would have had to do all that, she wouldn't have bothered!' Otto laughed.

Friedrich joined in, but his laugh was false. He knew that Otto was joking, but he also knew that his own mother certainly wouldn't have cared for him – she would have left his skinny naked body to cry until it died. He wanted to tell Otto what he thought, but Otto would simply try to make him feel better – say it wasn't true, and tell him his mother loved him. He didn't want to hear that; he just wanted to sit for a moment in the dankness of the wood, the earthy smell of mushrooms that grew in clumps at the bases of trees filling his nostrils, his best friend by his side, and listen to the caw of birds in the trees, and the little squeaks from the baby birds as they took the food from their mother.

Friedrich sat in the spare bedroom, looking out into the garden and to the camp beyond. The binoculars were on his lap but he hadn't used them just yet, his thoughts on the trees that swayed in the breeze, bringing him the memory from the previous year of his friend and the baby birds.

The blossoms had burst from their buds, dotting branches with white, yellow and pink. The bulbs that the gardener had planted in neat rows in the garden before he had stopped coming had begun to push up the dirt, lightening it with their green heads.

The house was busy. His mother had ceased to be a ghost that wandered the hallways, crying and moaning. Instead, she had emerged from her bedroom, her hair pinned back, her eyes no longer glassy and unstaring. She shouted at Friedrich to stay out of her way, then spent hours on the telephone. He kept himself out of sight but he could hear snatches of her conversations as she talked to friends, family, and to a company that she wanted to ship her furniture to another place.

Friedrich had tried to hear where it was being taken to, but her voice had been unusually quiet. He'd heard her talk about a date she needed them by, and then, 'the address, yes, of course,' before she tailed off, whispering so that only the company man on the other end could hear.

In the past days she had become a flurry of activity, muttering to herself with a pen and pad of paper in her hands as she walked from painting to painting, table to chair, scribbling something down and then staring blankly out of the window as if the answer to her writings would suddenly appear.

Friedrich desperately wanted to ask what was happening but knew he couldn't. His father had barely been home – he had meetings, he said, he was needed elsewhere. He was short with not only Friedrich, which was normal, but also with his wife, and instead of falling into a pool of tears when he spoke to her, she would stare at him with narrow eyes and then walk away as if he had never uttered a word.

A light rain spattered against the windowpane and Friedrich watched each drop as it tracked its way down the glass.

Then he noticed the lantern begin to glow its burnt orange in the shed window, alerting him to Isaac's arrival. Although his mother roamed the hallways, tiger-like, he could easily dodge past her and get to the shed.

He placed the binoculars on the floor and crept out of the spare bedroom, noticing each squeak of the dusty floorboards as he walked.

Reaching the top of the stairs, he looked down and saw two men, both wearing mustard-coloured overalls, wrapping the grandfather clock in cloth, a large crate next to them on the floor. Another man entered through the front door, carrying a large box. He shook his head like a dog to rid himself of the rain and trailed wet footprints into the dining room.

Friedrich descended the stairs, spotting that the photographs and paintings that had hung on the walls had now disappeared, leaving clean rectangular spaces on the dirty white of the wallpaper.

They were leaving. Of course they were. But where?

Suddenly Friedrich was excited – of course, they were going home! Back to their townhouse in either Munich or Berlin. He wanted to race to the telephone to call Otto and tell him the news – they would be together again soon.

He did not care if his mother heard him now, and ran down the rest of the stairs, almost bumping into one of the mustard-coloured men as he tried to edge the clock closer to the box, ready to lay it in its tomb-like case.

'Watch yourself!' the mustard man scolded him. 'You break this, and I'll tell your mother.'

Friedrich ignored him, but then he saw a postmark on the lid of the case that would be hammered into place to hold the clock still.

It was a strange postmark – one he had not seen before – but he made out the smudged word: *Argentina*.

He knew the name of the country and tried to place it, straining to remember those long geography lessons where he and Otto, instead of listening to the teacher, had drawn silly pictures in the back of their books to make each other laugh.

He could see the outline of his mother in the dining room – she was with the wet man – and Friedrich scooted past quickly, into the kitchen and out to the garden, heading for the shed.

Isaac was not alone when Friedrich entered. Anna was sitting on the bucket – his bucket that he would sit on when he came to visit. Stupidly, he wanted to push her off it and tell her that it was his, but then he saw that her eyes were red and tired, and her face seemed to have deflated, leaving cheekbones that jutted out, making her eyes look too big for her face.

'Friedrich.' Anna stood. 'Is everything all right?'

'We're leaving,' he cried. 'It's really happening.'

He saw Anna look over his head towards the house, a crease in her brow.

'When?' Anna asked him.

'There are men downstairs now, packing things, and I saw a postmark on a box, a label saying where to send the things – it said Argentina.'

'I must go – she'll be looking for me.' Anna did not wait for a reply and scurried down the path towards his mother.

Friedrich closed the door after Anna.

'Argentina,' Isaac said.

Friedrich sat on the upturned bucket. 'Where is it?' he asked.

'South America,' Isaac answered. 'It's very far away. It's very hot.'

Friedrich remembered now the comments about the heat from his father, how his mother had been upset by them – she did not want to go.

'What if I don't want to leave?' Isaac was smiling, a faraway look on his face as if he were dreaming. 'Isaac, what if I don't want to go!'

'It's really happening,' Isaac croaked, then began to cough, a hard cough that made him clutch his chest.

Friedrich stepped forward to support him. He wanted to run back to Anna, to get her to help.

'It's all right, I'll be all right,' Isaac said, as if reading his mind.

'What will happen if we leave? Where will you go, back to the camp?' Friedrich asked.

Isaac stared at him and did not speak.

'What if you come with us, what if we say to Father that you should come because you can fix things and we will need you. And maybe if Anna comes too then she can make sure we are all fed. We should ask, shouldn't we, Isaac? We should try?' Friedrich felt his throat growing tight, his eyes starting to burn.

'I have to stay here,' Isaac said simply, his voice tired, his movements slow.

'But then so do I, because if I don't stay, then how will you teach me how to fix things in your workshop?'

'Friedrich, when you are a grown man, when your parents are old, like me, you can do whatever you wish. And that will be the time that you will come to find me and my shop.'

'You promise?' Friedrich sniffed.

'I do.'

'I don't like it inside the house,' Friedrich said. 'I don't like our things being put in boxes or the way Mother and Father talk to each other – everything is so strange.'

'I understand strange. Things have been strange for me for some time.'

'Because of the camp?'

'Yes, because of the camp.'

'The gardener, he was in the camp too, wasn't he? He had stripy clothes like you, but he didn't come back when you and Anna did.'

'Levi,' Isaac said. 'That was his name, Levi.'

'Why didn't he come back with you?'

'Because he couldn't.'

Friedrich thought of the baby birds once more in the woods with Otto. How one day, when they looked in the nest, wanting to see the fluffy bodies of the birds as they sprouted wings, only one remained in the nest, lying as if he were sleeping.

'Did he die?' Friedrich knew the answer but wanted to hear it – he needed to. He needed to know what happened at the camp, and what his father had done.

'He did die, yes.'

'How?'

Isaac looked at his hands. 'I don't know. Perhaps from hunger, or perhaps from thirst.'

'He was hungry?' Again, Friedrich thought of the birds crying out for their mother, for their food. 'Why didn't someone feed him?'

'There was no food for someone to feed him with.'

'Like the baby bird,' Friedrich said.

'Like who?'

Friedrich could not answer and cried, allowing the tears to cover his face, allowing the sobs of confusion, of anger and loneliness, to finally spill out of him. He felt the arms of Isaac around him, holding him close, letting him cry for everything he couldn't understand.

CHAPTER TWENTY-NINE

Anna

The house was in disarray. Liesl's clothes were scattered on her bedroom floor, paintings and photographs stacked against walls, silverware laid out on the dining room table as if awaiting guests who would never arrive.

Anna, as directed, spent her time placing the silverware into royal blue velvet pouches, each fork, knife and spoon allocated its own special place. Strange, she thought, that the Bechers would worry so much about their eating implements that they should make sure they had their own special bed, yet she slept on a straw-filled mattress, each morning waking with a new imprint, or a new scratch from the rough stuffing.

She could hear Liesl's footsteps above her, heavy and angry as she stormed into her bedroom, into Herr Becher's bedroom and their bathroom, collecting things, trying to pack them, and then becoming so exhausted by the activity that she would lie down on her bed and scream.

'She's getting worse.' Greta was by her side, more cloths and sheets in her hands ready to wrap the artwork in. 'I thought at first she was getting better, when she stopped wandering round with that stupefied look on her face, but this, this is far worse.' Greta looked to the ceiling as the wailing began.

'When do they leave?' Anna asked.

'Who knows? Not that they'd tell me anyway.'

Suddenly there was a hum in the air, and the plates stacked on the sideboard began to rattle as the plane descended lower. Instinctively, Anna crouched down low, as if the plane would land right on top of them.

'Getting nearer,' Greta said, her eyes scouring the garden outside, waiting to see the Americans arrive.

'There were bombs all last night.' Anna stood. 'They are close.'

'You look worried?' Greta said.

'I heard they are evacuating the camp tomorrow. Making us march elsewhere before they arrive.'

Greta shook her head. 'They'll be here before they have a chance to march you anywhere. Mark my words – they'll be here to save you.'

Anna finished with the silverware and wrapped the plates, placing them carefully in boxes. A part of her hoped the plates would smash en route and that Liesl would open the crate to see her fancy china cracked and worthless. Smiling at the thought, she missed wrapping one, then two plates, giving them a chance to break.

'What are you smiling at?' Greta asked.

'Nothing.'

'Look out there, and here we are stuck inside.' Greta pointed at the garden where the grass had grown long, dandelions bobbing their yellow heads, daffodils and tulips colouring the borders.

'Come on, come with me, we deserve a break.' Greta pulled on Anna's arm and led her to the kitchen, where she instructed her to sit on the doorstep.

She came out with two cups of coffee, and squeezed in next to Anna.

'What about Liesl?' Anna asked.

'Her? Leave her to wail and scream. I've had it with that woman. Here, I'll lock the kitchen door, stop her from finding us, all right?'

Anna liked the feeling of annoying Liesl. She relished the moment of disobedience, feeling like the old Anna, the Anna before who would cheekily stay out later than she should, or play music when she should be studying.

'I like it better like this,' Greta said, as she sat back down once more. 'The dandelions growing, the grass taking over as nature meant it to. You know, when they first arrived, they had that poor gardener mow the lawn nearly every other day, in stripes. Up and down he went, up and down, and then he'd have to bend over and pull out each dandelion, treating the grass so they would not return.'

'Levi certainly worked hard,' Anna said.

'No, no, not him. The one before. He was a young lad, very quiet and polite. Half-Polish he was, so that when he spoke German, there was always a word he said with a different inflection – it was nice, sort of like hearing it anew. I always thought he would have made a nice singer; he had that kind of look about him.'

Anna took a moment or two before she realised who Greta was talking about – J. A. L. and the diaries and letters. 'Where is he now, where did he go?'

Greta looked at the top of her coffee cup. 'You know, they say that if you look at your coffee and the bubbles are in the centre of the drink, it will be a nice day. If the bubbles are at the side, it will rain. Strange, isn't it?'

'What are you talking about?' Anna looked at Greta who still stared into her mug.

'It was like that on the day the poor boy did not come back. I'd looked at my coffee that morning, and it told me the weather would be clear. It was clear – at least for that time of year, when it was getting cold and the branches were becoming bare. I remember being happy that day, thinking to myself that at least we'd have no rain. We'd had rain for weeks, you see, and that poor boy was almost covered head to toe in mud all the time.

'I was peeling vegetables for dinner, right there at the sink, as I do most days, when there was a crash through the side gate and three SS guards came marching in. They went straight to the shed and I heard the boy cry out, then a bang and then another.

'I ran to the door and screamed at them to stop, but they wouldn't listen to me – I mean, why would they?

'They dragged him out of the shed by his feet, and I saw that his face was bloody from the blows they had dealt him. It was a sport for them, I think. They seemed to delight in what they were going to mete out to him. Each one kicked at him, in the ribs, the legs, even his head. His whimpers were drowned out by the noise of their boots hitting the bone. I turned away and hid my face after a moment; I couldn't watch them kill him. Perhaps it was a minute later, perhaps two, when they stopped. I looked up and saw that each one was pissing on him. Actually urinating on his body, which was battered and bleeding. It was then that I noticed Frau Becher at the window, watching the whole thing, a blank expression on her face, and there at the side gate was Herr Becher, smoking a cigarette and leaning against the gate as if he were simply on a break from a busy day at work.

'Two of the men picked up his body by the arms and the feet, and took him towards a waiting truck. I shouted at the remaining guard, who had a prominent scar above his eye. "May you burn in hell for this!" I was crying, my hands shaking, stupidly hoping that Frau Becher had not heard my outburst.

'The guard just lit a cigarette, and blew the smoke into my face. "It's him who's disgusting," he said. "All this time and you had a homosexual working here – right here where Herr Becher lives. You can bet he'll burn in hell when we're finished with him."

'"He's not dead?" I asked, wanting to run to the truck and help him.

'"Not yet." The guard grinned. "Give us an hour or so, and he will be."

'He walked away from me and I think I stood there in that garden for an hour or more, staring at the bloodstains on the grass, the paving stones, and spattered on the floor of the shed. Eventually I found my breath and my mind came back to me once more. Inside I filled a bucket with hot, soapy water and scrubbed at the blood, washing the violence away.'

Greta finished, sipping at her coffee, then turned to Anna. 'I wish it had rained that day, I wish my coffee and its bubbles had been wrong. I keep thinking that if it had rained, maybe Becher and his guards would have waited, given him a few more hours, none of them wanting to get soaked in the downpour. It's stupid, I know. They wouldn't have cared about the weather; they would have done what they did regardless.'

Greta stopped talking. Anna could hear the squawks of crows in the trees then the flap of wings. She imagined J. A. L. here, in this very garden, the blows raining down on him, the fear he must have felt.

She shivered. 'What was his name?' Anna asked, her voice thin and tired.

'He never said. He wasn't like you and Isaac – he kept to himself, his head down. That was why I was so surprised when they came for him. He hadn't broken a single rule. Here, take Isaac a cup before we get back to work. If she comes looking, I'll tell her you're doing laundry – I doubt she'll want to come searching for you.'

Anna made Isaac a cup of coffee, taking with her a piece of bread that Greta had left on the side for her hands to find.

As she walked towards the shed, she heard Greta call out, 'I think it may have been Adam – his name. I'm sure I heard someone say that to him. Adam.'

Adam, Anna thought. His middle name, perhaps? She looked at the ground in a different way now, imagining that the blood which had spilled from his body was somehow still there.

Opening the door, she found Isaac asleep, his head hanging down to his chest, his breathing heavy. As she placed the mug on his desk, she reached over and rested her hand on his forehead, feeling his skin raging now with fever.

'Isaac,' she said gently.

He opened his eyes and tipped his head back, immediately rubbing at the back of his neck.

'You were asleep,' she said.

'I was? Where am I?'

'In the shed.'

He looked about him, taking in Anna, then the floor of the shed, then back to Anna; finally he realised. 'Of course I am. Yes. Herr Becher wants me here to check the cars. I must go and check the cars.'

He made to heave himself up out of the chair, and Anna placed her hands on his shoulders and gently pushed him back down, so he sat once more. 'Herr Becher isn't here. So you don't need to check the cars just yet. Drink this, and eat this.' She handed him the bread.

He ate slowly, and when he drank from the mug, his hands shook so much that he spilled the coffee, staining the whiskers on his chin. Anna felt a lump rise in her throat. She wanted to wipe his chin as she would a child, she wanted to cool his head from the heat, but she was unsure whether he would let her take care of him.

'You should go to the infirmary when you return tonight,' she told him.

'I've been sleeping here,' Isaac said. 'Herr Becher wants me here. I don't know why.'

Anna suddenly thought of J. A. L., of the way he had been dragged out of the shed. She had an image of the same fate befalling Isaac – his old body dragged across the paving stones whilst brutal kicks and thumps battered him.

'Perhaps it's a good thing,' Anna tried. 'Maybe you will get rescued quicker – maybe when they leave, they will just let you go?'

'Maybe,' Isaac said, his voice indifferent.

She tried again. 'Anyway, the infirmary in our camp has run out of medicine. No one is being fed there. So maybe it's better that you are here – it would do no good to show them how sick you are.'

'What day is it, Anna?' he asked.

'It's Friday.'

He nodded. 'Friday,' he repeated. 'I have lost track of the days. They are all disappearing from me.'

Anna could not bear to see him this way. The Isaac she knew was slowly being replaced by a sick old man, whose mind was starting to slip away.

'I think I know what happened to our mutual friend,' Anna ventured.

This time, Isaac's eyes opened more. 'Who? J. A. L.?'

'Yes.' She latched on to the fact that he seemed to brighten, if only a little. 'Greta thinks his name was Adam.'

'Adam – perhaps his middle name,' Isaac said. 'What happened to him?'

'He died,' Anna said simply. There was no need to tell him the details of the violence, the blood that had spoiled on the floor of this very shed. 'He was homosexual too.'

'Aha!' Isaac sat straighter now. 'So his letters, his love letters, they were to someone in the camp! I thought as much, but then I wondered how he had met a woman and fallen in love in such a way. Now, now it all makes sense. Here, Anna, get the papers. There are a few left – let's read them together.'

Anna scrabbled around on the dusty floor until she found the loose floorboard, picturing Adam doing the same as he tried to hide his writings to his love. She imagined the fear he would have felt as they dragged him out, the pain as he lay dying. Finding the papers, she pulled them out and sat on the upturned bucket. 'Shall I read?'

'Please do.' Isaac was brighter now – a mystery had been solved. He crossed his arms and leaned back, closing his eyes whilst Anna began to read.

CHAPTER THIRTY

J. A. L.

September 1944

They know.

I can tell that something has shifted.

This morning I was woken by a guard who had a scar over his eye. He grinned at me as I lay there and waited for the inevitable blow, but it did not come.

'Get up,' he told me. 'You're needed at the house.'

It was too early for me to come here – the sky was still heavy with sleep – and yet he marched me here and asked me to wait in my shed.

'What work should I do?' I asked him.

Again, that grin. 'No work for you today.'

As soon as he left, I needed to write. I think it is the last time that I will be able to. He saw us, you see, the guard with the scar, he saw as I kissed you behind the bunkhouse. A fleeting kiss – our first and our last.

Is he with you now, the guard with the scar? If they ask me, I will tell them I made you do it – I forced you – and perhaps they will leave you be.

Oh, why did we risk it? In all the months of talking to one another, of telling each other about our lives and dreams, we never took a risk – not even to hold hands.

Yesterday it was the stars, I know it was.

I told you how I loved to watch them, that each time I did it gave me some hope, however foolish, that since they were always there, a permanent scar in the sky, it was possible that I would exist too – although only for a part of their lives, it is enough for me.

You laughed, then ran your hand down my cheek, and our eyes locked. It was that simple and yet that complicated.

Do you think I am being paranoid? Oh God, I hope I am! I hope they have brought me here so early for some job that must start as soon as the sun begins to rise.

I will write as quickly as I can, just in case I am no longer here come tomorrow. I have foreseen the dangers of what could happen if you fall out of line – I have witnessed them first-hand. It would be foolish of me to think that if they did see us there will be no reprisal – there will be, and when it happens, I just pray to God that it is quick.

I have not prayed in some time. It is as though I have forgotten how to.

I told you the story of the day when I was young, when my father took me fishing and told me that God was everywhere. It was easier to believe that sitting on the riverbank, watching His creation. It has been harder here.

I went away with my father and we talked of God once more. I was perhaps fifteen or so, no more than that. It was summer, our favourite time of year. The days were long and warm, the garden overflowing with colour, and bumblebees hummed happily, filling the still air with a sort of music from nature.

Father had to go to Krakow to visit an academic friend of his who had some papers he was desperate to read. He asked me to accompany him, taking us on a train journey overnight, and to spend three days where we could visit the university and the bookshops.

Of course, I went. The thought of spending time with Father surrounded by learning, by books and fine architecture, appealed more to me than having to spend most of my days in the house with my siblings, as I had very few friends.

Krakow was the city I decided I would live in when I grew up. The Wawel Castle drew me to it, as though it could one day be my home! Oh, how I dreamt of wandering those streets at night, sitting at cafes and bars, talking with like-minded friends.

Father's friend, Mordecai, lived in Kazimierz in an apartment above a coffee shop. He was older than Father and wore his white beard long, his hair falling in knotted curls from under his skullcap, and wire-rimmed glasses that seemed too small for his large open face, which would perch almost on the edge of his nose so that he was forever pushing them back up with his index finger.

'Welcome!' He wrapped Father in a hug as soon as we arrived and then did the same to me.

'This is your boy – this is him?' he asked Father, who nodded.

Mordecai's apartment was full of books. They were stacked on the floor, on every available surface, so that it was almost a game to try to follow him to his tiny kitchen where he brewed us tea and gave us sweet pastries to eat. 'From Turkey, from Istanbul,' he told me, as I took one of the syrupy pastries from their box. 'Not that I went there to get them. I've a friend, Ismail, who makes them and serves them with his strong coffee. I will take you there to meet him – you will like him very much.'

I could only nod in reply as I chewed on the honeyed, flaky pastry that filled my mouth and made me feel exceedingly happy that I had agreed to come on this trip with Father.

Mordecai ushered us to his balcony overlooking the street on which he lived, full of bookshops, and cafes. The cobbled streets led towards a synagogue and beyond that, I could see a small square.

'It's quieter,' Father said to Mordecai.

Mordecai nodded. 'It's changing. That is for certain.'

This was the first time I had ever understood the rumours. It was 1937, two more years before Mordecai would have to leave his home, but even then, sitting on the balcony with red begonias trailing from his window boxes, I could feel the tension, see how people hurried down the streets, their heads lowered.

'It is the same in Posen,' Father said.

'They haven't said anything at the university yet, have they?'

Father shook his head.

'What are they meant to say at the university?' I asked him.

'Nothing. Don't worry.' Father smiled at me and Mordecai changed the subject.

'I went to Istanbul, you know, when it was still Constantinople. I much prefer the latter name and I have a mind to petition that they change it back, if for no other reason than it rolls off the tongue much easier!' Mordecai laughed.

'What was it like?' I asked, taking the bait.

'Oh my! What was it like?' He rubbed at his beard and I saw a few crumbs of pastry fall from it. 'Well, it is hot, hotter than here in summer. There are smells of spices all around, young boys on bicycles carrying loaves of bread on the back of them, shouting out and waving to their friends as they ride past each other. In the bazaars there are all manner of wondrous things – sweets, pastries, gold, brass, paintings, fine silk rugs. Why, that rug in there,' Mordecai turned to the living room, 'well, you can barely see it for all the books on top of it, but that there was from a bazaar. In the evenings I would sit with my friend Ismail – the one we shall visit later – and we would sip a pungent liquor flavoured with aniseed, then drink back cool water to take away the biting heat on our tongues. We would listen to the call to prayer that sang out on the cooling air of the night, the minarets seemingly touching the stars. On those days, I felt as though I were in a dream, or in a story at least, like *One Thousand and One Arabian Nights*. I told Ismail of this and one evening, as we sat, he bestowed on me a gold-plated lamp, with rubies on the side. He said it was a magic lamp, and a genie would appear if I rubbed at the sides to grant me wishes. Have you heard of the tale of Aladdin?' Mordecai asked me.

I shook my head.

'Well, now. Come with me.'

He took me into a room at the rear of the kitchen which I supposed could have been a bedroom, but he had made it into a study of sorts. It was filled with treasures from his travels, rugs that hung from the walls, gold, silver and bronze ornaments in a glass case, a heavy polished desk whose legs were made to look like tree trunks, the branches holding up the desktop.

Of course, there were books too. Red, blue and green leather-bound volumes, simple paperbacks, leaflets – it was as though Mordecai had collected every single thing ever written, and devoured the information. I decided in that moment that I wanted to be just like Mordecai.

He handed me a book he had been foraging for in a pile. It was bound in red leather, the pages edged in gold.

I held it to my face as I had always done with books, and smelled the leather, the pages.

I saw Mordecai watching me as I performed my ritual, and reddened.

'Don't be embarrassed,' he said. 'I do the same thing myself.'

He showed me the lamp that his friend Ismail had given him, and told me that he had rubbed its side every night for years, waiting to see the genie appear, but the genie had yet to grant Mordecai any wishes. 'I feel that he moved to a new house,' Mordecai said, as he placed the lamp back on his desk. 'Perhaps he jumps about into other lamps and this one which Ismail gave me was vacated.'

'Is Ismail your best friend?' I asked. I had heard his name so many times now, and I had not yet been in Mordecai's home an hour.

'He has been my friend for many years. I am not sure that when you reach my age you have a best friend, but he is certainly my dearest. Do you have a best friend?' he asked me.

I blushed at the question. I had had a best friend. But no more. And I did not want to talk about it.

Father was awaiting us on the balcony. He had poured red wine into three glasses, letting me have the smallest glass with barely a sip of wine in it, yet I was glad to be included as an adult.

'I've arranged for you to see our friend tomorrow,' Mordecai told my father. 'Best if you go alone.'

'Are you sure you don't mind?' Father asked.

'Oh, of course not! We shall go and visit Ismail, shan't we?' He nodded in my direction and I nodded back in agreement.

I am not sure whether it was the wine, or whether they were talking in code – perhaps a bit of both – but for the entire evening, I could not follow what each of them said. There was much talk of papers, of travel, of identification, and of the possibility that we would just have to 'wait and see what happens'.

Of course, now I know what Father was doing. He was trying to secure us a loan to leave as soon as we could, for he foresaw what would happen in a few years' time. I do not know whether he did not get the loan, but I know he returned to Krakow once more in 1939, to try to secure papers once more. But again, it came to nothing.

The following morning, I woke in Mordecai's apartment and my father had already left.

Mordecai told me to dress and that we would have breakfast with Ismail.

We followed the cobbled lane as far as the synagogue, then turned left down a narrower street. Here the shops were closer together, the buildings on each side almost touching, letting only a sliver of light peep through from above.

Although it was darker, it was brighter to me. One shop sold chocolates, a large black man standing at the doorway smoking, his white apron stained with smears of melted chocolate which he had been working with his hands. He smiled and said good morning to Mordecai, who greeted him by name and promised to be back later. At another, a small cafe, two men sat outside, sidelocks of curls escaping from their black hats, their arms raised as if in argument.

'They are scholars,' Mordecai told me. 'Always arguing about some translation or meaning – pay them no heed.'

A bookshop caught Mordecai's eye, the tables set out in front spilling over with books, but then he noticed something further down, a hand raised in greeting, and thankfully ignored the books.

We passed a jewellery store, all the emerald bracelets, diamond earrings and thick gold necklaces winking at us, then a French patisserie, the cakes displayed in the window so tiny and beautiful with their icing figurines and sugar-coated fruits that I wanted to stop. Mordecai noticed my glance. 'We'll visit here too,' he promised. 'My friend owns this – from France originally, he brought over his wares.'

It seemed as though everyone was Mordecai's friend, each of them smiling and waving, the smells of pastries, cooking stews, wine, tobacco, chocolate, all mingling together into one rich aroma so that for a moment I forgot that I was still in Poland.

Finally, we reached Ismail. He was the colour of the milky coffee that Mother made, his eyes wide and bright, his smile taking over most of his face as he fell about himself trying to welcome me.

He sat us at a table on the cobblestones. Two other men sat smoking from a long hose attached to a yellow glass bottle that sat on the floor, adorned with an intricate design of a dragon, the scales of which were made from green glass, its eyes red, and the flames coming from its mouth a rich gold.

'It's called a shisha,' Mordecai told me. 'Instead of smoking cigarettes, you can smoke that, with all different flavours of tobacco.'

From inside, I could see Ismail talking to a younger boy, then he looked at us, grinned and came straight out.

'It's all sorted – I have placed your order,' Ismail told Mordecai.

'Sit with us, Ismail, come and meet my friend here.'

Ismail shook my hand, even though he had only just done so when I met him, and he sat next to Mordecai, the pair of them smiling at me as if I were some prized possession.

'Mordecai has told me so much about you,' Ismail began.

I was surprised by this. I had heard of Mordecai maybe three or four times before we had come to visit, and I wondered what Father had said about me.

'You are very clever, just like your father.'

His voice was rich, his accent tinged with his own language. I liked it.

'Ah, here – breakfast!'

The boy placed three tiny coffee cups in front of us, the liquid inside a dense brown that was almost black. There were perhaps three sips of coffee in the cup, and I couldn't understand why it was so small.

'It's very strong,' Ismail told me. 'Very. So sip it as you eat, here.'

He took some bread from the tray that the boy held, still warm from the oven, then some cheese, olives, freshly sliced tomato, and some green stalks in a dish with lemon.

'Eat, eat,' he encouraged, building himself a sandwich of sorts – first the cheese, then a slice of tomato, a squeeze of lemon, and a few leaves from the stalky plant.

'Parsley,' Mordecai said, noticing my hesitancy over picking some up myself.

I made a similar sandwich and popped a black olive in my mouth, just as Ismail and Mordecai did. Then, like a mirror image, I sipped at my coffee. Although basic, the flavours were so exotic to me. I was used to porridge for breakfast.

'Your father told me that you were having some trouble at school,' Mordecai began. I felt my face flame as it had when he had asked the previous evening about friends.

'I know you probably don't want to talk about it, but you see, I think you will find we would understand.'

Ismail nodded along with Mordecai, his face serious. How much had Father told Mordecai, and how much had he in turn told this stranger?

'How about I tell you my story first, and then perhaps you will feel more comfortable telling me yours?' Mordecai asked.

I sipped at the bitter coffee and nodded. Ismail passed me a sugar cube and I dropped it into the drink, wondering whether he could read my mind.

'I was twenty-two, I think, when I fell in love,' Mordecai began. 'I was travelling for work with a professor at the university – I was his assistant, you see. His speciality was the history of the Ottoman Empire, which of course led us to Constantinople, to review some ancient manuscripts that were held in a library.

'I worked hard and barely left the library – only to eat, drink and sleep in the tiny hot hotel that was a few doors away. However, that time was all I needed to find love – those brief moments of sitting at a cafe, listening to the call to prayer, watching the world float by. In the evenings I would sit with my love, and we would drink alcohol spiced with aniseed, then drink water to calm the burning in our mouths.'

It was then that I realised I had heard this tale before, the previous night in fact. 'But you said that you sat with Ismail at the cafe?'

'I did,' Mordecai said simply.

It took me a few more sips of the coffee until I reached the sediment at the bottom before I realised what Mordecai was trying to subtly tell me – his love was Ismail.

I looked at them both and saw it instantly: the way they mirrored each other, the ease with which Ismail passed him a napkin or salt, neither of them having to ask – it had been learned from years of being together. How had I not seen this before?

'Now it is your turn,' Mordecai told me.

I twisted a paper napkin around my fingers, watching as it stopped the blood flow, making my skin go pale. Then I released it, feeling the sensation of my pulse pushing blood back once more.

'He was my best friend,' I said, not looking at either of them. 'We played when we were younger, and then as we grew, we studied together and laughed together. The other boys were always talking about girls and it was nice that I didn't have to do that with him – he seemed indifferent to them, as I was.

'One evening we were studying together in my room. I don't know how it happened, but I found my lips kissing his cheek. He didn't immediately pull away, so I tried to kiss him on his lips. It was then that he pushed me hard in the chest and stood up, his face red, his fists balled at his sides.

'He didn't speak, and neither did I. I didn't know what to say. I watched him gather his things and leave, and it was then that I cried.'

'But you told your father?' Ismail asked.

I nodded. 'The next day, at school, people looked at me strangely and my friend – my best friend – became my enemy. He punched me in the face on the way home from school to the shouts and screams of the others. Father found me curled up on my bed, crying into a pillow.

'I told him that I had been hit. He asked me why. I didn't want to tell him, to say it out loud, and he didn't push me to. All he did was hug me and tell me he loved me and was proud of me, and we never spoke of it again.'

'Until now,' Mordecai said.

'Until now.'

'Your father wrote me a while back and asked for my advice. I told him to bring you with him when he visited next and that perhaps I could help. You do see, don't you, that your father is not ashamed of you – he simply was not sure how to talk to you about it. His kindness and love for you meant that he could bring you here, to his friend for the best part of his life, so that we could let you know it is going to be all right – that you are perfect as you are.'

I bit my bottom lip to stop myself from crying. I realised at that moment how much my father and my mother loved me. How they had probably talked about it and decided to show me that they understood, knowing that my teenage anger and confusion would not allow a full conversation with them – would not allow me to be completely honest with them.

When Father returned that evening, flustered from the heat, I hugged him, and he patted me on the back and whispered, 'I love you.'

'What about God?' I asked, pulling away.

'He loves you too,' he said. 'God is love. Don't forget Him, as He hasn't forgotten you.'

That was our conversation about God – those simple few sentences, yet I wanted to write them, to remember them here, now, when I feel scared. God loves me, just as my father did, and I wanted to tell you that I love you – I wanted to end my story with love.

CHAPTER THIRTY-ONE

Isaac

That night, Isaac was sent back to the camp; the atmosphere in the bunkhouse was electric with fear and hope.

'I heard they are evacuating us tomorrow,' Jan said, as he and Elijah helped Isaac into his bunk.

'All of us?' Elijah asked.

'Who knows. That's just what I heard. A few have decided to hide in the infirmary.'

'You?' Elijah asked.

'I'm going to try,' Jan said. 'You two should come too.'

Isaac lay back on his bunk, his chest weighing heavy on him as if a boulder had been placed there. As Jan spoke, a scent reached him, pricking at his nose – lemons.

He turned on his side and closed his eyes, waiting for the lemon scent to get stronger, falling into a fitful sleep in which he imagined he was in the street that Adam had described, sitting with Mordecai and Ismail, drinking coffee, whilst all around them people were screaming.

He thought he had been asleep only moments when the guard with the scar over his eye woke him and half dragged him from his bunk.

Isaac started coughing but the guard did not care, and pushed him in front of him towards the door.

'Herr Becher needs you now,' he told him.

The sun was just breaking as he reached the house, birds waking up to sing for their breakfasts, the trees swishing and rustling as if telling secrets to one another. Isaac looked at the sky for a moment, marvelling at the world, at the nature all around him. He could not smell lemons anymore.

Herr Becher was revving the engine of the black car and asked Isaac to check it once more.

He fiddled with the petrol pump, as if it would help, and declared to Becher that everything was in working order.

'Thank you, Isaac.' Becher patted him on the back. 'You have done a very good job, very good indeed.'

It was then that Isaac noticed he had shaved off his moustache, leaving a clean top lip spotted with sweat. His clothes had changed too. Now he wore brown slacks, a white shirt, as if he were someone entirely different.

'You'll be rewarded,' Becher said, 'I owe you for this.'

'Shall I take him back?' the guard with the scar asked.

'No. No. Isaac will stay here. In the shed, Isaac, off you go. I haven't quite finished with him yet,' Becher told the guard, whose eyes never left Isaac as he hobbled away back to the shed.

He had one chance now, and this was it, he knew. He got on all fours and crawled, painfully, to the hiding place where he took out J. A. L.'s papers, placing the watch for Anna inside, then took a few sheets of spare paper and began to add his own story – one for Anna and Friedrich, the family that had been brought back to life.

As his hand began to scratch words on the paper with the pencil, he smelled them again – lemons. He needed to be quick.

CHAPTER THIRTY-TWO

Isaac

My dearest Anna,

I write to you with a hurried hand, to try to tell you things I have thought during our friendship.

To begin, I wanted to say thank you – you brightened my days by just being you, by talking to me, and by caring for me. I think often of our talks, of how I was able to tell you about my life, my losses, which has relieved me of a weight I was not aware that I was carrying with me all these years. The dance we shared is seared into my memory – a memory where I felt young again, hopeful and free. And I have you to thank for that too.

Now I feel lighter, freer. It has helped me to imagine a future – one which I am not sure I will see, but one that gave me hope. In my imaginings, you were by my side, just as Hannah had been before. You are so much like Hannah – not just in the way you look at me, but in the way you consider everyone, worry for everyone and try to help. You brought Hannah back to me and for that I am forever thankful, as my heart is full once more with love, and I did not want to die consumed with hate and sorrow.

I know that you are broken too – your fiancé, parents and brother all taken from you – but know that you can be mended once more. You can have new parts of your life, new memories to replace the old, which will keep you moving, keep the time ticking along.

Remember, dear Anna, that you are strong, and you can overcome anything.

To Friedrich,

I never spoke to you of my son, but I wanted you to know that you are very much like he was – kind, thoughtful and intelligent. I hope that our friendship has given you hope and shown you that there will always be someone who can be a part of your life, sometimes much more than your own family are.

Dear Friedrich, you brought me joy with your inquisitive nature, and gave me the opportunity to see how perhaps my son would have grown if he had had the chance.

To you both, these past few months you have given me my family back – you have helped me to become alive again, even in this place of death.

I am, forever yours and with all my love,
Isaac.

CHAPTER THIRTY-THREE

Friedrich

His bags were sat at the foot of his bed, packed once more. He had wanted to take his train set, but his mother had told him there was no room and he was to leave it behind.

The bed was stripped of its bedding, leaving the stark white mattress. He held the red engine in his hands, turning it over and over, trying to sear it into his memory – his toy that his friend Isaac had fixed for him, his toy that he was told he was not allowed to take with him.

He hoped a new family would move into the house, and that perhaps they would have a little boy who loved trains and had always wanted a train set. He decided that if he thought about it enough, if he imagined it, then it would become real.

Outside he heard the revving of the car engines, then his father's voice. He walked to the window and looked out, seeing Isaac standing near the open bonnet, his shoulders drooped as if he were about to fall over at any moment.

He watched him stare into the engine then straighten up, his father talking to him. Then, Isaac walked towards the side of the house – he was going to the shed.

Friedrich ran from his room and took the stairs quickly, feeling as though his feet were flying down them.

His mother was asking Anna to help her carry a suitcase to the car and he ran past them, straight out to the shed. He peered through the window and saw Isaac sitting on the floor, writing something on a piece of paper. He desperately wanted to go in, but he didn't want to disturb him either.

He'd wait, he decided. He'd sit in the trees at the back where no one could see him, and he'd wait a while and then go in.

The pine needles that had dripped from the trees littered the floor, and when Friedrich sat down, a few pricked him in his thighs, so he had to keep moving to try and find a more comfortable spot.

He could hear his mother shouting at his father on the driveway and wished they would forget they had a son and simply drive away without him.

A plane flew low overhead and there was a smattering of gunfire from near the camp. He knew he did not have long – his mother would come looking for him soon. He had to disturb Isaac.

Inside the shed Isaac was still sitting on the dusty floor, the paper from his hands gone.

'Friedrich.' Isaac's voice was low, and simply saying his name seemed to require a lot of effort.

'I wanted to say goodbye,' Friedrich said.

Isaac patted the floor next to him and Friedrich sat, letting Isaac place his thin arm around his shoulders, drawing him into his side.

'Do you smell lemons, Friedrich?' Isaac asked.

'No. Should I?'

'No. You shouldn't.'

'Do you smell them?'

'I do.'

'Where will you go now, Isaac? Will you have to go back to the camp?'

'I'll be going home,' Isaac said. 'I'll be going home to see my wife Hannah.'

'You never told me you had a wife!' Friedrich exclaimed. He had thought he knew everything about him.

'She's a lovely woman, Friedrich. She likes to cook, and she likes to garden, making beautiful things grow from the soil. We'll sit in the garden together when I get home, and we will talk and laugh, and I'll tell her all about you.'

'Can I come and see her?'

'Not yet. But one day.'

'I don't want to leave.' Friedrich sniffed and felt a tear roll down his cheek. 'I don't want to go with them. Can I please stay with you, and I will come with you and see your wife? I can help her in the garden, and I can help you in the shop fixing watches.'

'Ah, yes! The shop. Here.' Isaac gave him a scrap of paper with an address written on it. 'You keep this, and when you are older, I want you to go to my shop.'

'Will you be there?' Friedrich asked.

'Probably not. It may not even be a shop then. But, if you count eighteen floorboards from the front door and walk due north, you will find one floorboard that is nailed down with gold-tipped nails. Open this floorboard, Friedrich, for there is a treasure inside that is for you, and for you only.'

'What is it?'

'It's a surprise. Promise me though, promise me you will remember, and you will go?'

'I promise. I will memorise the address just like my Latin teacher taught me to do. I will memorise it and when I am old enough, I will go straight to your shop and I will find it.'

'Thank you,' Isaac said, and pulled him even closer to his body. 'Thank you, Friedrich.'

Friedrich heard his name being shouted – his mother. He didn't want her to come to the shed. 'I have to go.'

He felt Isaac relax his hold on him, then a light kiss on the top of his head. 'You take care of yourself now, Friedrich. You be who you are. Help people. Be kind. Always be kind.'

Friedrich stood, his mother calling his name louder now.

'Go, go – you need to go,' Isaac said.

Friedrich suddenly flung himself at Isaac and took him in an embrace, allowing Isaac to rest his head on his shoulder for a moment, not wanting to let go.

'Go, go now.' Isaac's voice was muffled, tears falling from his eyes. 'Go now.'

Friedrich stood, wiping his face with the back of his hand. He reached the door, then turned. 'I love you, Isaac. You have been my best friend. Even better than Otto.'

Isaac gave a watery smile, then waved. 'And you, Friedrich. And you.'

CHAPTER THIRTY-FOUR

Anna

Anna had been packing all night. She and Greta had stayed in the kitchen drinking strong coffee as they folded Liesl's clothes, boxed hats and sorted shoes. Liesl and Herr Becher argued most of the night, their screams at each other bouncing off the walls.

'If they make it to where they are going without killing each other, I'll eat my own hat!' Greta exclaimed, shoving a cream day hat into a box, denting the top.

Anna grinned – first there would be broken plates on her arrival and now a dented, unwearable hat.

It was Friedrich that Anna worried for. The boy was paler than usual, his face betraying every feeling that rushed through his body – fear, anger, sadness. She had wanted to hold him to her, to say that everything was going to be all right, but she couldn't, and she knew he would not believe her words.

As she helped Liesl carry a suitcase out to one of the cars, she saw the back of Isaac retreating to the garden.

When she returned to the kitchen, the back door was wide open and Friedrich was opening the shed door. She would give him a moment to say goodbye before fetching him, lest his mother find him in there.

As tired as she felt, there was a fluttering in her stomach, the same as when it was her birthday and she couldn't sleep with excitement. She knew it was foolish. She had been told that upon getting back to the camp, they were to be evacuated, led away by SS guards, all of them holding guns.

Why she thought she would see the Americans she did not know, but perhaps, just perhaps there was a chance.

Caught in her own thoughts, she did not hear Liesl calling for Friedrich and did not hear her footfall on the kitchen tiles. It was only when she was by her side, her cloying perfume taking the air away from her, that she realised it was too late.

Liesl saw Friedrich come out of Isaac's shed and her eyes narrowed. Anna held her breath and waited for her to scold the boy when he entered the kitchen, but she did not. Instead she grabbed him by the jumper and dragged him from the kitchen into the hallway, then told him to sit on the bottom step whilst he waited for his father.

'It's worse when she's quiet,' Greta said. 'I had chills all over me.'

'What will she do to him?' Anna asked.

'Probably spank him – what else can she do? Poor lad.'

Anna could hear Herr Becher's voice as Liesl explained where Friedrich had been.

'Well, what are you going to do?' she screamed at him. 'What? You're so useless – I never should have married you. I knew you had no backbone and I was right – look at where we are now!'

Herr Becher adopted his calming voice, one not heard for some time, and then he spoke to someone else – a guard at the door. 'Take him away,' he told the guard.

'I thought you said to leave him here?' the guard asked.

'It's his punishment for corrupting my son,' Becher added, then slammed shut the front door, leaving the family in the hallway. Anna understood then that the punishment was not for Friedrich.

She looked to Greta whose eyes were wide. 'Go – go now to him!'

Anna ran from the kitchen, beating the guard to the shed. Isaac was sitting on the floor, his eyes closed, his breath raspy, the writings of J. A. L. wrapped in a piece of cloth on Isaac's lap.

'Isaac!' she screamed at him.

He opened his eyes and smiled at her. 'Take these.' He tried to lift the papers.

'They're coming to take you – you need to try and get away!'

'It's all right, my dear Anna.' His smile was fixed in place. 'Take this.'

'No – I can help you. Please—'

'Hush, my dear.' His eyelids flickered as if he were about to fall asleep, then he opened them and placed his hand on her cheek. 'I love you, Anna. I am a silly old man, I know. But you have made me feel love again.'

Anna could barely see him through her tears. She held him to her. 'When we danced, I saw you, Isaac, I saw you as you were, as a strong young man,' she said. 'You can be strong again. You can. Let me help you.'

Then, just as Isaac started to speak, the guard grabbed Anna by her arm, pulling her upright, bruising her skin and dragging her away from Isaac. She kicked at his shin and took the few steps towards Isaac, holding him in her arms, her tears wetting the top of his head.

'Go to the infirmary,' he whispered to her. 'Pretend you are dead, or hide somewhere in there. That's where you need to go – trust me. Jan said it was true so it must be.'

As he spoke to her, her hand found the wrapped bundle and she held it to her chest.

There were arms around Anna now, pulling her away. She kicked and screamed at them, and all the time, Isaac smiled and told her it was all right, it was all right.

She hit the damp grass with a thud, and for good measure, the guard kicked her in the stomach. Lying there, clutching her sides, she saw another pair of shining black boots on the ground walking towards the shed. The wind taken out of her, she could barely move, but with each breath she tried to scream out for Isaac.

Hands were underneath her once more, pulling her upright. Greta. She helped her move towards the kitchen door, her arms around her waist to stop her from running towards the shed once more.

She waited, her vision blurry, the greens of the trees merging with the blue of the sky so that she did not know where the sky began.

The guards emerged with Isaac who could barely walk. His feet scuffed the ground, his head to the floor, unable or unwilling to raise his eyes.

'Pointless,' one of the guards said.

'You can do it,' the other said. 'But take your time,' he added as he walked past Anna, grinning at her, a scar above his eye.

Anna fell to the floor, her hands tearing at her dress as she had done when Piotr had died. Huge waves of pain overwhelmed her so that she could barely breathe.

'Hush now, come on, hush, breathe – in, out, in, out.' Greta's voice was firm.

'I can't…' Anna tried.

'You can – now breathe, come on, in and out.'

'They're coming – oh God! They're coming!' Liesl was scream-ing inside the house and grabbing for the handle to the front door.

Anna looked to Greta who already had her hands under Anna's armpits, pulling her upwards with a strength Anna did not know Greta possessed.

'Pick that up and hide it.' Greta pointed at the bundle of papers.

Anna, still sobbing, nodded, picked up J. A. L.'s writings and shoved them down her dress, holding them against her body with one arm.

The engines in the driveway started up, Schmidt's voice shouting for Friedrich to get in the car, then peppered shots rang out as if there were snipers in the trees at the back of the garden.

'Come with me.' Greta grabbed Anna's arm and made for the front of the house, down the gravelled driveway as the black car driven by Herr Becher, Liesl in the passenger seat, shot past them, the next car driven by Schmidt with Friedrich in the back seat, who, upon seeing Anna, turned and looked out of the rear window, his hand on the glass his goodbye.

'Isaac?' Anna mumbled to Greta.

'Isaac's gone, Anna. He's gone.' She held Anna's chin in her hand and made her look at her. 'You're in shock but you have to try, you have to still try.'

Anna shook her head and felt a wave of fear overcome her – Isaac, the planes, Friedrich, it was all too much.

'I can't!' Anna screamed now. 'I can't.'

Greta held her face in her hands once more. 'Look at me, Anna,' she commanded. 'Look at me.'

Anna tried to calm her breathing and stared into the old woman's eyes.

'Now, listen. You have to do as I say. You have to put one foot in front of the other and move. If Isaac were here now, if he were in this situation, what would you tell him to do?'

'I'd tell him to run – to escape,' she stuttered through thick sobs.

'Good. Now, calm your breathing. Good, that's it.'

Anna concentrated on Greta's eyes, on her voice, and found that her breathing slowed, the sobs becoming small hiccups.

'Good. Now come on.' Greta moved them on once more.

They had not walked for more than a minute when a car pulled up, driven by the guard with the scar above his eye.

'And where do you think you are going?' he asked.

'I was just taking her back to the camp,' Greta said.

'Is that so? Seems you are going the wrong way.'

'Oh, so I am.' Greta turned the other way. 'Silly old me. Can't tell my left from my right, can I?'

'I'll take her,' the guard said.

'No, no – it's no bother.' Greta still held on to Anna's upper arm.

'I said, I'll take her,' he repeated.

Anna turned to Greta. 'Thank you. I'll be all right.'

'You mind yourself.' Greta stroked Anna's cheek. 'You make sure you live.'

'Get in!' The guard was impatient – more shots were ringing out; a plane droned overhead.

Anna had no choice but to climb into the car and be driven away from her one chance at escape.

'Thought you were clever, didn't you?' he asked her.

When she didn't answer, he reached over, his hand on her thigh, pushing her dress upwards, just as Becher had done to her.

'You all think you are so clever, don't you? Well, I'll show you who's still in charge. Herr Becher is gone, so how about you serve me now, eh?'

He pulled the car to the side of the road and lurched over to grab Anna. In one moment, a moment she would never repeat again, she bit the side of the guard's face, so hard that she tasted his blood in her mouth. He pulled away screaming, and Anna did not stop, the fury inside her boiling over, her thoughts of Isaac, of Nina, of her brother all welling up. She punched him hard in the groin, then with deft fingers she pulled out the wooden baton on his belt and smacked it on the back of his head so that he slumped onto the steering wheel.

She counted to twenty and he did not move. She climbed out of the car and, hearing only her rough breathing in her ears, she ran to the camp, to Nina, to hide.

The camp was in disarray. New bodies littered the floor, blood seeping from them where bullets had mowed them down. Lines of women were being led towards the entrance to the camp, some of them falling as more shots from watchtowers picked them off.

Anna ran to her bunkhouse and screamed for Nina – was she in the line?

There was no answer, so she ran again. Following a line of women at the rear, she saw Joanna and then, yes – Nina. She grabbed Nina's arm. Nina looked at her with a mixture of shock and relief. 'Come with me!' She pulled Nina from the line, then saw Joanna fall to the floor, a bullet hole in her back, a bullet meant for her or Nina.

They dodged their way to the back of a bunkhouse and crouched low in the long grass.

'Where are we going to go?' Nina asked, her voice breaking.

It was then that Anna remembered what Isaac had said. 'The infirmary,' she told her. 'Come. Come on, quickly.'

The pair ran, tripping over bodies, ducking every now and again when a shot rang out.

They reached the infirmary. 'Undress, quickly,' Anna told her. They both undressed, and each climbed into two empty beds, pulling the covers over them. Anna slid the diary under the mattress.

'Look as though you are dying,' Anna told her. 'Look as though there is no point in taking us.'

'There isn't.' Nina was lying flat on her back, her eyes on the ceiling. 'We are already dead.'

EPILOGUE

Cornwall

1980

The snow had thickened by the time the clock struck twelve and she wondered whether it would keep them all from coming. She sat in an armchair facing the bay window that looked out onto a wide lawn and then further, to the Atlantic Ocean where the sea roughed itself into tall foamy peaks. She could smell the salt from here and loved the days in summer when she would sit in the garden, the sea calmer, bringing her the scent of freshness. Her nose was attuned to any bitter or foul smell, so that she swore she could tell when a vegetable had gone bad, even before it looked rotten.

Her children had got used to her ways, her husband, Frank, too, who even now was in the kitchen making sure everything was ready, not allowing anything to burn or spoil.

She drummed her fingertips on the arm of the chair, counting the seconds. Who had taught her to do that? Her hand reached for her wrist where the watch sat – ah yes, she knew who it was.

Katharina would be late. She was always late for everything, so it was not her car she was waiting to see pull into the driveway. Isaac would be on time – he would have no choice – and Jakub would be with him, keeping him company on the drive, making him laugh and annoying him with the silly songs that he made up.

'Someone's here,' Frank's voice rang out, and she saw him go to the front door as a taxi pulled up.

A taxi – had Katharina's car broken down again?

There was a hello, a man's voice, and then in the doorway stood someone she had not seen for ten years or more.

'I'm sorry I could not come sooner,' the man said. He had changed; his hair was a silvery grey, lines now appearing around his mouth and eyes, creasing his tanned skin.

'Friedrich!' She stood and took him in an embrace, marvelling at the change in him.

'I've got older,' he said.

'Almost as old as me now!' She laughed.

'Not quite! You've still got a few years on me yet.'

'I didn't think you would make it,' she said, as she directed him towards the purple flowered sofa. 'I didn't get a letter back, so I assumed you were away somewhere again on your travels.'

'I was, but by the time I got your letter, there was no time to reply. I simply got on a plane and now here I am,' he grinned.

'Drink?' Frank asked him. 'We've anything you can think of – wine, scotch, champagne even!'

'Scotch would be great,' Friedrich said.

As soon as Frank left, the pair fell into the language that came naturally to them, catching up on each other's lives since the last time they had seen one another.

'You still like it here then?' Friedrich asked her.

'What – England, you mean?'

'I always imagined that you would return home at some point.'

'I'm not sure where home is. I know it has been here, with Frank and the children. That's enough of a home for me.'

'I went back, you know, to the house and the camp.'

'When?' She sat straight now, her eyes on his.

'I couldn't help it. I was on a train platform in Munich and there was an announcement that the next train to Dachau would be leaving in five minutes. Before I knew what I was doing, I was running to catch a train I wasn't sure I really wanted to be on.'

'What was it like?' Her voice was quiet now.

'The house, my parents' house, is a museum now. My little red engine in one of the display cases – can you imagine that?'

'And the camp?'

'People go there and look around. I never saw it as it was, so I don't know how it is different, but I saw the photographs that the Americans took, watched the reels of films. I saw it as best I could through your eyes.'

'I knew it had become somewhat of a tourist attraction, but I have never met anyone who has been.'

'It's more than that though.' He leaned forward and took her hand in his. 'It's not for amusement, it's to educate – so that it is never forgotten.'

'And yet I have tried most of my life to forget.'

He nodded then sat back, letting the cushions behind envelop him.

'You look tired,' she said.

'I'm always tired.'

'Still have trouble sleeping?'

'Scotch helps.' He raised the glass that Frank had handed him and grinned.

'Your parents,' she ventured. 'They still haunt you, don't they?'

Fredrich ran his hand over the stubble on his chin, that too turning grey. 'I know they are dead, but yes, they do. Like ghosts. It's almost like I can hear them telling me I am useless, or Father berating me for not eating quickly enough. When Mother died, when I was what, seventeen? I thought then that my life would be easier – isn't that terrible, to be glad when your parents die and not grieve for them? Anyway. It was Father I could not leave. He was almost dead when we arrived in Argentina. He drank to escape what he had done, but it didn't work; it made

him a sad, useless man who soiled himself and needed his son
to wipe his behind.'

'And yet you think of them.'

'And yet I do.' He drank the scotch back in one go, and went
to find Frank to pour him another.

When he returned, she saw him playing with something in
one hand.

'Is that it?' she asked, her arms already outstretched, ready to
take it from him.

He handed it over and she read the engraving:

Isaac Schüller
remember me
January 1945

'When did you go?' She ran her fingers over the engraving,
imagining Isaac cutting into it all those years before.

'After I went to the camp,' he said. 'He was right. It wasn't a
shop anymore. It was a cafe – imagine that, me walking in and
asking to prise up one of their floorboards!'

'But you did it,' she said.

'I did. I should have gone sooner, but for years, like you, I
suppose I wanted to try and forget that part of me, that part of
my life. It was only when I was standing on the train platform
that I realised I had to face it. Strange, isn't it, that the way my
friendship began with Isaac was over a train, and the one thing
that made me return was when I was near a train once more.'

'It was as if he was talking to you, asking you to remember
your promise to him.'

'If you believe in those kinds of things, then yes, I suppose it
was. He told me, the day I said goodbye to him, to find his shop,
but also that he could smell lemons,' Friedrich said. 'He asked
me if I could smell them too.'

'It was his way of telling you that he was going to die – he knew it, you see – he was so sick; he knew his end was near.'

Suddenly Friedrich started to cry, fat sloppy tears that wetted his cheeks, making him look like a lost boy again.

She sat next to him on the couch and let him weep into her shoulder.

'He said something else too.' Friedrich sat up, wiping his nose on his sleeve. 'He said he was going home to see Hannah.'

'But Hannah died years before.'

'I know. But at the time I didn't. I remember asking him if I could go with him and he told me not yet.'

She wanted to grieve with him, to share his tears, but she could not – there was something holding her back, a part of her she worried would take over her and not allow her to return to the life she had built.

A crunch of tyres on the driveway as it negotiated the fresh snow gave them both a moment to compose themselves.

It was, as she expected, her sons Isaac and Jakub, soon followed by Katharina who looked as though she had just rolled out of bed, her hair wild, her clothes creased.

'Could you not have at least ironed them?' she asked her daughter, who made straight for the glasses of wine her father was handing out.

'I was busy. Studying all night for exams and then I've got that dance recital next month, so I had to practise this morning. I jumped in the shower and now I'm here, so I'd take that as a win!' She kissed her mother on her cheek.

Isaac was enamoured with the pocket watch of his namesake, whilst Jakub told tall tales of his first year at university – it seemed as though all the girls adored him.

She sat back in her armchair and watched the scene unfold around her, secretly drinking them in. The way Katharina tossed her hair back and how each time she turned, it was as though she was doing a pirouette. How Isaac wanted to know more about the watch – how old was it, where did it come from, how did it work? His inquisitive green eyes behind his spectacles, trying to take in every detail.

And then, Jakub. Her baby.

Three children in four years. She wasn't overjoyed when she found out she was pregnant with Jakub so soon after Katharina, but when she had seen him, his delicate features, his face that already looked too old, too wise for him, and then that smile, that smile she already knew – she fell head over heels in love with him.

His humour had come on naturally and was so much like his uncle's – the same teasing silliness and yet, underneath it all, soft and loving.

More people quickly arrived, filling her living room, bringing flowers, food for the buffet and bottles of wine. She meandered between them, talking, laughing, and then there was the tinkle of a knife as it tapped the side of a champagne glass – it was time.

Everyone duly stood or sat whilst she took her place next to the fire, the photograph of Anna on the mantel.

'I'm so grateful that you could all come today to say goodbye to our dear friend, Anna,' Nina began.

She waited whilst the murmur of acknowledgement died down. Then, with shaking hands, she picked up a bundle of papers she had left on the side table, ready to show them all.

'As you know, Anna and I were best friends for many years. She and I were lucky to find love with two brothers, Frank and Paul, and even luckier to find homes near one another. Anna was a second mother to my children; to Katharina, whom I gave my own name, which was also my mother's – to Isaac, whom I gave the name of the man who saved our lives, and to Jakub, named after his uncle.

Over the years, some of you have asked me about the war, about the camp, and I never responded. It was a time I wanted so much to forget, and yet when Anna died, I read these once more.' She held up the papers.

'I want to read something to you now: *She was the positive out of my negatives, and since then, she had given me three more positives which have filled my life up so much that no negative experience can ever diminish them.*

'These were the words of my father, who spoke of my mother to my brother, Jakub. My brother wrote this memory down to try and make sense of the love that he felt for a fellow inmate in Dachau, and it was this that made me realise that my life in Dachau will always be a part of me – it was my negative which brought so many positives, and I cannot ignore it any longer.'

She felt the tears come now, and Frank handed her a handkerchief.

'Mum, it's all right, we can stop there.' Jakub stood and wrapped his arm around her shoulders.

'I have to, I have to finish,' she said.

Jakub nodded but did not leave her side.

'Anna saved my life. It is that simple – I owe that to her, and when she lay dying, I told her I was angry with her that I owed my death first. She laughed at me.

'That day she saved my life – she took me to the infirmary, where she told me to pretend I was dying so that they would not force us to march with the other prisoners, so many of whom died along the way.

'I had given up. I had seen so much death around me for so long, and that day I had witnessed the unbridled violence of men and women who wanted one more chance to get rid of us, because we were Jewish, or Polish, or a gypsy, or gay. I wanted, in that moment, lying in the bed in the infirmary, to die. But Anna would not let me.

'All the rest of that day and night she made up stories, silly, funny ones, and she did not tire in reciting them to me. At first

I did not hear her, but bit by bit, she pulled me out of myself. She told me of Friedrich, of how he had given both her and Isaac the opportunity to dance together, of how in that moment of dancing with him, she had felt love once more – love that had been hidden from her since her family and fiancé died, a love she had not known she could feel again.

'By the morning, we realised that not one guard had come to check on us all night. Indeed, the gunshots had ceased; the cries from inmates disappeared into the wind.

'There were other women in the infirmary who had hidden just as we had, and one of them offered to sneak outside to see what was happening.

'When the woman returned, her face said it all – it seemed to be over. Just like that.

'There were American Jeeps and trucks pulling into the camp and we ran to them, ran, telling them we were inmates, begging them to help us.

'They wrapped us in blankets and placed us into the back of their trucks. I remember there was a young soldier, perhaps no more than twenty, who was vomiting on the ground at the sight of the piles of corpses heaped around him.

'Some of the SS guards had stayed and were being marched from the offices. I saw one, a woman who had overseen myself and Anna, Aufseherin Margarete Lange, smile at an American solider then giggle to the woman standing by her side. I felt a fury in me then – a complete anger that I had never known. Just like that she was flirting with a man, as if she had had no hand in our torment. I realised that in order to survive, in order to live, I had to forget.

'But it isn't so easy, is it, to forget one's past. Soon after we reached the hospital, Anna gave me these papers, my brother's writings – Jakub Adam Lietz, Kuba for short. She told me of how he had died by being beaten and then taken away, perhaps to be tortured, gassed or shot – that I do not know and I am thankful for it. We read the letters, the diaries together, and inside we found another letter, one from Isaac, the watchmaker. He had made a watch for Anna too, the one I wear on my wrist now, the one Anna wore for years and so loved.

'He wrote of his last moments; he told Anna and Friedrich how much they meant to him, of the love they brought to him in his final days alive. It was Isaac who found my brother's letters, it was Isaac who brought Anna close to him, and Friedrich too; it was Isaac who saved us after telling Anna where to hide on that day. Without Isaac, there would be no me, no Anna, and I would never have known my brother as I should have, and I would never have found such love in my life.'

There was a moment of silence in the room as everyone bent their heads and thought of Anna and Isaac.

Then Friedrich stood and made his way to Nina, wrapping his arm around her shoulders and leading her towards her chair.

'Can we go outside?' she asked him.

'It's snowing.'

'I don't mind. I just need a moment of fresh air to compose myself.'

Friedrich did as she requested and opened the back door where they stood, side by side, a carpet of snow in front of them, the briny waves peaking in the distance over the low garden wall.

'I'm so glad you found Anna,' Nina began. 'She talked of you so often that when you came to her – what, in your twenties? – she was beside herself with happiness.'

'I'm glad I found her too. And you,' Friedrich said, then blew warm air into his cupped hands.

'What will you do now?' she asked, not looking at him, but focusing on the waves that rolled one on top of the other.

'Travel some more, maybe? I don't know.'

'Make sure you have a family. Promise me that – make sure you find yourself a family.' She turned now to look at him, trying to imagine him as the little boy who had befriended Anna.

'I thought I already had,' he said, his eyebrows raised in question.

She took his face in her hands and kissed the tip of his nose. 'Indeed, you have. Forgive me. We are your family.'

That night, the snow stopped falling and a light wind cleared the clouds, leaving a perfect velvet pinpricked with light. Nina stood at her bedroom window and stared at the sky, remembering how she had done the same the last night she had seen Kuba, when they had buried their father.

She shivered at the cold, and for the first time in years, pulled the window closed and climbed into bed. As she did, she smelled something – something out of place, something that did not belong.

It was the tangy fresh scent of lemons.

A LETTER FROM CARLY

Hello,

Firstly and most importantly, a huge thank you for reading *The Watchmaker of Dachau*. I hope you enjoyed reading it as much as I enjoyed writing it.

 If you want to keep up to date with my latest releases, just sign up at the following link. I can promise that your email address will never be shared and you can unsubscribe at any time.

www.bookouture.com/carly-schabowski

 The Watchmaker of Dachau was a particularly hard story for me to write as this was not only inspired by a true story, it is based on the reality of what so many holocaust victims suffered. As such, I wanted to approach this story responsibly; without appropriating their stories, but still describing and bringing forth the reality of this time. It became important to me to then hone in on the characters themselves – their loves, hopes and lives prior to the camp – and show the relationships that they can build, even during the harshest of times. Friedrich, especially, became a conduit for this to happen – he was able to move about in places other than the camp, he was able to hear and see what they could not know, and of course, I was able to explore a relationship between the victim and what we deem the perpetrator to be.

It's always wonderful to hear from my readers – please feel free to get in touch directly on my Facebook page, or through Twitter, Goodreads or my website.

Thank you again,
Carly Schabowski

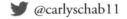 @carlyschab11

ACKNOWLEDGEMENTS

As always, my friends and family deserve to be acknowledged for their support during the writing of this book – it is a lonely and sometimes frustrating process, that of writing a novel, and their patience and kindness is something that keeps me going.

I would also like to thank my wonderful editor, Kathryn Taussig, for talking over suggestions with me, and correcting me when I am completely wrong! A big thanks goes to my agent, Jo Bell, who is kind, thoughtful and patient, and the best agent I could ask for.